EVANGALINE PIERCE

Sword of plated gold

A Rumplestiltskin Fairy Tale Retelling (book 2)

First edition

This book was professionally typeset on Reedsy.
Find out more at reedsy.com

Contents

I

A Sword of Gilded Thread

The conclusion of Gwen's story and an answer to the question:
Why do they always marry the prince?

Hope you love this baby girl!

Choices

The carriage swayed back and forth. Despite her best intentions, Gwen's eyes fluttered shut. She had told the horse to take her home, which he seemed to understand. He was a magic horse, after all. She had hoped to delay the decision the queen had forced upon her. She had had minutes to decide whether to return to Aurum or rescue Prince Aurius from the curse of his kind.

Perhaps if she had had more time to think, she would have returned the kindness Aurius had shown her. And the truth was, she didn't know where her home was, or what her heart desired. She didn't want to be a pawn in the game of politics. Princesses rarely got what they wanted.

When had she decided she was a princess? The thought drifted lazily through her mind as if she had all the time in the world to ponder such things.

Her mind drifted through thoughts of rescues in a restless half-sleep. Flashes of faces popped into her mind. Ryland, on the morning of their wedding, dressed in his crisp dress uniform. His broad smile revealed perfect white teeth set against his tanned skin. As quickly as his image appeared, it faded, and Avonlea took its place, forlorn at the thought of marrying a foreign prince. Even Captain Drake made an appearance in her dreams. The daunting man, who never missed a detail. But the image that pulled at Gwen's heart to the point of breaking was Aurius curled in a ball, suffering alone because she was too cowardly to admit her feelings. If she had just been honest with him, could she have avoided this nightmare?

It was too late for what-ifs. How could she find him now? In those few moments in the carriage, she finally admitted to herself what she could not have admitted to anyone else, not to the queen or even Aurius. Living without him would be dreadful. She already missed his easy smile when they were alone. The way he let her discover herself and her magic. The way he delighted in seeing her happy and did everything in his power to make it so. That's how her life had been for the past few weeks at his side. Until the elf ball. What had happened, she wondered. If she were going to look for Aurius, she would need to start there. "Am I going to look for Aurius?" she whispered to herself. There was still the contract between them. How could she ever know if it was true love when his father had manipulated them so egregiously?

The abrupt stop of the carriage nearly threw her to the floor. She grabbed the railing to keep herself upright and shook off the groggy feeling of sleep. Her chest constricted, making her breaths short and shallow. It was all she could do to keep from rushing out to see what had happened.

She felt the carriage tilt to the left as a footman climbed down. A few seconds later, a knock at the door.

"Princess Gwen?"

The use of the title by anyone other than Aurius startled her, still not sure it was believable.

She cleared the sleep from her throat. "Yes."

"We have arrived." The uncertainty in his tone caused Gwen to rise quickly to see where they were.

The footman opened the door. She took his hand, pushing back the carriage door to look at the area. It was not what she had been expecting. And judging by the look on their faces, the footmen hadn't either. Her suede slippers padded against the wooden step and then onto the grassy edge of the road. The train of the dress followed her until she swished around at the click of the carriage door behind her.

The footman bowed. "My apologies madam. We have no idea where we are. But the horses will go no further."

"That's alright. We'll just go another way," she said.

The footman cleared his throat, and Gwen stepped back.

She folded her hands together. "I guess you have orders to leave me."

"Yes, Princess. I'm truly sorry."

Gwen pulled her lips into a brave smile. "If this is where the horses brought me, this is where I'll stay. Please remove my luggage."

The footman obeyed orders. Fortunately, she did not leave with much. Her bags had been packed for her. A couple of bags made of upholstery. No trunk. She could trudge through the forest with two bags. It had been kind of the Queen to pack anything for her at all. She had entered the castle with nothing, so two satchels were actually generous.

There were worse scenarios to consider. If only she knew where she was. Was she close to the barrier? Close to Aurum? She turned to ask the footman just that. The carriage creaked as he took his seat behind the horses. He slapped the reins against the horses' bridles, turning them back toward the castle.

She pulled her hand back to herself and let it rest on her chin. "Ok. I can see you are in a hurry to get back. I'll just make my way through this very frightening forest by myself. Thank you for your kindness in giving me transport." The dust settled, and the forest returned to its chorus. A few birds trilled quietly at first, then more joined, building their symphony with chittering and chirps.

She placed her hand on the handle of each of the bags and lifted them. She took tentative steps in the direction away from the carriage. The horse must have misunderstood her. Home would not have been in the middle of a forest that was clearly not in Aurum.

Still, she prodded along an overgrown path. Giant reeds towered over her with bushy tassels shading her way. Animals had left small signs they used this trail. Trees lined the pathway, but a clear path cut through them, proving people had once used it. Whoever that was had been gone a while now. Much of their work had overgrown.

Her leg swung over a fallen log. The charcoal-grey wedding dress wasn't the best for climbing or hiking. Gwen took another step and heard it rip. She froze, turned and removed it from the snag, briefly wondering if Josie had planned this as revenge. How could she have known? Their choices

5

had been limited as almost every dress was a wedding gown. "I'd give a lot for a pair of trousers right now," she grumbled, gathering her skirts. She reclaimed her bags and trudged on through the overgrown passage.

The deeper Gwen's journey took her into the forest, the dimmer the light became. More trees filtered the sunlight. She trounced around a few more turns and up and down a couple of hills. The path sloped up again, and she groaned. "At the top of this hill I will take a break and reconsider my life's choices," she whispered to the trees. But as she crested the incline, a structure came into view. Familiarity rushed through her. Anxiety built in her abdomen, renewing her strength and energy. She dropped her bags and sprinted to the edge of the property.

Her smile broadened. "Home," she whispered. Deep within her, something told her it was so. She gathered her skirts and jogged to the door of an abandoned cottage. She stopped in front of it and stared at its stucco walls and steeply pitched roof. Though it had clearly not been lived in, it wasn't in disrepair.

The trees creaked with a rush of passing wind, casting shadows with their eerie dance. Gwen jumped at the sound, peering over her shoulder into the forest. Loneliness pressed in around her, building an empty dread in her heart. Ignoring her growing fear, she turned her attention back to the cottage.

"Have I been here before?" she wondered aloud. It was comforting to hear her own voice. The dense canopy of the trees and the decreasing light cast shadows around the porch. All the moisture in her mouth seemed to dry up. Wind rushed through the limbs of the oak and birch trees.

She stepped onto the front porch. It barely creaked under her weight. The wooden planks were damp and dark. Patches of light green moss covered a few. Gwen jumped at the sharp pop from above her. Her hand found her chest to keep her heart in place as something scurried across the roof. She traced the movement to the edge where an acorn dropped off the side and made its soft landing in a bed of dried leaves. She took a deep breath to calm her racing heart. Folding her arms over her chest, she made her way back to the front door.

Gwen's lips turned down in thought. "This isn't the same cottage as the enchanted forest." Her shoulders slumped at the thought. She couldn't hope to run to the elves. That probably was for the best, considering one of the elf princesses wasn't a fan at the moment. But they were her best hope for finding Aurius.

She tilted her head as she inspected the cottage. "No there is something different. It feels more deeply familiar."

She approached the wooden door and lifted a fist to knock, but tilted her head when she noticed a notch. Instinctively, her hand went to the locket Aurius had returned to her. She tugged it from under the dress and placed it in the notch.

Instantly, the cottage transformed. It didn't change into a castle as in the enchanted forest, but the sheen of abandonment fell away. The density of the air shifted, and the house brightened along with the surrounding forest. The impending dread lifted and her mood lightened.

The door clicked and swung away from the frame. Her mouth hung open in awe of the transformation. The joy and relief nestled in her chest. She closed her eyes and took a full breath for the first time since she had woken that morning.

Gwen took careful steps into the cottage. She felt the wobble as reality shifted through the magic bubble surrounding the house. The inside was as immaculate as any palace she had ever entered, though it was small and quaint. It was easily triple the size of the two-room house she shared with her father.

A noticeable difference between that dwelling and this was the staircase, just across the entrance from the door. Ornate oval carvings decorated the newel posts of the banister and were inlaid with gold filigree. The subsequent posts were delicate wooden spirals twisted to match the designs of the newel posts. It reminded her again of the evening she'd spent with the elves.

The rest of the cottage was tastefully decorated. To her right was a bright living area with dark shelves of trinkets and books on every wall. Beyond that, there was an area that was unfamiliar to her. It looked similar to a workshop, but it had instruments used to prepare food. A large hearth loomed on one side. Shelves held stacks of white dishes and clear glasses on either side of a framed window.

"What is this place?"

Gwen jumped when someone answered her. A wispy, transparent image of Aurius appeared in the center of the room. "This is your haven, Gwen."

She squinted and pushed her head toward him. "Aurius? Is that you?"

"Its a version of me. I'm meant to be helpful if I can. Ask me anything?" he said.

"Where are you?" She had to ask, even if she didn't expect an answer.

He pursed his lips. "That I'm afraid I can't answer."

"I expected that."

Wispy Aurius nodded in agreement.

"Why did the horse bring me here?" she asked.

"The horse?"

"Yes. The horse. I told it to take me home and it brought me here."

"Aw. Magic horse. You were trying to avoid looking too closely at your feelings, perhaps."

She rolled her eyes. He knew her better than she thought. "But why does the horse think this is home to me?"

Transparent Aurius looked at his boots. "I've been collecting things for you. Things I've found when I was searching for you. And the cottage is yours. Well it was your mother's. I've protected it for you and made some enhancements to make life easier. You won't have anyone to look after you here."

"I can take care of myself well enough."

He nodded in agreement.

She looked around the room. "This was my mother's home?"

Aurius nodded. "Her refuge when she was weary of court life."

"And these things?" She lifted her hands and peered at the items throughout the room.

"Some of them are from your mother. The items contain magical memories. Lift them and you will see a memory from your mother or yourself.."

"You saved all this for me?"

His chin tilted to his chest, and suddenly his boots were the most interesting thing he could find. He shifted one foot forward, then back. "Mostly. Your mother had saved some items. I just added to it. I wanted you to have it. It was meant to be a... gift."

"A wedding gift?"

He pulled his lips into a devious grin and looked up through his lashes. "We are betrothed after all."

"Yes," she said, her voice lowering to a whisper. Could that still be a possibility? The contract still wasn't broken, it loomed between them.

He straightened his body and lifted his chin. "I'll leave you to look through the house. If you have further need of my assistance, just ask."

Wispy Aurius blinked away into the floor. Gwen noticed a golden coin. She picked up and put it in the coin purse that rested at her hip.

Her footsteps echoed through the space as she continued her exploration of the house. A yellowed paper covered in dust lay on the table between the small kitchen and the living area.

Through the haze, she could just make out her name at the top. She leaned down so that her face was even with the table. Her lips pursed and parted. She pressed the breath out of her lungs, through her lips, and across the paper.

The text darkened with her breath and popped against the yellowed paper.

Queen Liora

Dear Gwendolyn,

If you are reading this, you have discovered who you are.

You are not the daughter of the miller. He is a good man, and I hope you are happy in his care. He was rewarded for his silence and his caretaking. If he has released you, there is nothing more you need to do for him. Although by now I'm sure you love him as your father, it's best for him if you put that part of your life behind you.

Her mouth gaped open, and she took a step back from the table. Were these her mother's words? She had read her mother's diary nightly. She recognized the handwriting as if it were her own. Her fingers slid over the rough edge of the paper where it had been torn. The same pattern as the missing page in the back of her mother's book. It was likely still lying by the hearth in the two-room cabin she shared with her father. She had examined the torn edge of the diary so often, imagining what the page had been used for.

She scoffed, placing the page back on the table and stepping away. "Put it behind me? I've only just left him and no matter what you say, he is my father." She shrugged and added a few mumbled words to herself. "My father who sold me to the king and told everyone of my secret magic, but my father none the less."

Gwen shook her head to clear that thought away and continued reading the words her mother had written twenty years ago.

I never wanted this for you. When your father, the king, found out what type of magic I possessed, he panicked. We were in love, and he wanted very much to protect me. But he was irrational. We both were. We made mistakes. Especially when I made a deal with the Goblin King. I knew what I was risking, but my freedom felt more important, and what he asked seemed far-fetched. I thought I wouldn't be able to conceive. We had tried for so long to have a child.

But Rumpelstiltskin must have known I had already conceived. And I thought we had won when we played his game. But foolishly, I hadn't read the terms of the contract. I'm so sorry you are now paying for those mistakes. I wish there were another way.

"You couldn't have left a clue in your diary?" Her quivering voice sounded foreign in the empty room. She curled her fingers into fists to keep them from shaking.

After your father died, abdicating the throne with the agreement you would be heir seemed the next best choice. Helen has the power to protect the kingdom from the death of magic. The vacuum created when the Earth swallowed up Rumpelstiltskin. She could erect the barrier when I could do nothing. The people of Mystrim will not follow a queen without power. Mine and yours had to remain hidden. But we used your magic to strengthen hers. You are a powerful catalyst, even as an infant. Fortunately, you were born with a head full of beautiful hair.

Gwen absently grabbed a lock of hair and curled it around her finger as she read the explanation. The missing pieces falling into place after so long and so many questions.

By the time you read this, the barrier may be weakening. While your power never gets used up, Helen's will. The barrier will fade, and all magic will die. The land will be barren; the commoner will starve. Unless you fulfill the contract. Rumpel's magic is taking power away. Your ability is to give power. There is an imbalance. Already I've seen the signs. Our barrier is blocking the curse, but it's killing other lands. If Rumpel's magic can't take power from magic users, it will take it from the land. It will take and take and if it doesn't find magic, it will take whatever it can find. I believe Rumpel kept the taking under control, but when he died, there was no one left to control it.

"What can I do about it? I'm just a Miller's daughter. I have no power in this world," she responded as if she were sitting across the table from her mother rather than being separated by the impossible span of time.

11

There must be a balance. A new Goblin King will arise. Rumpel's son, though I don't know who he is. "His name is Aurius, Mother," she whispered in answer. *The only way to satisfy the taking, the reason for the contract, is to marry and produce an heir. It is a dreadful position I've put you in. A perfect balance between the catalyst and the reagent. It is a sacrifice. But it could mean the death of all things if this doesn't happen. By the time you read this, you may have found a better solution, or a way to break the contract. If not, I hope for your resilience.*

Gwen placed the letter flat against the wood of the table. Her chair screeched as it scraped against the floor. She crossed to the water basin under the window. The contraption there allowed water to flow freely into the bowl. She stuck a glass under the flowing water and brought it to her lips. It was crisp and cold as if it flowed directly from the spring underground. She wouldn't be surprised if it were. A few weeks ago she would have given anything to be standing in front of a contraption such as this.

After clearing her mind, she steadied herself to return to her mother's words. Aurius wouldn't have left them for her if they didn't come from her mother. Her body lowered onto the chair. She took a deep breath into her lungs, preparing herself for the rest of the letter.

I don't know who you can trust. Helen seems nice enough, but if I had had another choice, I wouldn't have put her on the throne. She was keen to make this suggestion, and we needed her power. I wish I were there to train you in court politics and intrigues. But we must flee this place. Helen knows your power, and she will seek you out soon. Magic users covet the catalyst powers. Once they've used it, they crave it.

She may even take you from me. It is what your father feared. While no one can force you to use magic, she could manipulate you into it. But it would cost all the other lands dearly. Allowing Rumpel's magic to take while we prosper. It is all that we can do until the new Goblin King reveals himself. I fear that day for you, but you must be strong.

Gwen stood again, pulling the letter with her. She paced between the kitchen and living areas, absently wandering about the house as she read.

My thoughts are all over the place. But I have to get you out of Mystrim, protect you, and give you time for a normal life. The miller has agreed to take us in.

Aurum, the curse, will probably drain my magic. But I have to sacrifice this for you. If nothing else, it is my penance. I have had a token created for you. It will protect you from many things. But mostly it will hide your power so that no one knows who you are and protect you from the curse while you live in Aurum.

Once you return, you will be safe here in this cottage. It is a haven for you. Hidden. No one will know of it. But don't linger long. Be the leader I know you are. Do what I could not. You are more powerful than I could ever be.

I love you, sweet girl.

Forever and Always,

Mother, Queen Liora of Mystrim, 4th Degree Catalyst

Gwen slid to the dusty floor, folded her head into her hands and wept. Until this moment, she hadn't realized how much she missed her mother. A gaping hole widened inside her. Tears soaked her blouse. The letter only highlighted her mother's absence. She hadn't given herself the luxury of wishing for her mother. That required energy. Until this moment, she had needed all that energy for survival.

Her fingers curled around the dusty letter, wanting to crush it. Instead, she tossed it away from her with a sob. Immediately, she wanted it back, but she restrained herself. Wrapping her hands around her upper arms, she gently rocked. "It's just a letter," she told herself. But it wasn't just a letter; it was her mother's letter to her. Her mother, the Queen of Mystrim.

Gwen lifted herself from the floor and pulled her lip between her thumb and finger. Her mind whirled with all the information her mother had dumped on her in a single piece of parchment. Helen had wanted her to save Mystrim by marrying Aurius. Her mother wanted her to save two kingdoms by marrying Aurius. "Couldn't you have told me any of this? Clues, notes, anything." Her riding boots tapped against the hardwood floor, toward the basin in the kitchen. She watched a blue bird building a nest just outside the window. Turning her back on the scene, she rested against the counter and stared down at the letter again.

"And Papa... he's got a lot of explaining to do. How could he have let this slip at a tavern? Drake was right. Why would he let us live in squalor?" She said to the empty room.

She pulled the coin out of her pocket and cast it onto the floor. "Aurius, I have a question."

The wispy, transparent version of Aurius popped out of the coin. "Your wish is my command." He grinned, looking more handsome than he had a right to. It's not actually Aurius, she reminded herself.

"Why the scowl?"

Gwen lifted an eyebrow.

"Oh, you must have found the letter."

"Yes. Did you know the locket protected me from illness and hid my magic?"

"I tinkered with it a bit. I had my suspicions something was blocking us from finding you. I did not know until after you bargained it away. But it was convenient. I wouldn't have been able to spin the gold as well without your catalyst magic and the locket would have prevented it from working."

"It also would have kept me from dying."

Transparent Aurius's eyes darkened. "I kept you from dying."

Gwen rolled her eyes.

"You have the locket back now. No harm done," he said.

She lowered her voice and narrowed her eyes. "I wouldn't be here if you hadn't taken it."

"First. *Princess*, you bargained it. Second, you wouldn't be here, because you would be dead."

"And you would be free of the contract."

"I will never be free." His voice fell, laced with sadness.

A tear slipped down Gwen's cheek. How had this weight become hers to bear?

"It's a terrible burden, Gwen. I know it is." Aurius looked around the cottage, hands raised, palms out. "This place is your refuge. Take some time. Nothing has to be decided in the next two minutes."

"My mother wanted me to marry you. In her letter. She said it was the only way to stop the curse."

Aurius raised an eyebrow. "And what do you want?"

It was a question no one had asked her before. But one she didn't have an answer. Her fingers went to either side of her forehead, and she breathed in a lungful of cleansing air. Despite the dust, the air smelled sweet inside the cottage.

"How long do I have before I have to figure this out?" she asked.

He shrugged. "A few days, probably."

She wiped the tears off her cheeks and then dried her hands on her dress. "How long to save you?"

Aurius scowled. "I can't be saved."

"You've given up?"

"The goblin will take over soon. If you are communicating with me like this, it's too late for me."

"Is your father's magic draining Aurum?'

Aurius shook his head. "I've never heard of goblin magic doing such things. But…" He looked about the room as if he were standing in it and not just a magical hologram. "My father was special in his own way. No goblin has ever been swallowed by the earth because a bargain didn't go the way he planned. He didn't do things in any usual way so, I can't say it is or not."

Gwen swallowed the lump in her throat. "Queen Helen believes our marriage can save you."

"She's mistaken."

"What will save you?"

Aurius looked away from her. "Nothing." His image blinked out. Only the golden coin remained on the floor.

Gwen rolled her eyes. Even Aurius's magical persona was exasperating. "Of course he can still just shut down conversations that make him uncomfortable." She blew a golden curl out of her face and rested her elbows on her knees. "I'm not letting him give up." She stood from her spot on the floor. "Maybe there's something here that will help him."

She scanned the cottage, carefully avoiding the letter in the center of the room.

That conversation hadn't made her feel better at all. Everyone in Mystrim seemed to want her to marry Aurius, including her dead mother, who didn't even know him. Everyone except Aurius. He had escaped to who knew where to turn into the Goblin King without her. "What would it be like to be married to the Goblin King?" she wondered softly. Maybe it wouldn't be so bad. The chronicles made them seem gallant and benevolent. Everyone else feared the goblins, even hunted them to extinction. Maybe the trick would be keeping him from becoming the Goblin King.

She shook the thought away, continuing her scan of the cabin from her spot between the kitchen and living space. How could she accomplish anything if she didn't know where he was?

Trinkets covered the walls and every available flat surface, giving the cottage a cozy ambiance. Her steps echoed throughout the cottage as Gwen crossed the space and closed the curtains in the living area. The light in the cabin dimmed slightly. Lamps flickered on without a thought, bringing a smile to her lips. "Now that's practical magic." She closed the door and twisted the cold metal lock, then tiptoed back to the middle of the cottage.

There was nothing in the room that would help her find Aurius. Nothing stood out that would prevent his destiny from becoming the Goblin King or hers from marrying him.

She tapped her finger on her chin. "Maybe my magic could save everyone if I knew how to use it."

Sitting at the kitchen table, she lifted the delicate chain over her head. Immediately, she felt the difference, lifting her shoulders with a deep breath. She hadn't noticed until now, but it had almost always felt as if she were trudging through a muddy pond in thirteen skirts with a bushel of wheat on her shoulders.

Gwen's magic tingled, coming alive within her again. Until this moment, she hadn't realized she missed the buzz since Aurius had given back the locket. She rolled her hand over and held her palm up, thinking of one trinket on the mantel above the fire. The tiny statue of a horse.

She focused every ounce of her attention on it.

It mocked her from its place over the hearth. Tiny and weighing less than an ounce, and yet she could not move it. Her face strained with the effort.

Her breath rushed from her lungs. She hadn't realized she wasn't breathing until she remembered to do it again. Still, the miniature horse sat across the room. A tiny little smirk on its face.

"Maybe I was wrong about the book, then." Slumping in her chair, she glared across the room. If only one thing could work. She focused her will and intent again on the tiny horse again. The items on the table jumped when she slammed her hands against it, standing in frustration.

"Why can't I do this again?" Her hands found her hips as she paced. "I know I can do this. I need someone to train me." She squeezed her forehead. "But there isn't time for that now. Isn't this supposed to be innate? A part of who I am?"

She held out her palm. The magic danced just below the surface of her skin. She could feel it wanting to break from the prison of her body and spring out through the cabin. Allowing the magic out, controlling it, she didn't know how to do.

Instead, she stomped over to the mantel and plucked the trinket from its resting place. She wanted to throw it across the room, but she restrained her frustration, allowing it to rest in her palm for a few moments. It was cool against her skin. The moment it touched her hand, memories flashed in her mind.

Her mother playing with her in the living area. Gwen was sitting on the floor. Her mother cooed over her and played with the little horse. *"You had a horse like this at the palace. We called her Lady. She was so gentle."*

The memory ended. Air whooshed in and out of Gwen's lungs. A single tear traced its way down her cheek. Triggered by the forgotten sound of her mother's voice.

The sharp edges of the porcelain embedded in her skin. She released her fist one finger at a time and placed the tiny horse on the table next to her mother's letter, with a little tink.

Gwen looked over her shoulder, immediately eyeing other trinkets on the mantle. A giant tooth stood out among them.

Trinkets

The princess jumped over a log in the woods and raced along a stream. Her dress snagged on a notch in the log, halting her escape. She tugged furiously at the fabric, trying to release it from the snare. There was no time to reach for the dagger in her boot.

The ground beneath her feet shook. Once. Twice. Darkness shrouded her as she looked up at the beast standing over her. A scream escaped unbidden. She tugged again at the fabric, but a giant meaty hand swept down upon her. Her feet dangled back and forth, kicking against the air that suddenly filled the space below her feet. As she was being lifted into the air, she struggled against the enormous chartreuse fingers that held her, stabbing the troll with her sharp fists.

"Put me down, you overgrown meathead," she screamed at the troll, beating against his fingers wrapped around her.

"No." It was a simple answer from a simple beast. "You took food."

"I did not take it. I released it," she screamed.

"My food," the troll yelled back. Bits of mucus covered gunk drenched her face and hair.

She scrunched her face and wiped her hands over it. "Perhaps I should have told you first, but you can't just go around stealing farmer's sheep." She continued to struggle in the giant fingers of the troll.

"I eat you." His fingers tightened around her. Her breath forced itself through her lips.

She squirmed, struggling to pull breath into her lungs. "Let's not be too hasty. I'm sure we can come to another arrangement."

A giant, muck-brown eye loomed before her. "No. You look yummy."

"No doubt that I am, but I'd like to live to see a few more sunrises." She hit the troll with her fists, which were tiny in comparison to his, a few more times. He lifted her to his gaping jaw. She gagged at the smell. Bits of his last meal still clung to his teeth. That was going to be her in a few seconds.

Her feet wiggled back and forth as she dangled above his mottled tongue. She waved her arms trying to break free from his grasp. If she could twist just enough, she would avoid his mouth and make her escape.

Suddenly, she was falling. The troll's jaw moved from under her. His fingers clutched her apron, holding tight and taking her with him as he tumbled. He crashed through the trees and bushes. A dust plume rose into the air, covering the nearby foliage.

The princess wiggled herself out of the troll's now limp hand. His eyes were closed. He wasn't moving. An enormous arrow protruded from his back.

She stepped away from the beast. Too late, she heard hoofbeats. She had wanted this to be a simple in and out operation. Now she would have to face an inquiry at the nearby castle. She had a desperate urge to roll her eyes at the inconvenience, but her relief at being alive wouldn't allow it.

A man appeared silhouetted against the sun. "Are you alright miss?" he asked as he dismounted from his horse. His armor clanked with the movement.

"My neck isn't broken, if that's what you're asking." She moved her head from side to side for good measure. With a twist of her hair, green gunk plopped onto the ground.

"I was inquiring about your health due to being captured by a cave troll," he said, gesturing behind her, unaffected by the state of her dress. She continued to clean herself up. If she were going to have to present herself to their nearby royals, she had best try to look presentable.

She looked over her shoulder at the likely dead troll. "I had it under control," she said, re-braiding her hair into a long golden plait.

The prince removed his helmet and raised an eyebrow. "He was about to eat you."

"As I said, it was under control." She stomped away from both the man and the troll, bending to pick up the scarf she had lost in the tussle.

"I had rather thought you would thank me for saving your life." She wrapped

19

the scarf around her head and tucked her braid underneath.

"I don't thank pompous princes," she sneered. Pulling a knife from her apron, she bent toward the troll's gaping mouth. The front incisor wiggled back and forth easily. "Perhaps that was why you wanted an easy meal," she whispered and plucked the tooth from between its lips. She stood, wiped the tooth with her apron and tossed it to the prince. "You slayed the beast, so you get the trophy."

He caught it, bowed low. "I am but a humble servant to fair maidens in need of rescue. We don't normally take trophies, but I will accept it as a gift from the rescued maiden."

Her eyes shifted. "I think you misjudged the situation."

"You were dangling over his mouth." The droning tone of his voice suggested he didn't believe her.

"I had him right where I wanted him." She turned and took a few steps away from the prince.

"Then my apologies for impeding your quest by rescuing you."

She stopped, twisted her head to look over her shoulder, and narrowed her eyes. It was the first look she had taken at his face. She didn't let his handsome features persuade her to give him an inch. "What did you just say?"

A smirk crossed his lips. "Join me at the castle and I will repeat it."

She stomped toward the prince, with a finger pointed at him. "You will not repeat that to anyone at anytime."

His smile broadened. "Fine. Join me at the castle, and I will not repeat it. Say midday tomorrow? That will give you some time to be presentable to my father the king."

She rolled her eyes and let out a heavy breath.

He stepped closer to her and leaned in. His voice became a gravelly whisper. "But if you do not show up at this agreed-upon time, I will indeed repeat that I rescued the Rogue Princess, far and wide." He stepped back. The princess's eyes narrowed. "Your reputation would take a hit, I think."

She crossed her arms over her chest and ground her teeth as the prince strutted back to his horse. "I'll see you tomorrow at noon," he said as he swung his armored leg over the white stallion.

Gwen released the tooth, allowing it to tumble to the floor. It clattered along the boards. The memory faded. "That was extreme." She took a few deep breaths to clear the anxiety from her body. Gwen recognized the woman as Liora, her mother. If she were alive today, people might confuse them. She had been sorely mistaken to compare herself at all the Queen Helen. The prince she assumed was King Nolan.

She shook her head, trying to clear away the memory. Gripping the wall to keep from falling over. The effect of the memory was quickly fading, but it was going to be difficult navigating the cabin. Anything she touched could hold a memory. They were intense, as if she lived in those moments herself.

Her hand still gripped the mantel. She hardly remembered touching the tooth she could only assume had come from the cave troll. Absentmindedly, she wiped her hand on her skirt. And glanced at the offending object on the floor. After the effects of the memory wore off, she found she longed for more. Information about her parents and her lost past lured her into memory after memory. Filling in blanks. Holes in her heart that she hadn't realized existed. The more she got, the more she wanted. As if the memories had woken the beast of longing, which was never satisfied. She filled the rest of the morning absorbing the memories from the trinkets her mother saved for her, learning everything she could about her parents and the life she never got to live.

Plotting

Helen tapped the curved handles of her chair. The craftsman had styled them to resemble the talons of an eagle. This chair was her brother's favorite. She'd trained herself to ignore the hard edge where the cushion had worn away, so she avoided shifting to give herself some relief. "It seems she has made her choice," she said to the footmen, who bowed before her.

The footman lifted themselves after being addressed. "We left her in the forest ma'am as instructed."

The queen pulled in a heavy breath. "You were instructed to take her where she asked to go."

His eyes shifted to his partner beside him, who had resigned to keep his lips sealed. That was probably wise. But the queen demanded an answer, so someone must speak. "It was as far as the horses would allow. It seemed there was an invisible wall they couldn't cross." The muscle in his thigh twitched, and it took all of his training to keep from taking a step back. The queen narrowed her eyes toward him, delighting in his nervous energy.

She tapped the arm of her chair with her long manicured nails. "There has to be more there," she said. The footman looked about the room, unsure what to do or say next. Looking for a lifeline. The queen herself gave him his rescue, waving a dismissive hand. "You may leave, Andre."

He bowed again without a word.

King Aric appeared beside her when the footmen vacated the room. "So what of our wager?" His pointed tongue slithered over his lips.

Queen Helen sighed at his troublesome presence. Doubly exasperated by his question. "It hasn't played out yet. She hasn't truly made her choice."

"I am growing tired of these games, Helen," he said.

She remained still, though she wanted to slouch into her chair and rub her head. The dull ache grew between her shoulder blades, up the back of her neck and into her temples. It was a familiar ache from a rigid posture. "Then return to your kingdom and let's see how that goes for you. But remember you can only pass through the barrier because I allow it." Only her eyes followed his movement toward the wall on her right. Though his form had filled out in the last couple of years, he still had a stature that allowed a swagger. His movements were slow and graceful, as if he were not merely invited, but belonged.

The king raised an eyebrow and poured a drink from the refreshments table. "We had an agreement," he said, swirling the liquid around.

Helen allowed herself a head tilt and narrowed her eyes. "It might be time to renegotiate," she said.

The king sipped from his crystal glass. He winced as the liquid slid down his throat. "You have plundered my kingdom for twenty years. And now when my payment is in hand you want to renegotiate." He drained the glass and poured another.

Helen stopped her hands from gripping the wooden arms of her brother's throne. "You've squandered the penance I've given you. Payment to the people for their plight and now you've allowed Ryland to raise an army against me."

His lips pulled into a half-smile. "I have the boy well in hand, but its best you remember what might happen should the barrier fall."

Helen didn't grind her teeth, though she wanted to. Instead, she waved a dismissive hand. A few quick seconds later, a black bird the size of her forearm perched on the open windowsill. Its wings beat the air in a chaotic rhythm as it hopped from the sill to the perching stand beside the throne. The queen's fingers stroked lazy circles around the raven's head. "Relax King Aric, I won't betray you now. I'll send someone to look in on her. Perhaps they'll encourage her along in her choice."

"And what of the goblin? If she doesn't choose him and she chooses Ryland.

Their heir will belong to him?"

"The contract was a surprise to me, but my scholars have discovered a possible way to break it. You should probably hope she doesn't choose your stepson. Otherwise the goblin will have rights to your grandchild." Already Aurius seemed dead to her. There was little hope Gwen would arrive in time to prevent the transformation.

The king swirled the liquid in his glass again, peering into the bottom as if it were the only thing that interested him. "How do you break a blood contract with a goblin?" he asked.

Her fingers continued their lazy strokes on the bird's head. She watched her fingers follow the path of the silky feathers. She didn't move her head to answer his question but met his gaze with a sideways glance and a half-smile of her own. "There are a few ways. One is the death of the goblin, but the contract passes to any living goblins until the terms are met. And there's no way of knowing if he really is the last. If there are others, they may be worse."

"Don't kill the goblin. Message received."

"There may be an object that will nullify the contract."

He took another sip, turned from the queen and refilled his drink with slow, methodical movements. "Do you know where the object is?"

The bird hopped back onto its perch. "We had assumed it was hidden among Aurius's things. We're searching."

"See that you find it," he growled.

"Another option is to renegotiate the terms. Are you ready to fold?"

He shook his head. "The wager doesn't matter. Either way I win."

The queen pulled her lips back into a flat smile that didn't reach her eyes. "Those are always the best bets."

The king tipped his glass into his mouth until its contents were empty. The glass clinked loudly against the marble table. "Get this over with Helen. I have better things to do."

He walked through her suite and stepped behind a marble statue. Exiting through a passage hidden by the sculpture.

Helen's knuckles whitened as her grip tightened on the chair under her. She met the raven's black, beady eye. Her thoughts and will pressed upon his until his wings fluttered and sent his body back to the windowsill.

"If you find it, bring it to me," Helen commanded, reinforcing the silent instructions she had given him moments before.

The raven gave one loud caw as it pitched itself off the window and flew south.

Helen relaxed against the back of the throne and brought her hand to her eyes. A moment was all she needed, just a moment to catch her breath. When she opened her eyes again, the light had faded from the room. Had it been hours? Her back became rigid again. "Was it a mistake to let her go?" She looked down at her shaking hands. Power danced below the surface. "More," it whispered. "You are fading. We need more."

Helen ignored the whispers as she had thousands of times. It was always the same. Her constant companion for over twenty years. Until recently, the whispers hadn't bothered her. She learned to live with the quiet taunts until the catalyst was so close. They recognized her niece, and the magic she hid. It became impossible and exhausting to drown their voices. So she did the next best thing. Sending Gwen away infuriated the voices. But not even the voices in her veins were strong enough to interfere with her plans.

Memories

"I need clues about magic and how to save Aurius," Gwen said to the trinkets in the room.

She stooped to retrieve the preserved tooth, gripping it with only the tips of her forefinger and thumb. "Perhaps it has some kind of enchantment to keep it from decaying," she said. Her head tilted toward her shoulder as she examined the artifact. It didn't pull her back into the memory when she touched it. "A warning might have been nice," she said to the tooth.

She placed the tooth on the mantel where she had found it. Curiosity had gotten the better of her, and now that she knew anything could hold a memory, she would be more careful. She picked up the horse trinket again. No unwanted memories assaulted her. "Hmm. They must only work once." The items she had touched appeared dull now, next to other items on the mantel.

"I see the enchantments now," she whispered. The golden shimmer she had seen in Aurius's suite was now obvious on the trinkets around the cottage. There were so many objects and so much magic that Gwen hadn't noticed it before.

She released a heavy breath. "At least now I can choose the objects I want to remember. I don't have to worry about every little thing pulling into a memory."

She slumped at the thought of the lifetime of memories that surrounded her, exhausted and grateful simultaneously. "This is going to be a long day. I'll need to start a fire."

As she spoke the words, the hearth whooshed with a blaze. Gwen yelped as she jumped away from the flames. With a hand over her heart, a giggle escaped as she realized she was okay. "A hearth that lights on its own with a spoken word." She shook her head. "How have I ever survived without magic?" She silently thanked Aurius for thinking of the most mundane things.

"What of food? Will that simply appear as well?"

She waited for a cauldron to bubble, or a plate to appear on the table. Nothing of the sort happened. Gwen reached for the coin that contained Aurius's likeness. As her fingertips touched it, she pulled back. "I'll figure it out on my own, later," she whispered. "I can't rely on him for everything."

* * *

Gwen heard wings flapping coming from the kitchen area. She tilted her head around the corner to investigate the sound, not realizing the shutters of the window over the kitchen basin had blown open. A crow the size of a chicken perched on the sill.

"What do you want?" Gwen asked.

The bird turned its head sharply, the way birds do, in response. A rapid blink. A hop. Another head tilt. As if Gwen could read its mind.

"I'm looking for food myself. So if you think I have any you can move on. I don't."

The bird hopped, turning its body in the other direction. "Oh. Don't be like that. If I find it I'll leave some out for you."

She stroked its silky black feathers that gleamed a dark blue and green when the light hit it just right. "We could make a pact. If you find food you could bring some to me."

Gwen poured some water for the bird into a shallow bowl she found in the cabinet. The bird hopped to the liquid, stuck its beak in and lapped it up. After a second, it tilted its head back and allowed the water to slide down its throat. Then, repeated the process.

"I hope that helps. I'll just continue my search for that food I told you about. Make yourself at home, but please do your business outside."

Gwen searched through the cabinets around the cottage looking for anything edible. If she found nothing, she would have to forage in the forest soon. She released the door of a cabinet near the hearth, jumping back as it folded down into a desk.

As her heart rate slowed and nothing else seemed to jump out at her, she took a step toward the desk. Parchment, inkwells, and quills lined the shelf. One thing stood out among the other items. A golden quill. It shimmered with magic. Though she knew she shouldn't touch it, she couldn't help it. Her fingertips brushed the soft, blade-shaped feather.

Gwen's eyes fluttered closed as another memory assaulted her.

Rumpelstiltskin pulled several instruments from thin air and laid them on a small table in front of the queen. It was fortunate her husband had allowed a small kindness in giving her space and light to write by.

The lid of the jar scraped against the glass as Rumpel removed it. Then he selected a small silver knife. It glinted in the lamplight as the goblin inspected the blade. Once he was satisfied, his lips pulled away from his elongated incisors and he unfurled his knobby fingers. The queen was reluctant to place her hand in his. As she did, his yellow pointed claws wrapped around hers, extending her arm toward him. His hands, though, were unexpectedly soft.

The queen gasped as Rumpel slid the blade over the skin of her finger. Deep red blood rose through the cut. He wrapped his green, knobby fingers around her wrist and pulled it to the jar. Her body jerked forward. Squeezing her finger over the opening, he captured the drops of precious liquid in the amber glass.

"If I sign this contract you will take my first born child?"

"Well yes," Rumpel made it sound as if it was the most natural thing in the world to give up a child.

"And if I never have children?"

"Then you have nothing to worry about." His words were quiet.

"I won't be in breech of contract?"

"No. The risk is all mine it seems. I will warn you though, often what we think is impossible tends to become possible and with the worst timing."

Queen Liora lifted her chin. "This is the consequence of magic."

Rumpel pursed his lips and shook his head. "This is the consequence of power."

"It's the same thing."

Rumpel smiled. "Now you get it."

The queen sighed and took the quill, dipping it in the thick, dark red mixture of her blood and the goblin's blood.

As the quill scraped across the parchment, the liquid sparkled with gold, which was absorbed into the paper. By the time Queen Liora's finished her name, the magic set.

Rumpelstiltskin stood by, giggling in that cruel little way of his. He snatched the contract away, wrapped his fingers around it one by one, and opened them again. When his palm was flat, the contract was gone, and Liora couldn't tell where it had gone.

Queen Liora plucked a hair from her head and handed it to the Goblin King. "Your end of the bargain," she implored.

Rumpel flipped his coattails behind him and lowered himself onto the stool at the spinning wheel. He fed her hair through the spools a third time. Liora hoped it was the last. She had nothing left to bargain. She bargained all she had, and some of what she didn't have. The wheel whirred to life as Rumpelstiltskin fed the machine the straw on the floor. Passing through the maidens, it stretched into a golden thread.

Liora sighed her relief that the task was being accomplished and sat on the wooden footstool near the bars of her cell. Freedom was a breath away. But it had cost her everything. Her delicate fingers gripped the cold iron bars. Was it worth it? "Only if I never have a child," she whispered, leaning her head in the space between metal rods.

Gwen stumbled away from the desk and wrapped her hand around her abdomen. "Ugh, I need a drink."

She laid the quill back with the others and curled her fingers around the bottom of the desk to close it. The raven, which had been watching closely, glided across the room, snatched the quill in its beak and flapped back to the windowsill. Gwen swiped her hands at the bird, but it easily avoided her flailing arms. Perching for a few seconds, it took one long glance back.

Gwen turned toward the kitchen, her hands spread to her sides. "Look, I know ravens like to collect things. But you can't have that." The raven didn't release the quill from its beak, but it didn't fly away either, so Gwen continued to reason with it.

"I'll give you another quill. Any other really, but please just let me have that one."

Gwen took a step toward the little beast. "It was my mother's... sort of. And I'd like to keep it." Another step. The raven turned toward the forest and crouched. Gwen raced toward the window, arms out to snatch the bird. Wings spread and the bird flapped away into the sky. Gwen watched it for as long as she could, hoping it would drop the quill. But the black bird disappeared into the noonday sun moments later.

She lifted her hands to her forehead. "Well that's that I suppose." She turned to lean on the counter, noticing for the first time that food had finally appeared. Dread built in her belly, quelling her appetite. She couldn't help thinking the quill was important beyond the memory.

Berries, pecans, and cream spread out by some magical force, ready to be eaten. Determined to put the bird incident behind her, she pulled another bowl from the cabinet. Careful not to touch things with gold shimmers, she scooped the food into it. In the drawer, near the bowls, were silver spoons. The berries burst with sweetness over her tongue. She groaned quietly and added more to her mouth. The food soothed the ache from the battle she had just lost with the bird and the memory she saw. Her mother signing her life away.

"Actually, I'm glad that bird took the quill. I never want to see it again." She buried the dread.

When her belly was finally satisfied, she began her exploration anew, seeking the memories the cottage held. Her eyes landed on a rose in a vase beside the sofa, carefully tucked into a shadow. It shimmered as other artifacts had. It wasn't an old memory from her mother, though. She knew that rose and that vase. Aurius placed it on her tray when she was recovering from the assassination attempt. She shook her head and stepped away. That was the kind of memory she needed to avoid for now.

She explored the cottage and found that it had several rooms. A sitting room, living room, and kitchen on the first floor. Four bedrooms upstairs down a single hallway. The porch spanned the length of the front of the house. Most of the shimmering trinkets were on the lower floors.

Another interesting trinket caught her eye. A wooden carving of a throne on the bookshelf. She extended her body to the tip of her toes. Still, she barely brushed the item with her fingertips. Her tongue darted out as she concentrated on her task. Another little stretch and it tilted off the shelf and fell toward her face. She caught it before it caused permanent damage.

As her fingers touched the wooden legs of the figurine, the memory began.

The king twirled his hand. Roses, chrysanthemums, and hydrangeas grew from the ground. All for the princess who stood in the middle of the courtyard. Her arms crossed over her chest, and a frown on her lips.

"If you think you can impress me with magic you are sorely mistaken." Liora pressed her nose into the air.

"I'm not trying to impress you with magic. I'm trying to impress you with flowers," he said.

"Oh?" Liora shifted her body slightly but still held her shoulders away from the king.

"Are you impressed now?"

She laughed. "You think three flowers will impress me? No. I think I would require a whole garden."

"Is that so?"

"Yes. But I haven't time to wait. I'm late for an appointment." She gathered her skirt and swished back to the door.

The king laughed. A deep, amused sound. "Who would keep you from my company and I shall have a word with them?"

"You can barely expect me to say after that threat."

The king skipped in front of her and grabbed her hand, bringing it to her lips. "Very well. I'll let you go. We'll meet again tomorrow and you'll have your garden."

Liora lifted her chin. "We'll see."

The memory shifted. *Liora sat on a garden bench reading a book. The garden had grown into a magical forest. It was a constant, perfect temperature, not too warm, not too cool. There were splashes of color in every direction. A brook trickled in the background. Liora lowered her book to watch a leaf float on the water, twist*

31

around a small river rock, and continue its trek down the stream.

"Are you impressed yet?"

Liora jumped, startled at the sound of his voice. The one that caused her stomach to flutter. Her hand pressed over her heart, forcing it to calm down. She lifted her chin as if he didn't affect her.

"The only thing that impresses me is your willingness to fling magic around like confetti. Some of us weren't born with magic and we have to make do with what we have."

"Some of us must use magic to be impressive. We can't all be like you. You don't need magic to impress anyone. You are magic."

The book in Liora's hand slapped closed as pressed it between her fingers. She sighed. "Very well. Since it seems I cannot frighten you, disgust you, or will you away. I suppose I'll let you call upon my father and ask for my company from time to time."

The king's lips parted into a wide smile. "Liora you honor me with your affirmation!"

"Don't let it go to your head."

The image shifted once again.

Queen Liora's mouth rounded in a scream while a lady behind her begged her to push once more. Her hand squeezed the king's. Sweat dripped from her chin. Her cries were joined by smaller screams as a new life entered the world. Another woman placed the baby in Queen Liora's arms.

"What's her name?" she asked.

"Princess Gwendolyn Marie of Mystrim," Liora said.

King Nolan beamed as he knelt beside the birthing bed. He wiped his wife's sweaty brow and kissed her on the top of the head. King Nolan smiled down at their new family member. "A beautiful name for a beautiful daughter," he said. Liora's smile faded as she watched her husband fawn over their daughter, not knowing when Rumpelstiltskin would return to claim her firstborn.

The memory faded. Gwen put the tiny throne back on a lower shelf and stared into the corner. "Princess Gwendolyn of Mystrim." Her name came with a purpose and a price, one she had been paying since the day she was born.

Princess Gwen

Gwen ran her hands through her hair and squeezed the base, tugging slightly. The silky strands slid through the creases of her fingers. "I'm just a miller's daughter. I'm not a princess." The chant became her mantra. Over and over, she said the words to herself until her brain remembered her place in the world. That place was not the throne.

Until recently, her place had been in a cottage a tenth the size of the one where she now stood. Loneliness had been her constant companion. Aurius had been her protector for a few days until the elf ball, and there was Avonlea before the assassination attempt. Their absence pressed on her heart as if it were a physical weight.

Aurius had said to take some time. She stood and paced in front of the sofa, nibbling on her left thumb. Urgency bubbled in her belly.

The sofa beside the door filled the wall with soft tufted cushions. Not typical of a cottage. Normally, there might be a bench and some wicker chairs for seating. Gwen lowered herself onto the cushion nearest the door and slouched against the back.

Perhaps a book would help.

There were a few books on the shelf near the staircase. Nothing like the library in Mystrim, of course. That library would take up the entire house. But there might be a few books that could help her relax.

She tilted her to the left as she read the titles. *History of Mystrim, Princesses of the Courts, Court Etiquette, Suitable Suitors.* She sighed. These were great for princesses. Certainly, Queen Liora had provided these books to a daughter who would need to learn princess things. They were useless to her.

She turned to move upstairs and explore the rest of the cottage, but an item in the kitchen caught her eye.

It wasn't out of place exactly, but it didn't belong in this cottage. There was no way it could be here. Her feet carried her to the counter near the hearth. She lifted the cup, cradling it in her palms. No magic was needed for memories to flood her mind. This little silver cup was the very one she held at the fairy ball only a short while ago.

Her hand trembled, and she placed it back on the counter, backing away from it as if it held all the secrets of her past. How did it get into this cottage? There was only one answer. Aurius had to have brought it here. It had to be here for a reason.

She forgot to breathe. Something told her there was more to her memory loss that night than the fairy wine. A flash of memory invaded her mind. The cup was back in her hand in a moment, then she was transported back to the fairy ball. An outsider this time looking in. The edges were blurry, as if it were a dream.

Aurius walked away with the Elf King, disappearing into the shadows under the balcony. She exited the dance floor, not wanting to give the impression that she was available.

She pressed her back against a wall, and the cup was handed to her. She took it with a polite smile. The music swayed over her. The intensity of the music had died, and so her heart had stopped its racing beat. She told herself it was the music that caused the palpitations and not the dark prince. Her throat was parched from the excitement of the dance and meeting the Elf King. She sniffed the liquid inside. It seemed innocent enough; one sip wouldn't hurt.

A petite young elf marched to her.

"You are Aurius's betrothed?" The music stopped, and every elf eye turned in their direction.

Gwen shifted her eyes from side to side, searching for an escape or support. But she was alone and out of her element.

"We are contractually obligated to be wed. So I guess," Gwen stammered.

Gwen held out her hand to the elf. "Gwen Miller of..." She didn't even know who she was anymore.

The elf slapped her hand away.

"Elora, you are behaving poorly," Elanil said from behind them. Her head was held high on an elongated neck. She whispered, but firmly.

"Aurius is mine," Elora insisted.

"He is not and Gwen is under Aurius's protection. If you hurt her, you will suffer consequences you cannot bare."

Elora's voice was shaking. "We had an agreement. If neither us were married before our twenty fifth birthday we would marry each other."

"That's ridiculous. You know what happens when he turns twenty four in a few days?" Elanil said.

Gwen wanted to reassure the elf. "I'm sure it will work out. He's talking to the king right now about breaking the contract."

Elora scoffed. "Aurius clearly loves you."

"I don't think it is clear at all," Gwen said, peering into the drink in her hand.

"My brother can't break goblin contracts. And yet Aurius is willing to bargain with him to do so. FOR YOU." She screamed the last two words. Gwen covered one side of her head with her free hand to protect her hearing.

Elanil put a comforting arm around Elora, steering her away from Gwen. "It's ok. We'll find you someone to marry. And you won't have to be married to the dark prince," Gwen heard them say as they shuffled away. Sobs echoed through the dance hall. The elf princesses disappeared around a corner, and soft music began playing again. Everyone went back to their conversation ignoring the human under the balcony.

Gwen lifted the cup to lips again and gulped the liquid inside. "What's so bad about being married to the dark prince?" she whispered into the cup. The liquid tingled as it slipped over her tongue. Warmth spread over her chest, and her arms and legs felt looser.

Another girl approached her, splitting away from a group of young elves. "That was a close one... I thought she was going to turn you into a toad."

Gwen's eyebrows lifted into her hairline.

The group of she-elves giggled. Gwen could only tell them apart by the color of their hair. Silver, purple, pink, blue, green.

"That's something she could do?" she asked.

The elf nodded. *"You're lucky the Prince is here to protect you or you might be spending a day or two on a lily pad."*

Gwen shuddered. *"I'm not sure luck has anything to do with it. Bad luck seems to be my fortune."*

Another of the girls chimed in. *"The dark prince only has eyes for you. I'd call that lucky."*

She giggled. She didn't know why. The statement wasn't all that funny.

"The dark prince is far more concerned..." Gwen paused because she couldn't think of anything Aurius had been more concerned about.

The elf with purple hair chimed in, *"Betrothed or not it's obvious he is at least infatuated with you."*

Gwen protested. *"But I'm just a miller's daughter."*

"Oh? I heard you were a princess," Green Hair said.

"Well I might be... It's... complicated." Trying to explain the mess she was in was not as easy as it seemed in her head.

"How about some more wine?" Violet liquid flowed out of the pitcher that appeared in the elf's hand. Once her cup was filled, the pitcher disappeared again. *"Tell us about the dark prince."* The group closed in around her.

Gwen took the drink gladly, though something niggled at the back of her mind that she shouldn't. Unable to recall, she shrugged and sipped the bubbly liquid at the edge of the cup.

"There isn't much to tell. He doesn't seem dark to me," she said.

Another elf with silver hair pressed in. *"That's pretty telling. To everyone else he is terrifying."*

Gwen shook her head. *"He isn't. He's kind and gentle."*

"But he can travel through shadows," Blue Hair said.

"Oh yes, but that isn't terrifying."

"You are strange, Gwen Miller," Silver Hair commented.

Gwen shrugged her shoulder.

"Aobet don't be rude. Gwen ignore her. Tell us more about your betrothed."

"I would think you know more than me," Gwen said.

The girls peppered her with conversation, and she lost track of who was asking.

"He is so reserved we haven't gotten to know him."

"I suppose it is that whole Goblin King thing, but he really comes out of his shell," Gwen said.

"How did you meet?"

"Well he saved me from the dungeon, and another time a room full of straw and then he showed up at the banquet and then when the dress tried to kill me."

"That sounds like quite the adventure," Pink Hair said.

"So he invoked the rule of three?" Green Hair asked.

Gwen shook her head again. "No. He rescued me but never asked for anything in return." Gwen paused. "Well he did at first, but after a while he just kept showing up when I needed him."

The elves shared a sidelong glance with each other.

"But he had the contract. I didn't know about it at the time. But he didn't need the rule of three because the contract had already been in place for years."

"It's a blood contract though."

"Yes."

"It would have called you to him. He didn't need to come to you."

"You would have made your way to him eventually," another girl agreed.

Gwen squeezed her eyebrows together. "Does he know that?"

"He's a goblin dear. Of course he knows that."

Her free hand reached for her locket, remembering Aurius still had possession of it. "Then why spend all those years searching for me?"

"That would be something you would need to ask the prince. My question would be why is he going through all this trouble to break the contract."

Gwen groaned. "He's doing it because I asked him to." She emptied the liquid out of the cup.

"That's a big ask."

"It didn't seem sooo big to meeee. I'd like to marry someone I loooove," Gwen slurred.

"Well, breaking the contract would kill him," the silver-haired elf dropped that nugget on her.

Her mouth suddenly felt as if it had been filled with cotton. "What?"

"That's the only way to break a blood contract. Through death. As long as there is a living goblin the contract can't be broken."

"*That can't be the only way. Why would Aurius sacrifice himself for me?*" Gwen pushed her hand to her chest and swayed on her feet.

"*There's only one reason a man goes to the end of the earth for a woman,*" Pink Hair said.

Gwen's look of confusion caused her to continue. "*Love, silly.*"

"*Aurius doesn't love me.*" *She offered a small smile and took another sip. How did her cup get refilled, she wondered.*

"*Are you sure?*" *Purple Hair asked.*

But suddenly Gwen wasn't sure. Everything he had done could be seen as acts of love. Except for the first two times, when she had to bargain away her most prized possessions. But they could also be seen as desperate acts of a Goblin King. Wasn't love desperate sometimes? Nothing Aurius did served him. And if it were true that breaking the contract would kill him, that could serve as an act of love.

"*Do you love him?*" *Aoebet asked.*

The question startled Gwen back into the moment.

"*Aoebet, she just realized the prince loves her. Give the poor girl a minute to process.*"

"*Poor princess Elora. She will need at least a year to recover.*"

Purple hair scoffed. "*She isn't in love with the dark prince. And the king would never allow her to marry a goblin.*"

"*Half Goblin,*" *Gwen corrected.*

The ring of elves exchanged knowing glances as the beat of the music picked up again. They grabbed her hands. "*We'll help you take your mind off it.*"

They pulled her onto the dance floor. Between the music and the giggling, the twirling and twisting, Aurius was forgotten.

Until he appeared in front of her. Then, breath eluded her.

The memory spell on the cup broke, and she was back in the cottage. Alone. She set the cup down and picked it back up. Nothing happened. There was nothing else to remember. "How did I get back to my room?" Her fists beat against her temples, urging her brain to recall the events of that night. Everything until she woke up in the castle was a blank. Her eyes darted to the vase she had been avoiding.

She started pacing again. The cottage walls closed in, and suddenly the air was too thick.

"Aurius will be the Goblin King. Why would he be in love with me? When did he fall in love with me?" Her fingers pressed against her temples.

Gwen pulled out the coin again. Did she want the answers to these questions? All she had wanted from the moment Captain Drake had pulled her from her home was to live one more day. She had lived weeks since that moment. Mostly thanks to Aurius.

She shoved the coin back into her pocket. A prince, even a dark one, had to marry a princess. That was something she wasn't sure she could be.

Even if her birth gave her the legal right to claim the title, her upbringing did not. She had done nothing but struggle to survive since, well, her birth.

She didn't know how to behave at court, the proper etiquette. Avonlea had to give her princess lessons before she could walk through the castle in Aurum.

Marrying either prince was out of the question. Prince Ryland deserved someone who could rightly rule by his side. Someone worth fighting for, who truly loved him. If Gwen knew anything for certain, it was that she did not love Ryland.

And even if she could admit her feelings for Aurius, there was the contract. She wished more than anything that they had met for other reasons and not because of some dark agreement between their parents. He deserved to marry a genuine princess. Someone who would be an expert at navigating the courts of many kingdoms and negotiating peace. Someone who could temper a goblin's nasty persona.

While Elora was willing and would fulfill some of those duties, there was another who was a much better choice. It would broker peace in the land as well. Avonlea.

Gwen's shoulders hunched. "But the contract wouldn't be fulfilled." She sighed and shrugged. "I'll just have to remain childless so that we can break that stupid parchment." Disappointment fueled her rage at the unfairness of everything. She hadn't thought about motherhood much, but losing the possibility was maddening.

She paced in front of the sofa again, tapping her finger to her lips. "Even if I accepted that fate, and I must, how do I get Avonlea to fall in love with Aurius?" Her lips pulled into a soft smile as she pictured Aurius's sharp features. "That won't be hard. He's easy to love. The hard part would be getting him to fall in love with Avonlea? A love spell maybe? If I new one." Gwen's eyes lit with mischief. "He likes to save things. Avonlea just needs saving." She nodded to herself. "I need to get Aurius to Avonlea and make sure she becomes a damsel. Somehow."

She found herself absentmindedly gravitating toward the vase and the dried rose. She plucked it from the vase behind the sofa, her fingers tightening around the smooth stem. One she remembered. There was a familiar shimmer of magic, but it was different from the other memory tokens.

The memory didn't pull at her like the others. It seemed reluctant. As if Aurius didn't really want her to remember this. And yet, he left it here. Hidden among her mother's memories of times long past.

She pushed her will into it. Of all the things that were in this small cottage, this was the memory she wanted. The one that Aurius gave her.

The night of the Elf Ball came rushing back to her. The dance with Aurius, the kiss, the shaking of the earth. His confession that he loved her, the heat of his lips pressed against hers, his arms firmly around her waist. Deep longing settled into her heart, threatening to shatter her resolve. It all settled back into place as if it had never left. As if he had never taken the memory at all.

The plans she made to push Aurius and Avonlea together fizzled. Her heart cracked. It wasn't fair of him to take this from her, but she longed to find him now. Somehow the memory gave her the courage to admit her feelings. Knowing he might feel the same. But she couldn't get to him. She didn't even know where to look. And something stood between them. The contract. How could she ever truly know if he would have loved her had it not been the contract that brought them together and bound them?

"Is it selfish to want love that discovers itself instead of being forced upon you?" She put the vase back on the table.

"Of course that's selfish. I should be thinking beyond myself and helping others if I can."

The lump in her throat formed unexpectedly. A sob tore from her chest as gasping cries wracked her body. Through her tears, she looked over the cottage. Trinkets of memories in every direction pressed down on her, crushing her. "I can't do this," she whispered.

The fawn

Gwen ran from the cottage. She doubled over and put her hands on her knees. Her chest expanded and contracted rapidly as she tried to relieve the pressure building in her lungs. Her hands shook with the weight. The memories were too much. Everywhere she turned, memories meant to be treasures assaulted her.

As she let the cool, damp air fill her lungs, she placed her hands on her head. She let the scent of cedar and moisture calm her. Closing her eyes, she focused on her other senses. The sound of a songbird in a nearby tree, the chittering of squirrels fighting over an acorn, a gentle breeze on her face.

Her breathing slowed, and her hands moved to her sides. Her shoulders relaxed. She stayed like that for a while, building her courage to go back into the cottage and face the decisions she needed to make. The ones she was not equipped to make alone.

She straightened her spine and pulled her shoulders back. Turning toward the cottage, she nearly jumped into a nearby cedar tree. The bleating had startled her so badly that her breathing had increased again, and she was looking for something to hold on to.

Beside the front steps, a baby fawn was curled in on itself so that it looked no bigger than a tiny boulder. Fawns were camouflaged while their mothers searched for food. It was a wonder Gwen hadn't stepped on it in her haste to escape the confined space of the cottage.

The fawn bleated again, and Gwen relaxed enough to take a step toward it.

Gwen squinted her eyes. It reminded her of her adventure with Aurius in the enchanted forest. "Grinhelda?" But this was a different forest and a different cottage. Surely this wasn't the same witch she had met before.

She chewed her bottom lip, reluctant to involve herself. The last time she met Grinhelda, she almost died. Too many were relying on her to save them, and she didn't have much left to offer.

But her heart won out. She knelt beside the baby and slowly reached a hand toward its head. She noticed the deer was rather dirty and disheveled. It looked exhausted, as if it had just been in the fight of its life. There were some cuts on its back, proving her thought.

Gwen immediately felt sorry for the poor thing, letting her heart win her over, but she had been tricked before. "Grin. I know that's you. Turn back now and tell me why you are here."

The fawn blinked its dark, round eyes as if it understood nothing. It opened its mouth to release another bleat.

Gwen sighed and scooped it up. Even though everyone knows that a fawn should be left alone for the mother to find when she returns. If it were Grinhelda, it would be even riskier.

"Grin. If this really is you, you better not bite me."

She laid the fawn in a basket of blankets neatly folded by the sofa and ran to fill a cup with water from the well out front.

She turned to the tiny, sharp footsteps in the kitchen. When she stooped to offer the cup of water, the fawn limped over to her. It lifted its snout over the edge and let its little pink tongue loll out into the cup.

"You are very adept at drinking from cups for a deer." Gwen squinted her eyes again. "But if you are Grin, why have you not taken your human form?"

She allowed her hand to press against the fur on its head and smooth down its back. It trembled at the touch. The deer continued to lap water, ignoring Gwen's touch.

"Perhaps you are too weak to return to your human form," she said, continuing her soft strokes down the fawn's back.

When the fawn had its fill of water, it walked through the cottage on shaky legs. The clip-clop of her footsteps echoed in the silent house. Her head tilted up toward the bookshelf, seeming to read the titles of the books stacked against each other. The tiny deer sneezed, which seemed more like a scoff, and looked at Gwen as if to say, how boring.

She trotted over to the sofa and stood there expectantly, tilting her head. The fawn was not very fawnlike. Still, Grinhelda would have changed back by now, wouldn't she?

"Perhaps she can't," Gwen reasoned again. The fawn leapt onto the sofa, lay down and crossed her front legs over each other.

Gwen pulled at the top of her head and gently tugged a strand of hair. She knew what Aurius would say. He would warn her not to, but would stand back and let her do it, anyway. And if it went poorly, he would never say, "I told you so." His warnings were only meant to protect her, not to win points. And even though Aurius would warn to be careful, she wouldn't heed that warning, and she would do what was right.

If she gave this fawn her power, all of Mystrim might seek her out. And yet. She didn't care. She was a little tired of expecting the worst of everyone.

"Grin. I'm doing this. I understand what the cost could be, but please don't hurt me."

She placed her strand of hair on the fawn's head. It didn't have a mane like the unicorn, so she wasn't sure if this would work.

The fawn folded its legs and curled in on itself to sleep.

After a few minutes, Gwen stood and allowed the blood to rush back into her feet. Maybe this was an ordinary fawn after all. With that thought, Gwen moved to shoo the animal outside. The fawn's snout sparkled. Soon the sparkling took over the whole fawn. Slowly, a woman lay where the fawn had once been. It was different this time. For one, she wasn't clothed at all, and second, she was asleep.

As Grinhelda stirred, Gwen threw a blanket over her. There was no need for this to be awkward.

She stretched her arms wide and yawned. Her eyes remained closed until she froze. She drug her hands over her face and finally opened her eyes, staring at her now human appendages. She pulled her ruby lips into a broad smile and released a cheerful laugh. "I'm back. I've finally transformed."

Gwen cleared her throat.

Grin looked up, surprised someone else was in the room.

"Oh. You're still here." Her posture slumped at the revelation.

Gwen didn't let a smile touch her lips. "Yes," she said, putting a hand on her hip. "This is my house after all."

"Well, do be a dear and find me some clothes. Something extravagant."

Gwen crossed her arms. "No."

Grin's eyebrows pressed together. She looked as if Gwen had slapped her. "Do you know who I am child?"

"Yes. And until I helped you, you didn't have enough power to return to your human form. So I doubt you can smite me. Not that you would after I helped you."

Grin turned her head and lifted her nose. "No," she admitted. "I wouldn't."

"Why did you seek my help?"

"I know who you are. What you can do. And I never forget a bleeding heart."

Gwen rolled her eyes. "Obviously."

"I couldn't change back myself, I didn't have enough power left. I underestimated the strength of the curse in Aurum."

Gwen tapped her foot, waiting for the rest of the story.

Grinhelda rolled her eyes and tucked the blanket under her arm. "I went to Aurum to meet my betrothed. A king from a distant kingdom. I was looking for passage and my fawn form is much less threatening to most people. So I changed. But just being in Aurum is a drain on magic. It is worse than its ever been. I couldn't find nourishment in the land due to the drought and once I lost energy I couldn't return to my human form."

"How were you injured?"

"Oh, a wolf might have chased me and got a swipe in."

Gwen's eyes rounded. "I'm so sorry that happened."

"Well? Does that earn me enough goodwill for some clothes?" Grin asked.

"Why did you come to this cottage?"

"I took a chance you might be here."

"How did you know about this place, when I didn't know it existed myself."

Grin pursed her lips, and Gwen thought she might not answer. She turned from the witch on the couch, taking a step toward the kitchen. Had anyone

45

ever turned their back on Grinhelda? Gwen didn't know, but it seemed to have done the trick and loosened her lips. "I might have helped Aurius acquire some artifacts."

Gwen took a deep breath. "Fine. Follow me."

They walked down a narrow hallway with a few rooms branching off each side. She twisted the knob of the first door and stepped inside.

Grin followed her in with a slight limp. She had wrapped the blanket around her body and trailed over the floorboards behind her.

Gwen pulled open the wardrobe that stood in the corner.

"These are the only clothes that exist in this cottage. Take your pick."

Disgust plastered Grin's face. "They're all black."

"Yes."

"I can't wear black."

"Then you'll be naked. I was sent here with barely a moment's notice. Nor did I expect visitors."

"He must love you very much to clothe you only in black."

"Assuming the 'he' you speak of is Aurius, I understand the meaning of the color. It was explained to me just this morning. But I don't even know if *he* loves me at all. He is always so distant. And I've only ever seen him wear black, perhaps it is his favorite color."

"No." Grin shook her head. She had stepped toward the wardrobe and sorted through the dresses. She pulled on a black floor-length dress. This one had more ruffles than the rest and a few sequins around the collar. The sleeves were black lace. Grinhelda looked over and shrugged a shoulder as she threw it on the bed.

"He was distant because he wanted the choice to be yours. He didn't want to seem like he was manipulating you. But think about all he's done for you. He disguised himself and scoured Aurum to find you." Grin shivered as if the thought of it disgusted her.

Gwen placed a hand on her hip and narrowed her eyes. "You literally disguise yourself as a baby deer to trick people into helping you."

She smiled back. "You fell for it twice." She crossed to the dresser and chose undergarments. Gwen turned away as she dressed, though Grinhelda

46

didn't seem to mind an audience.

"There's a dressing room," Gwen motioned to the screen in the corner of the room.

"Oh?" Grin spun about the room. "Yes I see." She grabbed the clothes she had selected and stood behind the divider that covered her, continuing her tirade about the virtues of Aurius.

"Then when he found you, he rescued you."

"He bargained my most prized possessions to perform magic for me."

"He did it in the most goblin way ever, I'll give you that. But if he had popped in and said hey I'm a goblin and we have a secret, not-so-secret contract to be married what would you have done?"

Gwen perched herself on the edge of the bed. Her shoulders slumped. "I get it."

"But he showed up at your wedding to save you from an assassination, brought you to his home, clothed you, fed you, healed you. Showed you the most amazing library in existence. All while preparing this place for you to escape if you needed to. He is willing to hide himself away and become something he despises because you want to marry for love. Now that's irony dear."

"The contract is in the way of that."

Grinhelda emerged from the dressing room. "And he's gone to the ends of the earth to change that. To try to do the impossible for you." She looked at herself in the mirror. Smoothing down the dress. "Well," she sighed, "It will have to do until I get my magic back." She turned a meaningful look to Gwen.

Gwen threw her hands into the air. "What would you have me do?"

"Marry Aurius and fulfill the contract. We need you to bring balance to magic. Only you can do it. There is more at stake than just Aurius. All of magic will die if the balance is not achieved."

"How can Rumplestiltskin's death do all of this?"

Grin sat in an armchair. Though she looked better fully dressed, her hair hung limp over her shoulders, and dark grey circles underscored her eyes. Dressing seemed to have drained her energy. "I'm not sure Rumpel expected his magic to go haywire." She breathed. "I'm sure he didn't intend to die at all. It's strange for his death to create a magical vacuum. But I agree that until you marry the Goblin King, something will keep sucking all the magic from everywhere. It's unstable. And while it started in Aurum, there's nothing left. Mystrim will not be safe forever. Something has to fill the power vacuum."

As if to punctuate her speech, the ground beneath them grumbled. Grin raised an eyebrow.

"So the only way to save magic and the kingdoms is to let Aurius become the Goblin King?" Gwen asked.

Grin shrugged her shoulders and twirled a ruffle over a finger. "We need someone who can break Rumpel's curse. Our best hope is you and Aurius."

"Does anyone know how any of this is supposed to work? I'm just supposed to marry a man because my mother signed a blood contract with a goblin? Somehow that's going to make everything right?"

Grin shrugged as if that weren't important. "Rumpelstiltskin made it easier for Aurius with the contract."

"It's rather unfair, actually."

Grinhelda met Gwen's eyes. "There's nothing to be done. Accept who you are and fulfill the contract. It's certainly not going to make anything worse."

Gwen scoffed. "If I do anything, it will be because I love Aurius. Not because I'm bound by a contract and not to save your magic."

Reflection

G rin admired herself in the mirrors. She didn't have enough power to change the color of the dress she had chosen. In true Grinhelda fashion, it was one of the more ornate dresses.

"Of course, I'll owe you for the dress, and room and board and helping me in the first place." She pinched the bridge of her nose. "I've got to get out of here before I owe you more than I can pay."

Gwen remembered how leery Aurius was of Grinhelda's gifts.

"It's really ok. Think of it as a gift. No need for payback."

"I'll give you some advice."

Gwen pressed her lips together before saying, "I'm sure it will be sage."

Grin glared, but continued anyway. "You can't stay here. You have seven days before Aurius becomes a goblin and you've already wasted hours."

Gwen lifted her hands in frustration. "I have no idea where he is."

"So you've made your decision?"

Gwen pressed her brows together. "How did you get that from what I said?"

"You've at least thought about going to Aurius."

"What choice do I have? Prince Ryland and I... we weren't a thing. He spent most of his time..."

A shrill laugh stopped Gwen's musings.

"Oh I'm sorry. I can see where my question might have signaled that I care. But I truly only care about one thing."

"Yourself?"

Grin's eyes shifted up and to the right. "Okay. Two things." She stepped away from the mirror. "You must restore the balance to magic. There is only one way forward."

Grin waved her hand toward the mirrors. "Look more closely at the reflection."

Gwen hesitated, but stepped toward them. It was a trifold mirror, like anyone might find in a dress shop. She could have even mistaken these for being from George's shop. The frame on the mirror was extravagant, though. It was silver-plated and carved into loops and swirls that looked as if flowers had wrapped themselves in the design.

Grinhelda stepped behind her, and their eyes met in the reflection.

"Thank you for the dress dear." Grin wrapped her slender fingers around Gwen's shoulders, slipping her fingers through strands of golden hair. Gwen was suddenly wary of the sharp red nails at the ends of each of them. Gwen imagined them piercing her skin. Perhaps Grinhelda would enjoy licking her blood from the ends. But Grin smiled sweetly, and Gwen let the image in her mind go. Until Grin's smile changed ever so slightly. A smile that hid more knowledge than Gwen could ever hope to learn in a single lifetime.

"Look closer." Grin laughed quietly.

Gwen immediately noticed that the surface of the mirrors wasn't solid. Did they look like that before? She tilted her head and stepped closer. Grinhelda did not let go, stepping with her. But the mirror no longer held their reflection. The silver rippled as if it were made of liquid.

The ripples faded, and Gwen could see Papa, the miller, pacing in front of the fireplace. "Papa?" Gwen whispered. As if he could hear her, he turned to the door. His expression said he expected her to walk through it. He shook his head and began pacing again. Nothing had changed at the cottage. If he had gotten gold, he hadn't spent it on the house.

The image in the mirror changed. Prince Ryland stood before her in his finest regalia. Avonlea, too, was dressed in a stately gown adorned with banners, standing beside him. There was always a political banquet or ball. But something about the way Ryland held himself made her imagine him being weighed down. Was her disappearance a burden? Or the war? She hated feeling responsible for causing more stress. The captain entered and held out an elbow to Avonlea, who took it gladly with a smile. Drake rubbed his neck and turned, looking directly at her.

Gwen knew he knew she was spying on them, but before she could say or do anything, the mirror rippled again. This time showing her Aurius. He was in the same clothes he had worn when he left. But they looked filthy. He lay in a dimly lit room that looked as if it had been carved out of a rock. Perhaps a cave. Part of the rock formed a bench. Aurius had made it his bed. The walls were a shade of dreary white. His hair, which had always been neatly combed, was a mess. His arms wrapped around his midsection.

Gwen gasped and tried to step back, but Grin held her firm.

Aurius raised his head. His eyes were a bright shade of moss green and glowed slightly. A sharp tooth protruded upward over his lip.

"No Gwen. Do not come here." He practically growled. "I don't want you here."

Gwen's eyes rounded in shock and concern. "Aurius what have you done?"

"Go to Ryland. He will make you happy."

"I…" Gwen stuttered. In that moment, she knew. She knew what her heart truly wanted. She didn't love Ryland. He could never make her happy. And even now that Aurius was rejecting her, how could she go to Ryland?

Grinhelda's breath tickled the tiny hairs that lined the inner walls of her ears as she whispered next to her. "Don't listen to him dear. He's just trying to protect you."

"Protect me from what?"

She could feel Grin smile. "Go to him and find out."

Gwen shifted a shoulder to discuss that statement with Grinhelda. Simultaneously, Grin's pointed nails poked her in the back, hard, causing her to spin as she fell toward the liquid mirror. Grin wiggled her fingers in a wave goodbye, her red lips pulled into a wicked smile.

"You'll thank me later," Gwen thought she heard Grin say.

Gwen continued spinning. The liquid wrapped around her like a cloud. The silver fluff pressed against her in every direction and pushed her toward something she hoped was an exit. Pushing lasted so long, time had become irrelevant. With every press of the fluff, her body tensed. She had no control over her direction. Again, she waited to see what would become of her. She rolled her eyes. "This is getting a bit old," she whispered. And vowed to make her own choices as soon as she escaped this squishy torture session. It wasn't unpleasant, but being trapped here forever was a growing fear.

Just as she was wondering if she would ever escape, she fell through a break in the fluff. Arms flailed as she struggled to stay upright. The light silver clouds faded into inky darkness. The tips of her toes touched a solid surface. And then she was falling. Her hands flailed, and legs slipped out from under her.

Darkness stretched in every direction.

The Goblin

Strong fingers wrapped around her throat and pressed Gwen against a rock wall. The sharp jagged edges dug into her skin. A small whimper escaped as she winced.

Even in the darkness, with her eyes closed, she knew immediately who it was. His scent, the smell of earth just before a rain shower, wrapped around her as he entrapped her with his body. He caressed the center of her neck with his calloused thumb. It crawled to just below her jaw. She knew by the movement he could tell her pulse had kicked up a notch. Her breath matched it, making short, rasping sounds through her nostrils. She pursed her lips together to keep from screaming. His other hand pressed against the stone just beside her elbow.

He leaned toward her, holding her in place, but not hurting her. His lips hovered just above the soft flesh where her earlobe met the side of her face. Her heart felt as if it would beat out of her chest. Had Aurius ever been this close to her before? The air wheezed through her nostrils as it rushed in, preparing her body for a fight. Gwen willed her body to remain calm, reminding herself that Aurius would never hurt her. The Goblin King? She wasn't so sure about him.

"Is this what you want Princess?" His voice was just above a whisper, but the deep growl tickled the tiny hairs on her skin. "Do you want to fear me every day for the rest of your life?"

Gwen swallowed and slid her eyelids open. Her pupils dilated, adjusting to the low light. A faint ember glowed in the hearth nearby. Not as dark as she thought when she fell through the portal.

The man before her wasn't Aurius as she remembered him. His eyes had turned an eerie shade of green, and his hair looked as if he had been pulling at it for days. He had become someone dangerous. Gwen rejected the thought as soon as it registered. Aurius had always been dangerous. It had risen closer to the surface.

She realized it wasn't fear that drove her heart to a staccato. It was something far more terrifying. Now she wasn't sure she could admit it to herself, let alone say it out loud.

"I'm… not afraid of you," she whispered, even as she pressed her body into the brick. Her lungs wouldn't allow more than a short, quick breath.

Aurius's lips moved against her skin, pulling into a smile. "You're a bad liar."

He nibbled the edge of her ear. Gwen released a long breath and tilted her head, exposing more of her neck.

Aurius pulled away but didn't take his hand away. He narrowed his eyes and searched hers.

For a few long seconds, his eyes locked with hers. Then recognition. His fingers sprang away, and he took four silent steps back.

This was what she feared. What she couldn't admit. She wanted to feel Aurius's lips against hers. Her heart beat harder and faster when he was near because she wished he were closer.

Her breath caught. His rough beauty held her captive as the shadows danced over his torso. His white shirt was dirty and torn. It hung loosely over black slacks. His feet were bare and covered in filth.

Gwen stood taller as he stared at her. His eyebrows pressed together, and his eyes widened. He took more pained steps away from her. As the crack in her heart widened, she lifted her chin and squared her shoulders. For so long, she had expected death. Daily lived with the threat that it would be her last. She had never longed for it. Until now, she hadn't admitted her feelings, and must accept the rejection staring her in the face.

She schooled her face into a practiced expression and motioned to the space she must have just fallen through. "I thought I would never find you, but you left me a portal in the cottage," she said, deciding to ignore Aurius's brusque repudiation.

Even while dealing with his pain, Aurius had been there to catch her as she stumbled through the portal.

Now he turned away from her, sitting on a stone outcropping. "Yes." Aurius grunted, laying his body on a stone slab that must have been serving as his bed. "So that you could go home. Not come here and watch me fade away," he grumbled.

She crossed her arms and jutted out a hip. "According to the horse that was home." She sighed, taking a step toward the space and examining the rock ceiling. "Can we go back?" The only way would be with magic, if he were willing.

"It's a one way, one time use. No one has enough power to recharge it."

Gwen grumbled. Obviously, Grinhelda was holding back on how much power she had left. "I could help them," she offered instead of moaning about the witch. Why hadn't she used the mirror to go to her betrothed, the king she had gone on and on about?

"But you're here now and the mirror is in the cottage." He stared at the ceiling of the cave. "Gwen, you shouldn't have come. I can't control the goblin. He will force the marriage."

"And shadow magic?"

"Will only speed up the change and gets us nowhere."

"Why are you changing? Your birthday isn't for a few more days."

"I admitted." He turned away from her. "Something and it sped up the change."

She reached for his shoulder but stopped just short of clutching him and spinning him back toward her. "Can we stop it?"

"The marriage would slow it. Allow me use of the magic without fully changing, but it can't be stopped fully. From what I understand marriage is a stop-gap, but not a cure." Surely he wished his father were here. The only knowledge he had was from books.

"What can I do?"

"Did you bring someone to marry us?" Aurius asked, though the answer was obvious.

"No."

"It's fine. I don't want to marry you."

Gwen's jaw dropped, and she took a step back from him. He had confirmed her fear. After everything she had seen and all he had done, he didn't love her. She placed a hand over her chest. Was her heart rupturing?

He looked over at her, and his face softened. His gruff tone turned gentle. "Unless the goblin curse is broken," he added.

Gwen released the awful breath she had been holding to insulate the pain of her broken heart. "You just said fulfilling the contract won't break the curse?" she whispered.

He shook his head with a grunt. "I've read that it slows the change. I don't know how long or how much. Even if delayed it would continue on to the next generation." He wrapped his arms around his stomach, groaning. "But when I was searching for ways to break the contract. I found a few manuscripts that mentioned a magical sword." His arms tightened around his middle. "It can cut through curses." His words were strained, as if everyone caused him pain.

"And without it any child we had will be cursed as you are?" she asked.

"All goblins are cursed. It is in their blood." The gruff tone was back. As if he had two minds and they were at war with each other.

Gwen pursed her lips. "Of course. I read that in the Chronicles of the Goblin Kings."

Aurius rolled his head from side to side and rubbed his neck. "I don't want to be a Goblin King. If the sword is powerful enough it might end the goblin curse."

Gwen folded her hands in front of her. "And the race of Goblins."

"It will save the world a lot of pain if none existed."

"Would you lose your magic?" Gwen hardly knew what it was like to have magic, but to someone who had it all their life. That might be like losing a limb.

Aurius shrugged, but he wouldn't let his eyes meet hers.

A deep breath escaped her lips. Her fingertips touched his chin, and she tilted his face toward her. The rough stubble poked her fingers. "Whether you become a goblin or have magic is no matter to me."

"He will take everything from you."

"Stop talking as if he is not you."

Aurius grabbed his chest. His cry of pain pierced her heart with another wound, but Gwen could tell he was holding back. She didn't think. Her actions were purely instinctual. She placed her hands on either side of his head and sunk her fingers into his silky hair. Her lips pressed to his. When the shock of her actions wore off, his arms tightened around her, pulling her down to him. Desperation controlled his movements as if he were parched earth and she were the rain. His body relaxed, and the spasms faded. His breathing evened out. He broke away, only to pull her back a second later for two more quick kisses.

He pushed a strand of golden hair away from her face. "The goblin is a part of me and I'm a part of him, but on my 24th birthday he will take control. My body will change as you can already see. I'll become cruel and uncaring. I will take and take until there is nothing left," he said.

"That was your father. It doesn't mean you will turn out the same way."

His eyes widened in surprise. "What do you know?" He raised himself to a sitting position, bringing her with him. His shoulders hunched. He gripped the edge of the rock with one hand and her waist with the other.

"When Rumpelst…"

Aurius groaned.

"When your *father* died, his death created a void of magic. It devours any magic it can find. It seems that every goblin's magic is different." Aurius confirmed her suspicion with a nod.

"So my mother and Helen erected the barrier to protect Mystrim, using my catalyst magic. Unfortunately, the curse has no magic left to consume so it turned to the land of Aurum causing the drought. It's why so many are sick, dying, or have simply given up. My mother gave her life to keep the people, those with magic, from succumbing to the curse, at least in Mystrim. Everyone seems to think that if I marry you, the curse will end."

"It can only end when there is a new Goblin King," he said.

"If I marry you to fulfill the contract, you don't become the Goblin King."

Aurius shook his head.

She scrambled off his lap. "The curse would still continue to our children?" He didn't move, but he didn't deny it.

"So marrying you would actually delay the end of Aurum's curse, and pass the goblin curse on to our children."

He nodded. "If we meet the terms of the contract, I will never become the Goblin King and the curse in Aurum continues."

"And if we don't fulfill the contract, you become the Goblin King, the curse is lifted and everyone in the two kingdoms is saved. But the blood contract passes to the next generation."

He tilted his head. "We could fulfill the contract and let our first son eventually become the Goblin King and save Aurum, if it still exists," he said with a shrug.

"I can see why you don't want to say his name."

Silence.

"He wasn't trying to make you stronger. He was making you weaker."

His knob of his throat bobbed. "So I could never challenge his rule."

"Why have a child at all?"

"It is required for the king to produce heirs. And he could control you through me. I think that was his plan, but I can't really know."

Gwen shook her head. "He really was a terrible little imp."

She sighed and shoved her fingers into his ebony locks. His eyes fluttered closed as his chin lifted. "Looks like our best bet is this sword. We can end your father's curse, your curse and break the contract," she said, her voice barely a whisper.

The right side of his mouth pulled into a half-smile. "Hmph. So you're finally going to save the world?"

She shook her head. "No. *We're* going to do it."

"I'm afraid I can't go. The Goblin is too volatile."

"You have to come with me. I don't know anything about the sword. How long it will take to find it, how long it would take to get it back, or how to use it. And it seems you're doing a little better with me by your side."

Aurius sighed and rubbed his chest. "Yes. He does seem a bit more settled.

But you never know when he will appear."

She took his hand. "It will be too late. We have to take this risk."

"Fine. Fine. I'll get my coat." He stood, bumping into her as if he had forgotten she was there.

Recovering her balance quickly, she asked, "Are those the only clothes you have with you?"

He looked down at the ragged shirt, pulling it out with his fingers and thumb.

"It's better than a wedding gown."

She rolled her eyes. "These are the only clothes you left for me." Taking his hand, she continued. "Thank you for providing for me even when you thought you couldn't be there."

Silence passed between them for a long moment; they found themselves lost in the other's gaze. Wondering if the other felt the same. Gwen thought he might kiss her again as he leaned toward her. Instead he said, "You can't travel in a wedding dress. We'll have to find you some clothes." He pushed past her into the darkness.

"He knows I can't see in the dark?" she whispered to reassure herself.

"He knows," his voice echoed around the chamber where she stood. Light burst out from a torch near the tunnel. Aurius clutched the wooden post and held it up for her to see where to step. He held out the other hand. She grabbed it, and allowed him to lead her through the twists and turns of the cavern.

Making Do

Gwen and Aurius emerged from the darkness into a pit. Light filtered down through the green canopy. Natural steps formed from the base of the cavern up to the outside world. Rock outcroppings sheltered the cavern from the rest of the earth, providing a sense of peace and security. Gwen hesitated to leave it. This beautiful quiet. Beyond that promising green light, was a destiny she wasn't sure she still wanted along with so many unknowns.

An anguished moan from Aurius interrupted the tranquility of the karst window. Her attention went to the way he held his arms folded over his torso as if the Goblin was trying to claw its way out of his chest.

"Aurius!" She rushed to his side to help if she could. But what was there to do other than find the sword? "How can I help?"

He waved her away. "I'm alright. The change is just a little more painful than I thought and I've had no one to guide me through the process."

Gwen pursed her lips. The breathy flutter of anxiety traveled through her veins. Wanting to help and not being able to was a new kind of torture. She placed a hand on his upper arm, but she didn't know if it was for his comfort or hers.

She waited for Aurius's posture to straighten and said, "All right. Where is this sword?"

"You aren't going to like this," he whispered.

Gwen didn't react. She hooked her arm in his elbow and trudged up the stone steps beside him. "Where?" she asked again.

"It's in Aurum. In King Aric's vault."

Gwen stopped and looked at the canopy. The sound of birdsong stopped as Aurius emerged from the stone outcropping. Now, only the wind rustled through the trees. Rushing through the leaves as if it were a wave about the crash into them, then at the last moment changing course and rushing to the other side of the forest.

"Of course it is." She shook her head, stepping into the forest, her arm still looped through Aurius's elbow. "That does complicate things. Can you perform magic and shadow us into the vault?"

Aurius shook his head. "I am capable. But using my magic will speed the transition. Even if I wanted to, Aric's vault will be guarded against it."

Gwen tapped her lips. "So we'll need to sneak in?"

Aurius held up a finger. "We'll have to walk to Aurum" then another, "cross the barrier," a third finger, "get into the castle…"

"That's the easiest. There's an underground lake. Uncle George, the tailor, was sneaking in dresses to me." She tapped her finger on her chin. "I wonder if he has a secret entrance to the castle?"

"And an underground tunnel network?"

"Yes. He does have an underground operation."

"Who knows you know this?"

"Avonlea. Possibly Drake."

"And if they know, Prince Ryland knows."

Gwen was silent for a few steps more.

"He gave me a choice, Aurius," she said quietly.

"And you chose me? How sweet." His voice was flat.

The need to defend her choice rose in the wake of his tone. "In a manner of speaking. You needed me the most."

He sneered over his shoulder. "No one needs you Gwen. If you weren't here we would all get on fine without you."

"Wow. It's so nice to be wanted."

Aurius spun sharply and drove her against the nearest tree. Even though he didn't touch her, the space between her body and his was barely negligible. His eyes dipped to her lips as he leaned in. His voice lowered to a gravelly whisper. "Two different things, Princess."

61

Gwen looked up at him through her lashes. Her breath hitched as he leaned in, his lips barely brushed hers.

He spun away.

His back hunched as Aurius struggled to get the goblin under control again. His shoulders lifted once. Twice. Then he straightened to his full height. His shoulders dropped. He looked over his shoulder. "You should make choices based on what you want, not what anyone else needs."

"Maybe they're the same thing." Gwen pushed away from the tree.

"Maybe they shouldn't be." Aurius turned to her and took a single step in her direction. His hands became fists. His sharp nails were driven into his palm until blood bloomed. "You can still go home," he said through clenched teeth.

Gwen threw her hands up and let them fall to slap against her thighs. "And where is that Aurius? Is that a place? A cottage in the woods. Should I sit there safe in my little forest sanctuary while everyone I know and love wastes away or turns into goblins? Because that's not who I am Aurius."

He took another step toward her. Fire flashed in his eyes. "Who are you Gwen? Do you even know?"

Her slipper grazed his boot. Their noses nearly brushed. "I am a catalyst with dual powers, marked for death."

Aurius stepped away with a warning growl. He had forbidden her ever speaking of it.

She closed the distance again. "I am the daughter of Queen Liora and King Nolan."

The fire in his eyes died as they turned from their light chocolate brown to pitch black. "Yes. *Princess,* but who are you in there," he growled. His finger curved until it resembled a gnarled claw. He used it to press against the center of her chest.

The pressure almost caused her to wince. Instead, Gwen lifted her chin. Her hand pressed over his and held it there. "In here, Aurius. I'm just a miller's daughter, yanked out of the life I knew, betrothed to two princes, doing the best I can with what I have."

Aurius's upper lip lifted into a snarl. He wrapped an arm around her thin waist, producing a quiet whimper of surprise from Gwen. "You are not betrothed to two princes."

"I suppose Prince Ryland may have moved on by now. Aunt Helen negotiated with him to allow me this choice."

Aurius sat her down and took two measured steps back. "He'll never go along with it," he said.

"I'm here aren't I." Her hands were back on her hips.

"He's a dragon. He's laid a claim on you. The only way he allows you to leave him now, will be through death. His or yours."

Gwen blinked rapidly. "I'm sorry. Ryland's a what?"

"Draaagon," Aurius raised his eyebrows and drew out the word as if she were stupid.

She shook her head. "There is no such thing as dragons."

Aurius shrugged a single shoulder as if he didn't care one way or another if she believed him. He turned and looked toward the sky, shielding his eyes against the sun shining through the sparse canopy of trees. "Ryland's a dragon the same as his father." He swiped his finger over his tongue and held it in the air, sniffed like an animal, then started walking again.

Gwen followed him, high-stepping over debris in the forest. "How do you know that? His father died before his mother. She remarried."

He kept walking as if he weren't pulling the rug out from under her feet. "It's complicated for sure. His stepfather is his uncle, brother to the late king. His uncle is a dragon, hence the greed and affinity for gold. And his father was a dragon." He found a fallen tree and lowered himself onto it, then pulled his knees to his chest. If he hadn't just blindsided her with the dragon thing, she might have noticed how more unrefined Aurius behaved.

Gwen placed both hands on her forehead and paced in a tight circle. "Dragon's exist." She turned. "Ha. Of course dragons exist." Turned again. "I mean I believe that my mother is a heroine in a children's story, goblin's exist, why can't dragons exist."

Aurius tracked her movements with animal-like eyes.

"Not much difference between the two really." Aurius's eyes turned up in thought. "Although, goblins are more cunning, better looking. Gifted with magic. All the things that count."

Gwen's voice turned flat. "You forgot humble."

Aurius squinted his eyes, turned his lips up in the middle, and shook his head. "Never been accused of that."

Gwen threw her head back and groaned. "Aurius. How are we going to break into a dragon's hoard?"

"Well… look who knows so much about dragons now."

"I've read books."

He jumped off the fallen log and patted her on the head. "Of course you have." The scent of wet decaying leaves hovered with them. She almost didn't notice the scent he had kicked up.

She pushed his hand away. "Aurius, I'm serious."

All humor drained from his face. "The same way you were going to do it five minutes ago. Only now you know the risks."

"That we can be eaten by dragons?" Leaves rustled as she stepped around him.

He put a finger up. "Not until we break the curse."

Gwen stopped. Her mouth dropped open with the realization. "They can't change into dragons."

He shook his head. "Probably takes too much magic. They will have protections over their horde. Somehow there is a barrier around the magic of the castle. An object perhaps that protects the magic within, but the people can't access their own."

"Ryland thinks his great grandmother's grave feeds the magic in the castle that was in place."

Aurius shrugged. "Never heard of such a thing, but I haven't been everywhere."

"Is it important?"

"Could be."

Gwen closed her eyes and tilted her head to the sky. "So this just became twelve times harder than five minutes ago?"

"Yes." Aurius moved in a flash, grabbed her hand and dragged her along, stepping over logs and brush. Twigs snapped and leaves rustled under their footsteps. Trees were the only things seen for miles. Gwen didn't know how Aurius knew where to go; she simply trusted that he did.

"Want to give up and just marry the Goblin King?" he asked.

Her lips pulled into an insincere smile that matched her tone. "Sorry my wedding dress is having all the fake gold removed from it."

Aurius cut his eyes at her and growled. The attempted assassination was still a touchy subject, apparently.

"You will not be wearing gold to our wedding." His voice was low and gruff.

She pressed a hand to her chest and bent at the waist. "My mistake. I had forgotten about the entire closet of black wedding gowns. Still, as far as marriage proposals go, its a bit lacking."

Aurius turned on her with fire in his eyes and grabbed her by the elbow. "When I propose, Princess, you will know it."

Supplies

He dropped her arm and stomped away with a growl.

Gwen gasped and clicked her mouth shut. She knew better than to poke the goblin, waiting until Aurius turned again to breathe. She continued stepping over logs and debris.

"Is Drake a dragon?" she asked when she was sure Aurius had the goblin under control.

"Unknown." He lifted his other hand, palm up, with a shrug. "Though the name suggests."

"Avonlea?"

"Likely."

"Why didn't they tell me this?"

"Don't think they know," he said, inspecting a tree. Having found what he was looking for, he quickly stepped around it and continued the hike.

"How do *you* know?"

"I spent some time spying on the Aurum royalty while I was searching for you."

He dropped his voice to a whisper and put his finger to her lips. He crouched lower in the foliage, looking into the distance. Gwen watched him for a few seconds. She trusted Aurius's instincts.

"Aurius. What are we…" she whispered. But Aurius cut her off with a finger to his lips and a boop on her nose. She leaned away from him and scrunched her face. Why was he acting weird? He had never booped her nose before. *Maybe he's overcompensating for the goblin?* She wondered. Silently.

Still crouched to the ground, they crept through the woods. The damp leaves clung to her dress. Gwen stepped on a twig, which snapped in two. The humidity quieted the sound, but Aurius froze, turned, and glared. How did he creep through the fallen debris without a sound? The birdsong stopped. Even the buzzing of insects stopped in his presence.

Her mouth opened into a silent "Sorry."

After a few more steps, Aurius pulled back a limb from a tree to reveal a small farm. Water dripped down the leaves onto his sleeves.

The leaves rustled under her feet even as she moved slowly and methodically.

"Oh my gracious, woman, has no one ever taught you to walk silently?"

He released the tree branch. Water droplets flew in every direction, sprinkling them with the cool liquid. Aurius threw her over his shoulder as if she weighed nothing. She had eaten more in the last few months than in the previous two years, but she still had a long way to go to recover a healthy weight. A scream tore its way up her throat, but it died as a whimper before it could escape. Aurius stepped between limbs and debris on the ground to avoid being heard.

Gwen could only see the ground from her perspective on Aurius's back. The earthy aroma of horses overtook her senses. As she bounced, straw strewn about on the ground came into view. It had been weeks since she had seen a single piece. Seeing it here now broke the dam inside of her holding her fears. Her hands shook. Her body went rigid.

Aurius lowered her to the ground without a sound, just at the edge of the forest. A structure, small and modest, stood between the trees. A wooden fence surrounded it. Two horses grazed on the hay in the open. They didn't stop their chewing even in the predator's presence.

He looked down at her trembling hands and covered them with his own. Then up to her wide, round eyes. He ran the tips of his fingers around the edge of her face. He followed her line of sight to the trough of hay hanging from the fence nearest the trees.

Then, his face blocked her line of sight to the barn. He took her head in his hands, drawing her eyes to his. He raised his eyebrows. "Do you trust me?" They asked silently. She nodded, because she trusted him more than anyone in the world. He would never betray her. But would the goblin? She wasn't sure.

Before she had time to consider it, Aurius motioned to her hair, asking for permission to take some. She reached to her temple and plucked a strand of her hair and extended it to him.

The strand wound around his ring finger, and he slipped away without instructions to her. She decided his intention was for her to stay hidden. Away from the straw that could kill her.

She sighed and sat on a log in the forest, focused on Aurius's advance on the barn.

He had already exited the copse of trees and sauntered to the groom, who had appeared from inside the barn. Aurius snatched a few pieces of straw. Finally realizing what he meant to do, she jumped to her feet. He couldn't use magic.

Allowing her fear for Aurius to overtake her fear of death, Gwen caught up to him. A moment later, she wound her arm through his.

He tensed, but only she could tell. "And this is my betrothed," he said without missing a beat.

Gwen gave a little wave. She hadn't heard the conversation Aurius had begun with the man, but decided it was better to say something. "We've gotten a bit lost and are in need of horses to get back to our home," she said.

The groom gave Gwen the once-over. "It looks like she's not all that in love with you."

She wondered what had given him that impression. Aurius positioned his body between the groom and Gwen. "Actually she's running away from her other fiance. You know how it is... everyone loves a love triangle." He waved his free arm wildly.

The groom looked as if he had no idea what he was talking about, but Aurius kept smiling and talking, charming as he was.

"I'm sorry. I can't help you. Bruce and Gerdy are plowing horses."

Aurius looked over his shoulders at the horses. "They'll do."

Gwen opened her mouth, but before she could stop him, she felt the magic swirl around him. It was a foreign zing, but one she had felt many times.

She hadn't recognized it as magic before. This feeling, the zing in the core of her abdomen, took her breath away. She grabbed her chest, struggling to breathe. Too late. She was too late to save Aurius from using his magic and taking one more step toward the goblin.

Aurius's eyebrows narrowed as he raked his eyes over her. The groom also looked concerned.

She waved them both away. "How do you live in such stifling weather?" She asked, an attempt to explain her sudden ailment.

The man nodded. "It is a might bit humid in the forest but you adjust. Not from around here I see," the groom said.

"No. From somewhere a bit drier."

The groom's eyes narrowed and his head tilted just slightly. Aurius reached for his hand and slapped five gold pieces into it. "For the horses and a year's wages to get the farm running when you find new ones."

The groom looked at the gold and back at Aurius. His mistrust hadn't changed, but it was hard to argue with that much gold.

He shrugged. "Saddles in the barn," he said and leaned the pitchfork against the wooden fence. Walking back toward the house, he ran his fingers over the gold pieces in his hand. He stomped his feet on the front steps to get the dirt and muck off his boots and let the door slam behind him. Gwen shook her head. Men would give up a lot for a few pieces of gold.

Aurius turned to her, his lips flat.

"I was trying to save you from using magic," she said.

He stomped toward the barn, then turned with a finger pointed toward her. "Stay."

"It would have worked too, had you included me on the plan," she mumbled.

He ignored her as her feet retreated away from the straw strewn about in the horse pen.

He returned moments later with a saddle. His biceps bulged with the burden as he leaned against the weight of the saddle. Throwing it over the fence, he left and returned a few minutes later with a second.

He led the red horse out and secured it to the fence. They were already bridled, so there was no work there. Aurius brushed her with care. The horse didn't seem nervous at all.

"Say what your thinking princess,"he grumbled.

"I thought the horses might be skittish of you."

"Like the animals in the forest?"

"Yes. I thought that might be your doing as well."

He kept brushing and didn't meet her eyes. "Perhaps." He finished brushing the mare, placed the blanket against her back and swung the saddle over her back. "I've been visiting these horses every night."

"You knew this was here. You were conditioning the horses to the goblin."

He nodded silently and went back to the barn, repeating the process with the Bruce.

"So you were expecting me?"

"I'm not immune to hope, princess."

Gwen folded her arms across her chest. This was more than hope. It was a plan. "How long have you been planning this?" She tilted her head, watching him trail the brush over the back black horse. He ignored the question, lifting one hoof to chisel out the debris.

"We'll have to sneak through the barrier. We can't risk Ryland seeing you so we'll have to go through the mountains in the north and cross the barrier there," Aurius finally said, indirectly answering her question.

She let it go. Another question replaced her concern. "Won't the barrier react to me as the catalyst?"

"Maybe."

"You seemed really adamant that it would when I wanted to ride out and see Ryland a few weeks ago."

He shrugged. "I don't remember."

Gwen crossed her arms over her chest and tapped her foot.

"Are you going to question everything?"

Gwen narrowed her eyes at the Dark Prince.

He grumbled low in his chest. "Ok. Fine. I honestly don't know how it will react. I just wanted to keep you away from the front lines and that seemed the easiest."

"Lying."

"Yes." He continued grooming the horses.

"You are as bad as your father."

"I've been trying to tell you this."

"Fine. No more lies. What do you think will happen when we cross the barrier?"

"We can hope for nothing. Since we know for sure now that your hair was used to create the spell, I think it is likely that your presence simply strengthens it. That is not going to do anything terrible. Worse case scenario it strengthens it and we can't get through. Or maybe it overreacts and blasts everyone away from it might be worse."

She shook her head. Her eyes found a bit of blue chiseled in the spaces of the light green canopy above her. "This is impossible."

He shrugged. "We can go find a minister to marry us and have goblin babies."

"You are the one refusing to do that. And it won't really solve any problems. What if we can't get through?"

"I would have to shadow us to the castle and get closer to becoming a goblin forever."

Gwen stepped next to him and squeezed his hand. "I'm not going to let that happen."

His eyes found hers, searching for the lie. Aurius flattened his lips and nodded.

"Thank you for sharing the plan with me," she said.

He grunted and went back to preparing the horses.

Finally satisfied the horses would be comfortable with the tack, Aurius lifted the saddle over their backs. The brass latches clicked together as he slid the leather straps through and fastened them down. He jiggled the harnesses and triple-checked the latches. Once he was happy with the rigging, he offered her his hand. Her hand slipped over his as she slipped her boot into the stirrup and wrapped her other around the saddle horn. She threw a leg over her red horse and settled into her seat. Aurius mounted his black mare with a white star face and led them into the silent forest.

71

Magic

The soft pound of the horses' hooves hitting the dark earth tapped a beat on Gwen's heart. They had traveled in relative silence since the farmhouse. The birds didn't chirp in the presence of the Goblin King. Animals didn't scurry. They knew there was a predator lurking and froze to stay below his attention.

Leaves littering the ground dampened the hoofbeats, but provided a new crispness to the cadence. The air turned cool and breezy the further north they rode.

This area of the Mystrim was safe according to Aurius. The skirmishes were much further to the south, near the castle, where a bridge had been built over the chasm. There hadn't been a highway robbery of late either. Probably because all the men of robbery age had been conscripted to the fighting on both sides of the border.

Gwen wrapped the borrowed coat around her as tiny specks of white fell from the grey clouds, dampening her spirits further.

Aurius pulled a tiny piece of paper out of his pocket. "Here."

"What's this?" Gwen asked, unfolding the paper. She turned it one way and tilted her head and then turned it another.

"A spell."

She held it back toward him. "I can't do magic."

"The magic is already done, you just have to activate it."

"How do I do that?" she asked.

He moved his reins into one hand and motioned with the other around it. "Wrap a strand of hair around the paper."

Her eyebrows pulled together. "That's it, no magic words?"

"As I said the magic is done," he said, turning his attention back to the path.

"What does this spell do?"

"Warms you."

"And can anyone use this?" It was a silly question. What did it matter if others could use it? But she was desperate for the conversation, for his voice to soothe the despair that grew inside of her as they trudged back to the country where she had so recently survived an assassination attempt.

He shook his head. "Only people with magic hair."

Gwen must have imagined the smirk because he replaced it with a scowl so quickly it couldn't have been real.

Her eyebrows pressed together, creasing the space between them. "So you made this just for me."

Aurius remained silent.

"Will this speed up the change?"

"No. I made it weeks ago." The gruff tone had returned at the mention of the goblin.

"Thank you. That was very kind," she said as she plucked a hair from her temple.

"You may need to remove the locket for the magic to work."

"Oh. Right." The stiffness in her fingers made it difficult to remove the necklace and then wrap the hair. She almost dropped the paper twice. But as soon as the last of the strand touched the paper, the words lit with a soft white glow. They lifted off the paper and floated into the air in front of her, flowing and swirling all around her. As the words washed over her, her body warmed. She no longer felt the chill.

"This is nice, how long will it last?"

"Long enough."

"Do you have another for yourself?"

"I don't feel the cold and it will only work for you."

"Why?"

"Because I'm a goblin and that's how I designed it."

"Aurius."

SWORD OF PLATED GOLD

"I have what I need," he snapped.

"It seems I'll never stop needing to thank you," she said. Her voice was quiet, and she had meant for her words to be carried away on the wind, but of course, goblin hearing is much different.

"Your pleasure is thanks enough," he said, and a moment later, he turned in his saddle. "This is the perfect place to practice your magic."

"My magic is fairly simple to use."

"Not your catalyst magic."

"I..." Her mouth opened but no words would come out. She had read that holding two types of magic, and not being a goblin, would get her killed. Though King Aric didn't seem to mind. He had been hoping for her to have more. Unless he had wanted to kill her all along. There was the time she expected to die of starvation, and the other time King Aric would have killed her for not having magic. She swallowed the lump in her throat. "I'd like to not lose my head, Aurius."

"Which is why you need to learn to control it. Learn subtlety so that others don't recognize you are even using magic."

Gwen shifted in her saddle, earning her a head shake from her mare.

"I can teach you," Aurius offered.

"What happened to 'I don't teach magic'," she said, mimicking his gruff tone.

Aurius's eyes narrowed and his shoulders hunched forward. His head whipped toward her. "Fine. Die for all I care." He nudged his horse into a canter and quickly widened the gap between them.

Gwen's little horse was having none of that. She sped into her own trot to catch up with the lead. Gwen jostled at the unexpected change. Her head fell toward the horse's rump, and she lost her grip on the reins. Her feet slipped out of the stirrups and went over the top of her head. She nearly landed face down on a muddy trail, but just before she hit the ground, her body stopped its descent. She hovered just inches above the ground.

Black hooves crowded her view. "Aurius. We said no magic."

"I think you will find, Princess, that I'm not using magic."

"If you are trying to teach me a lesson, this isn't funny."

He lifted his hands, with his wide palms toward her. "I've done nothing."

"Well do something!"

He dismounted and knelt beside her. "Do you want to learn to control your magic?"

She raised her head along with her eyebrows as much as she could from her position near the ground. "Did you plan this?"

"No. But it is working in my favor."

"Fine. I'll learn magic."

Aurius's fingers slid between hers, and her feet lowered to the ground. As soon as they touched the dirt, she could control her body again and stand.

Gwen pulled her hand away from his. "What happened?"

Aurius lifted his lips into a radiant smile. His eyes had returned to his natural chocolate brown. "You did this on instinct. That's good."

"No. I mean what happened to you. Why did you run away?"

He tilted his head. "The goblin doesn't have much patience. And when he takes over, he's a bit harsher than I would be."

"I realize that. He hasn't made an appearance in a while. Is this because you used magic? Is it speeding up the process?"

He put a hand on her shoulder and offered a slight smile. "I'm not struggling more than before. It's better now that I'm close to you, but he does escape when there are very strong unexpected feelings."

Gwen nodded reluctantly.

Aurius crooked a finger under her chin and tilted her head up. Her eyes locked with his. "But I think you are avoiding the subject," he said.

"I'm not avoiding it. I'm just making sure we are still together on this issue." She stepped back. Away from that look, away from the desire to throw all her plans away and kiss the Goblin King again. Her hands swished down her borrowed riding pants, wiping the dust away.

"And what is that?"

"That you aren't going to use magic. If you do, you might as well just shadow us to the castle."

"Here's your first lesson." He held up a finger. "Different types of magic require different amounts of magic. Shadow jumping requires a lot of magic.

An illusion requires much less."

"Still, using magic will speed the process." The volume of her voice increased.

Aurius matched it. "Yes, but it was necessary and it wasn't going to speed it as much as shadow jumping."

Gwen's hands slapped her legs. "It wasn't necessary. But you just do things without telling me and you don't include me in your plans."

"I was trying to keep you away from the straw that almost kills you every time you are near it." Aurius's volume increased to match hers again.

"I know, but you can't always protect me. Especially not if it hurts you in the process."

The yelling stopped. Aurius took a deep breath.

"I will gladly exchange my life for yours Gwen." He said so quietly she almost didn't hear it. "That will never change. Don't ask me to do otherwise. It would be like asking me not to breathe."

A tiny bit of air rushed into Gwen's lungs. She took a tiny fraction of a step back. "I wasn't expecting that."

"How could you not?" His eyes met hers. She wanted to rush into his arms and squeeze him. To ask him to hold her and take her away from this endlessly frightening journey. They could be happy. But that happiness would be tainted by the fact that everyone else was suffering. And a curse loomed over their children. Maybe she could damn a world that had been nothing but cruel to her, but she could not pass on that curse and responsibility to her future children without first trying to solve the problem herself. So instead, she chose the hard path.

She pulled his hand into hers. "No more magic, ok?"

He lifted an eyebrow and one corner of his mouth. "No promises, princess."

Narrowing her eyes, she pulled her hand away and stomped away with a groan. Looking toward the sky, she gritted her teeth and pulled her hands into fists.

Aurius folded his arms over his chest, waiting for her outburst to subside. "Are you sure you aren't part goblin?" he asked.

She whipped around and stomped back toward him. "Fine, teach me how to use magic so I can worry less about you using it." Gwen returned to her horse and put her foot in the stirrup to mount.

Aurius's lips moved.

She swung a leg over the saddle and held the reins. "And wipe that grin off your face!"

A laugh erupted from behind her. It was the best thing she had heard all day, but she didn't let her face show how much it relieved her to hear it. Instead, she pursed her lips and narrowed her eyes.

Aurius approached her horse. "Lesson two. Practice. No special words, no gestures. Use only your mind. Start small. Try lifting the horse's mane. Then move onto bigger things."

"That's it. That's your magic lesson?"

Aurius shrugged and backed away to his horse. He mounted and turned the horse back toward the path. "For now."

Gwen rolled her eyes and took a heavy breath. She clicked her tongue to get her horse to move again. Aurius turned his to lead the way. "Practice princess." He said as he passed her.

Gwen looked at him out of the corner of her eye. A low growl rumbled in her chest. "Fine," she said.

The journey began again. Sunlight sparkled through the golden leaves. She let the glittering light calm her, looking down at her horse's mane. The red hair shifted with the horse's movements. Gwen put all her energy into making the hair move in a different direction. It paid no attention to her demands.

The sun blazed a trail across the sky as the pair moved through the forest toward the place Aurius wanted to cross. The longer the horses trotted along the path, the less likely it became that she would be able to lift the horse's mane at all.

"I think this becomes harder the longer I'm in this saddle."

Aurius grunted. "You're trying too hard."

"I don't know how to not try."

"Just relax and let your magic do it's job. Stop trying to force it."

"That's easy for you to say. I wasn't born with magic."

"You were born with it. Powerful magic. The time you needed to learn to control it was stolen from you. You don't have the luxury you should have had to learn this naturally. So I get that this is hard, but you have been doing hard things your entire life. Compared to what you've been through just in the last few months, lifting the mane of a horse is easy."

Her lips stung as she pressed them together.

They rode on in relative silence until Aurius pulled on the reins and his horse shimmied sideways. "Whoa girl." He patted her neck. "It's ok." He gently shushed her. The horse calmed under his touch.

"The barrier is just here. Do you see the shimmer." He pointed through the trees toward the green hills. "This is one of the few points where there isn't also a chasm."

She squinted and placed her hand on her forehead to shield her eyes, noticing a golden sparkle indicative of magic. "Didn't Ryland try to break through weeks ago? Wouldn't the chasm have prevented that?"

He nodded. "There's a bridge. Someone from each side built it many years ago. But it's still separated by the barrier. It would need to come down to connect both sides, but only a few feet separate them. It can be easily crossed."

"If the barrier came down would the chasm close?"

He shrugged. "The chasm was created when the earth swallowed up my father. Me becoming king is supposed to undo the magic and break the curse. Anything's possible I suppose."

"Well nothing is exploding. I guess that's a good sign."

"We're still a few miles away. Let's see what happens when you try to open it." He clicked his tongue to the horse and turned her back to the trail leading out of the mountains.

"I love that positivity, Aurius," she murmured.

The Barrier

The horses trotted on and on. Trudging toward the barrier that proved to be further away than she had imagined. It was dusk when they arrived at the shimmering translucent wall.

Gwen moved her leg over the saddle. The leather creaked as she lowered her boot onto the hardened soil with a thud. Her fingers spread wide and curled over again. The muscles in her legs burned. She ignored it and slapped her hands together. They made a weird brushing sound as she rubbed them against each other. "How do I do this?" she asked, looking up at the barrier. The dim light of the setting sun barely highlighted the sparkle of the magic separating them from Mystrim.

He stepped in front of her and put a hand on her shoulder. "We can't cross until you can use your magic without being detected."

"Why not?"

He lowered his brow. "You might not have the ability to practice on the other side."

"We don't have time." She tried to move around him.

He stepped into her path again. "We'll make time for this." He motioned to a clearing.

"No one can make time, Aurius. Time is what it is and we are running out of it."

"We'll use time for this," he said.

"If I can't use magic over there, what difference does it make?"

Aurius crossed his arms over his chest and leaned into his heels, displaying every muscle he had in his upper body. He lowered his chin to his chest.

"You need to be prepared for anything." He released a heavy breath. "If this doesn't work, as it likely won't, and I become the Goblin King. Your magic may be the only thing to stop me. I need…"

He stopped. Aurius needed nothing. He was never vulnerable.

Gwen pressed the tips of her fingers lightly onto his elbow. She tilted her head up. Her eyes met his. "I understand."

His lips pressed together, and his throat bobbed. He nodded and walked away.

"Sit princess. I'll make camp. You need to get some rest," he called over his shoulder. His voice reverberated through her chest. Minutes later, she was met with a sly smile and arms bulging with firewood.

The wood clanked together as Aurius dropped it into the center of the clearing. He patted a few pieces of down into a fluffy ball and placed it under the stacked wood. A few clicks of rocks tapped together sparked a flame. His cheeks puffed as he added air to the flame. A task she had completed hundreds of times. Moments later, the whoosh of heat that hit her took her back to the small cottage she grew up in. The acrid smell of smoke and ash drifted over her. Before she knew it, her head was bobbing forward, and she was asleep.

"Gweeeeennnndolllllyynn…. yooooo've coooommmeee hooooommmee," an eerie voice called on the wind. She lifted her head. The voice was familiar.

"Did you hear that?"

Aurius had found a place on the dirt against a downed tree stump. One ankle crossed over the other, fingers folded together over his abdomen. His chin touched his chest. He lifted his head. "The crackling fire or the same silence that's followed us since we left my cave?"

"No a voice calling to me."

"There were no voices."

Gwen shrugged and laid her head back on the knapsack she was using for a pillow. "I guess it was a dream."

Aurius leaned back against his stump. "Being called in the woods in a dream is dangerous. A lesson you might have learned recently."

Her lips pulled into a grin. "I won't chase down any sickly fawns. Besides

Grin is resting in my cottage right now."

"Making friends with a witch is dangerous. I'll only warn you about her once more."

"Between witches, dragons, and goblins it seems all I have are dangerous friends."

He ignored the implications. "You haven't eaten." He handed her a plate of roasted vegetables and meat.

"What's this?" She pulled the plate to her chest and picked through the food with her fingers. She wasn't about to waste food, but she did want to know what it was.

"Wild carrots and protein. You don't want to know the source."

"Not a house cat?" Should couldn't abide eating cats no matter how hungry she was.

He shook his head, his lips pursed at the memory of her previous dire situation.

She sniffed the meat. It smelled sweet and savory all at once. Her stomach rumbled with the sudden attention. Gwen had in fact eaten, but it had seemed like days ago when food appeared in the cottage. Much had happened since lunch. Picking apart the meat, she pushed it over her lips. Flavors exploded in her mouth to rival the cook in Aurum.

"This is delicious," she said between mouthfuls. She narrowed her eyes toward Aurius. "Did you use magic again?"

He smiled and lifted his hands in defense. "No magic. I swear." The fire popped once and drew his attention back to the flames. "Just some herbs I gathered in the woods."

Gwen slurped the juice off her fingers. Not very princess-like. "Well done. My compliments to the chef," she said, wiping the tray with a cloth and setting it aside. She nestled back against the stump again and allowed the warmth from the crackling fire to lull her to sleep again.

As soon as her eyes closed, the world tilted, flipping her reality. The surrounding light was deep amber, but it was daytime. She pressed her eyebrows together, swearing that she had just been about to fall asleep. There was something important she needed to do with someone. She struggled to remember, but the thoughts were like trying to grasp a bar of soap. When she let those thoughts go, she realized she was in the embrace of a woman she had never met. "Gwen. I'm so glad you've come home."

"Home? I've never been to this place," Gwen replied.

The woman took her hand. "Don't be silly. It has been many long years but you have been here."

"But this is not my home."

The woman's long slender fingers dropped her hand. "Where is your home then?"

Gwen turned away from her. "It's…" Her shoulders slumped forward. "I don't know." She pointed toward the forest behind her. "Back there maybe."

The woman took her hand and pulled her back around. Something about her smile was warm and comforting. Gwen wanted to snuggle into another embrace and never leave her side. "This is home," the woman said. "Show me how you use your magic."

Gwen wanted nothing more than to please her. Long, light-blond hair hung down her back. Gwen lifted it without a thought. She blew out a breath, having finally succeeded, though she couldn't remember who had given her the task.

The woman kept her smile, but Gwen could tell the trick had disappointed her. The woman clenched her teeth. "That dumb goblin has you doing parlor tricks when you are the most powerful catalyst the world has seen in a thousand years," she grumbled.

"What was that?" Gwen asked.

The woman pressed her lips together and waved a dismissive hand. "Nothing dear. But you are capable of much more than that."

Gwen nodded. "Yes, sometimes. But it requires my hair."

"No." The woman cut her off. The smile had faded. "Your magic is not bound by your hair as most catalysts are, though it is an option."

Gwen tilted her head and pressed her brows together. "What do I need then?"

The woman's face softened. "Nothing."

"Will you show me?"

With a nod, she held out her palm. A crystal blinked into it. "Pull the energy from this crystal into yourself."

Gwen scrunched her face. "What?"

"Connect with the crystal Gwen."

She shook her head. "I don't know how."

The woman stepped closer. Her hand still stretched out with the crystal in the center. "Your magic does. Close your eyes and stop holding it back."

Gwen rolled her shoulders and shook out her hands. Her eyelids slid closed.

"Good," the woman was saying. "Now relax. Let your walls down."

Gwen's head tilted back. Something within her started to stir. She recognized the feeling. It was the feeling of performing magic with her hair. But this was different. Stronger. Wilder.

Immediately, the inner gates that held her magic wanted to slam closed. If this magic ever got out, Gwen knew she wouldn't be able to control it.

"Don't be afraid. It won't hurt anyone," the woman whispered. Her gauzy white dress lifted in the breeze as if to emphasize her words and calm Gwen's spirit.

"Easy for you to say," Gwen grumbled.

"It is Gwen. Your magic isn't going to hurt me or anyone else."

"But it has before hasn't it?" Gwen didn't know where that had come from, only that it was the truth. She knew it as well as she knew the patterns on her palms.

"That was long ago. You were a child. Let go of the fear."

Gwen's hands balled into fists. "I don't want to hurt anyone." Why couldn't this woman understand the risks?

"This is a dream. You can't hurt anyone." Cool fingers gently pressed on her forearm.

With the touch, the movement in her chest resumed. A golden sparkling stream. It seeped out of her chest and mingled with the crystal. "You can take the magic or you can borrow it."

"There isn't much to work with."

"No. Crystals aren't magical on their own."

83

Gwen allowed herself to feel what little there was, but left it there. It didn't feel right to take it. She coaxed her magic away from the gem. It was like forcing lightning into a bottle. Gwen pulled it back, but it wanted to remain out. Cool fingers caressed her forearm.

"Don't panic. You feel the power, be gentle with it."

"It's wild."

"Would you want to go back into a cell you weren't sure you'd be able to escape?"

A crack ripped through the ground in front of her. "Not really."

"You control the magic, it does not control you," the woman said more firmly.

Wind roared around them, twisting Gwen's hair over her face. The woman's dress pressed against her legs. "I don't know what I'm doing," she yelled, barely able to hear her own voice.

"There is no difference between you and the magic, Gwendolyn."

"But..."

"Call it back," she commanded.

Gwen's mouth snapped closed. Sweat beaded on her forehead. She tugged at the golden magic with every ounce of effort she had. "Leave the crystal and come home," she said.

Her magic made a slow retreat. The golden shimmer crept back toward her, flowing back and forth until it had fully retreated.

"Good."

Gwen opened her eyes. "Good? I didn't do anything."

"You just learned to make the connection. And you learned to recall the magic. That's all you need." The woman lifted the corners over her mouth. Her face glowed with happiness. The desire to please this woman blossomed in Gwen's heart. "A bit of advice. The more you use it, the better you can control it."

Somewhere distantly a horse nickered. Her eyes popped open. She found her palm tracing a path down her horse's neck. Her forehead pressed against the coarse hair. Relaxing her shoulders, she allowed a bit of the magic coiled within her to escape. It reached out to the horse.

"Shh. Shh. Shh. I won't hurt you," she cooed as Gerdy reared away from her. Her hand continued to move over the horse, allowing it to get used to the feel of her magic. As the horse calmed, the magic trickled over the horse's thick red mane. Gwen opened her magic gate a fraction more; the horse's hair lifted from her neck.

Gwen returned to the fire and laid her head opposite Aurius. "How did you figure it out?" he asked.

"I think the barrier helped me."

Aurius grumbled something about listening to inanimate magical objects more than to him.

She reached her hand toward his and let the tips of her fingers brush his rough knuckles. "Thank you for believing me."

"Magic opens many doors. Not all of them good," he mumbled.

Before she could respond, he was snoring again. Her body shifted until her back was to the fire, watching the golden shimmer of the barrier in the moonlight. Tomorrow it promised. There would be more magic tomorrow.

* * *

She popped up and looked around, finding Aurius's place empty. The sky had lightened to a dull blue. They had lost too much time. A quick scan of the campsite revealed his hunched form close to the horses. His hand tightened around a wooden brush. A dark color revealed the path the brush had taken down the horse's body.

Relieved to have found the dark prince, Gwen poured herself a cup of the warm liquid she found brewing over the fire and joined him beside the horse.

"What do I need to do to get through the barrier?"

"Right to the point. No use in waiting I guess." He nodded and stored the brush in his pack again.

"We're running out of time."

Aurius nodded.

"Wrap a hair around your hand and place your hand into the barrier."

85

"At this rate I'm not going to have any hair left."

"You have plenty to spare, but you don't have to remove it from your head. It's long enough to use as is."

Gwen nodded and pulled the hairpins from her hair.

Loose locks fell over her shoulders to her waist. Choosing a strand, she wound it around her palm and approached the barrier.

Gwen took a heavy breath. In through the nose and out through the mouth. She pressed her palm into the barrier, which passed through easily. Now, she was about to exit the one place she never wanted to leave to go save a kingdom that wasn't her home.

The barrier shimmered and rippled all the way to the sky. Higher than she could see.

Gwen's mouth dropped open as she felt the tug of magic in her core. More than ever before. She had just recognized that tug as the use of magic. The barrier pulled at an unseen string in the core of her being. Something she didn't know existed, but now that it felt it was being yanked out of her body, she knew she would miss if it was gone. This was the source of her magic. She could hear someone. It was muffled or distant; she couldn't tell, and it didn't matter. She had to focus everything she had on resisting the urge to allow the spell to take everything she had. The barrier could do it. She knew instinctively it wanted it all and more.

Something hit her from behind, pushing her forward through the barrier. As soon as she was no longer in physical contact with it, the depletion stopped. She pulled herself to her knees and then slowly to her feet. The sound of horses stamping and a man yelling finally caught up with her. He was at her side. Gwen's eyes widened. She would swear the ground had become liquid and was rolling like waves on the lake. Not that she had much experience with waves or lakes. But it was firmly established that she read books. Maybe it wasn't the ground that had liquefied but her legs. Clutching the man beside her to steady herself, she gave him another smile as her knees buckled and she collapsed into his arms.

As he carried her away from the barrier, she allowed a moment to appreciate having him by her side. Her fingers found their way to the stubble on the edge of his jaw. Sharp points pricked her in reward for her effort. She smiled anyway. "I'm grateful you are always there to catch me."

He looked down, with concern etched on his eyebrows. "It is not a service I'd like to get accustomed to."

He laid her down near a felled tree. Even this far north, King Aric had depleted the forests.

"I'm sorry that happened," Aurius said, his voice barely above a whisper. "I should have known and taken precautions."

"How could you have known?" Gwen's eyes wanted to close without her permission. "I feel so weak."

"The barrier took a lot from you, but I think it is time you put the locket back on now. The curse could be draining your magic too."

"It's in my pocket. I don't think I can get to it."

Aurius gently searched the front of her coat with excruciating gentleness. Gwen barely felt the pressure at all.

He pulled the locket up slowly and let it dangle before unhooking the clasp. It took only a moment to place it back around her neck.

As soon as it was clasped, she sat up, placed a hand on her neck and rolled her head from side to side. Aurius's palm was on her cheek. One of his bottom teeth protruded over his upper lip as he pulled his lips back into a pleased smile.

"Better?" he asked.

She nodded and allowed him to pull her up to standing.

"Aurius. I think we ought to consider that it might not be your father's curse that is depleting the land."

"Ridiculous. Of course it is his."

"But just now... I felt this soul sucking."

"That could be because it recognizes your magic. I've never heard of anyone else experiencing that as they cross the barrier."

Gwen agreed reluctantly and shook off the nagging sense that their assumptions were horribly wrong.

* * *

Aurius hadn't wanted to stay close to the barrier for long. He had said he didn't trust an antique magic trinket to protect her, but he had seemed rattled. An uncomfortable weight had settled on her after they had crossed over, that lightened with each mile they put between themselves and the barrier. The horses had to be let go. Aurius wouldn't risk leaving her alone to get them across. The rest of the journey would be on foot. Dread built in Gwen's gut. It would take twice as long on foot. They would need more food and rest. Gwen did at least. Aurius seemed more invigorated the longer they walked.

He found what once had been a meadow in a copse of young trees. With the drought and the cutting of forests, everything was young and dry. There were no old-growth trees to be found.

Gwen rested between a rotten log and a prickle bush. Still, it wasn't difficult to fall asleep.

"Gwen?" a quiet voice called to her.

She rolled over with a groan? "Is this another dream? I thought we were too far from the barrier now for this."

"I need your help."

Gwen opened her eyes a crack at the familiar voice. "This is a dream. Prisma is in the enchanted forest." Gwen reminded herself.

"I am."

She opened one eye and gave the unicorn a drowsy acknowledgement. "You can visit me in my dreams?"

"Its become much easier lately for me to visit dreams. Bruce and Gerdy send their regards. They are grazing in the purple meadows," Prisma nickered.

"I'm so glad they made it home."

"But something's wrong."

Gwen sat up in her sleepy dream state. "What's happened."

"I'm fine. But the forest is dying around me." Scenes of withered fields and meadows flashed before her. Sick animals dotted the landscape.

"The curse has made its way to the enchanted forest?"

"Yes. But not in the way we thought it would." The unicorn bobbed her head. "Do you remember the gift you gave me?"

"I braided my hair with yours."

"Yes."

Gwen's mouth gaped open as if she were a fish trying to breathe out of the water. "It's me. I'm literally causing the death of magic." She pressed her thumb and forefinger on either side of her temples.

"Rumpelstiltskin caused the death of magic." Prisma shook her head, but Gwen wasn't convinced.

"How do I stop it?"

"I'm afraid I don't know. You understand the role of a catalyst?" Prisma asked.

Gwen nodded.

"It lowers the energy needed for the reaction to begin and makes it easier for the reaction to take place."

"So the hair I braided in with yours is allowing the curse to follow you." Gwen said.

"Maybe you need to revoke your permission for use of your magic."

"But I did that to help you."

"It's hurting everyone else!"

Gwen patted the unicorn's neck. "I understand." She wound her hand through the braid in Prisma's mane. "I revoke my permission to use my catalyst magic." The words were a sad whisper, but she felt the power break away from the unicorn. Prisma's sparkle dimmed a little.

Gwen's eyes met hers. "We are going to fix this."

Prisma mane shook as lifted her head up and down. "Of course you are. The enchanted forest awaits your success."

"Aurius and I, we're hoping to find Inauratus. We'll fix this."

"Hurry Gwen. Time is running low."

"I'm no hero. But I'll do what I can."

Prisma's image faded into the mist of her dream. "If I die travel to the east to find my replacement." Her haunted words floated through the fog.

"You aren't going to die Prisma. We'll fix this."

Prisma didn't respond. Gwen turned on her side on the ground and shivered. What if she couldn't fix it? She'd die, her friends would die, and now the enchanted forest and all the amazing people would fade into oblivion. They had to be rescued. She had to get the sword, break all the curses and save the world.

Time was running short. She had a unicorn to save, while Aurius slowly morphed into the Goblin King, his father's curse now threatening the enchanted forest.

Network

"We cannot walk into the streets of Aurum in the middle of the day. You will most certainly be recognized," Aurius argued.

Gwen rolled her eyes. "Supposedly they put my picture up and sing ballads of my incredible beauty."

"They aren't wrong to do so, but you are definitely recognizable."

"I suppose the green in your eyes and that protruding tooth might give you away as the Goblin King as well."

Aurius grunted in agreement.

"Very well. We'll wait for the cover of darkness and go in the back way."

Aurius raised an eyebrow.

Gwen shrugged. "I might have learned a thing or two. When I escaped the castle I discovered Uncle George's underground shop backs up to the forest."

"You escaped? But then you went back."

"I thought I could make a difference. That I could help in some way."

He cupped her face. "It might have happened. Had you married the prince, he might have become less likely to restart the war. But he's still a dragon. You would never have been happy and the curse wouldn't have been broken."

"They would have discovered my secret."

He nodded.

She took his hand. "I never would have gotten to know you."

He shook his head, looking down at their joined fingers.

"Even if we fail, if I die…" she paused when Aurius growled at the thought of her death. "If I die and you become the Goblin King. It will have all been worth these few weeks I've known you."

Aurius's eyebrows pushed together. "I can't believe this to be true."

"You can't believe that I value our time together?"

"No one loves a goblin."

Gwen swallowed. With all her might, she wanted to say the words. To reassure him that she did love him. She opened her mouth to say the words. To admit her feelings were true and cage her heart forever to the Goblin King.

"Aurius... I"

"Halt!" the shout echoed around them.

Gwen looked over her shoulder, as did Aurius. They were surrounded. Men, women, even a boy, held spears toward them.

"Did you know they were there?" Gwen asked.

"Why do you think we stopped?" he said.

"We have you surrounded," one of the men, the leader Gwen assumed, said.

"We mean you no harm," Aurius proclaimed. "We've come to meet with George the tailor."

"Says the Dark Prince."

"He's never harmed anyone," Gwen said.

Aurius pursed his lips and shook his head at her as if to say she wasn't helping.

"I'm not the one you should be afraid of," Aurius shouted back at him.

"Our future Queen would never harm us."

Aurius tilted his head to the side and shrugged. "So much for our anonymous arrival through the forest."

Gwen turned to the surrounding villagers. "The dark prince was escorting me through Aurum. He is my rescuer, not to be harmed."

"He's evil!" a woman shouted.

"That may be so, but he's my evil escort and he will not be harmed."

The people whispered among themselves.

"We have important business to discuss with Uncle George. Will you continue our escort to his shop?"

The group turned to the leader, who had spoken first. "We will escort you."

"George might not be happy about this."

"I will gladly sacrifice his happiness to break the curse and bring peace to this land," Gwen declared.

The leader nodded and motioned for them to follow. The king had left a few trees in the capital near the castle. They soon gave way to the structures of the city. The group stayed on the edges and walked beside back entrances and alleys. Gwen thought these places would be dark and dangerous, but with the midday sun bright in the sky, they didn't seem frightening at all. Twenty people formed a line without words. They stayed close to the walls of buildings as if on instinct.

When they approached an opening that led to the main street, they halted. The leader leaned around the corner and kept watch for activity. When the clank of metal armor echoed down the narrow corridor, he snapped back around and pressed himself against the wall. The others followed suit. Gwen held her breath to keep from making a noise. Seconds ticked by.

A young boy darted into the corridor, yelling insults at the guard. Gwen opened her mouth to protest, but Aurius's hand was over it immediately. Holding her firmly in place to keep from chasing the boy. When the sounds of marching soldiers faded, the leader motioned for them to move along. "Don't worry. He's fast," he whispered as Gwen passed by. He rejoined the lead once everyone had gotten safely past the intersection.

After half an hour of walking, Gwen realized their group was down to only five or six. In another half hour, they were standing in George's underground shop in front of an angry tailor. Gwen allowed the tension in her shoulders to relax a fraction.

"Uncle George.. this is..." She motioned to the man standing behind her. Calm. Relaxed Aurius. He seemed to have the Goblin under control now that they were in the city. Or perhaps the Goblin had settled on their journey, satiated by her presence. There hadn't been many disturbances on their way. But Gwen didn't trust his absence. Was the goblin biding his time and lulling them into a peace, waiting to surprise Aurius into losing the last scrap of himself altogether?

"The Dark Prince."

"Prince Aurius."

George remained stiff. He didn't take his eyes off the prince. "Why have you come?" he asked.

Gwen popped her head in front of his face, blocking his view of Aurius. "I need your help."

Uncle George rolled his eyes. "Usually."

"We need a way into the castle."

"No."

"No? Why not. You've helped me before."

"I helped you when you were running from Ryland. You would never have eluded him. But I cannot in good conscience help a traitor."

Gwen leveled her eyes at him. "I have escaped him. With a little help. But I'm not a traitor."

"Perhaps not. Are you delusional? Stockholm's syndrome perhaps?" George asked.

"I'm not sick."

"Have you fallen in love with your captor?" he asked again.

Gwen looked at Aurius, who leaned against a desk. Relaxed. Arms crossed over each other. Legs crossed at the ankles. Waiting for her to work this out.

She knew Aurius would not harm her. Not even the goblin would hurt her. That part she was less sure of; maybe she had been persuaded by the book she had found under Aurius's bed when she was recovering. She couldn't guess what he might do to others, but she wasn't afraid of him. Aurius only ever allowed her to choose her fate unless it endangered her life.

But George wouldn't understand that, and there was no time to explain. "Which captor?" she asked.

Uncle George groaned. "Are you choosing Ryland?"

"I haven't," she cut her eyes toward Aurius, "made my choice yet."

"You know… you would think by now you would be good at the lying."

"Maybe you've always been good at seeing through them."

Gwen had lied a lot to many people. Maybe the fact that George could see through it was a good thing. Or maybe this was penance for all the lies she told.

"Look. If I can get into the castle and get what I need, there might not be a choice to be made. I can end the curse and everyone can go back to a life with or without magic. Aurum will be restored and I can go home."

George leaned in. His voice was barely a whisper. "Very rarely does everyone get everything they want. You will have to admit your feelings eventually. The one trying to please everyone, usually loses the most." He spoke with the confidence of experience.

Gwen shrugged. "Maybe. but today… my choice is to try to free Aurum, Prince Ryland, Prince Aurius and myself. And then we can make choices based on our own free will and not some curse or contract forcing it upon us."

"Ryland is a good man." The assertion came in a fatherly tone.

Gwen squinted her eyes at him. "Define good."

Aurius stepped toward them and spoke for the first time. "You mean the man who purchased her from her father, kidnapped her, threw her in a dungeon which almost killed her, bought her a pretty dress…"

"I bought myself that dress actually." She was proud of that purchase.

"With the money he gave you."

Gwen shrugged.

"Then locked her in another room, which almost killed her again, left her alone to fend for herself in front of hundreds of people, which nearly killed her again. Then allowed an assassination attempt via dress."

George's lips twitched at the mention of the dress assassin. "You know, most of those things were done by the king, not Ryland."

Aurius's scoff echoed through the empty room. "Then at best he is ineffectual."

George looked at Gwen. "Will this mission help Ryland or not?"

Gwen took a moment to release a deep breath. "If we are successful it will help everyone."

His eyes turned toward the floor. "Then you had better go now."

Aurius straightened his body at the change in tone. "What have you done?"

"I sent a messenger to the royal guard. They will be here any minute."

"I... I trusted you," Gwen said.

"The first rule of being a leader Gwen... Trust no one." He sighed. "I'm sorry I betrayed you. But my first responsibility will be Ryland and Aurum always."

George was patriotic, and he loved the royal children as if he really were their uncle. She couldn't blame him. She wished her own father had protected her so fiercely. Maybe that's why she had trusted him so fully. Something she could examine later. When she wasn't in danger of being imprisoned again.

George rushed her through the office to a different entrance than he had given her last time. He motioned to a boy with a single finger. "Rat will take you through the tunnels."

He patted her on the back. "If you have magic, use it. The tunnels are dangerous. I only allow my most skilled down there and only at certain times."

Gwen's breath hitched. "I take it this is not the best time."

"No."

"What's down there?" Aurius asked.

"Nothing you want to meet. Do not let the boy out of your sight and if he says stop you stop. If he says go, you go."

Gwen and Aurius shared a look. He held out a hand as if to say, after you. "What a gentleman," she replied.

He shrugged. "You're the one that wants to save the world." He turned to George. "If she dies because of your cowardice, I will hunt you down and sever your toes, grind them into a powder and feed them to the cats that sit on your stoop."

George blinked twice at the threat and swallowed hard. "You should go now. I'd like to keep my toes on my feet."

Gwen pulled Aurius into the tunnel. "Come on, your highness, we have a curse to break."

He lingered just a second longer to let his threat settle and then stepped through the opening. Uncle George sealed them into the darkness.

Rat

"I think that threat was a bit unnecessary," Gwen said as the trio passed into the tunnels.

"Entirely necessary. And not a threat." Aurius's eyes flashed with a hint of green and then turned back to their rich brown.

The tunnels were dark and damp. Not black as pitch. She could see a couple of steps in front of her thanks to the glowworms living in the crevices of the rocks that formed the arched structure. Gwen wondered how George had gotten the dresses into the castle before they mildewed.

Rat was stealthy, as his name implied. He didn't speak but motioned with hand gestures to follow, stay put, left, right. No one had said not to talk. The atmosphere implied it.

After walking for half a mile, taking twists and turns, Gwen tried to build an image in her head of the underground system. She sighed when that failed, receiving a dirty look from Rat and a sharp poke in the back from Aurius.

Rat held up his little fist for them to stop. He turned to them with wide eyes.

"I leave you now."

"What? No. We can't get out," Gwen said in a harsh whisper.

But it was too late. The space where Rat had stood filled with darkness.

She moved to follow him. Aurius pushed her against the wall and pressed his hand over her mouth. He shook his head, indicating that there was no way they were going to find the little boy.

The darkness pressed in on them. An oily dread crept toward them, suffocating any hope of escape. Gwen could feel the stifling presence of a creature drawing nearer. The glow worms dimmed as if they were afraid a predator might see them.

Gwen pressed into Aurius, ready to grab him and run. His eyes widened when she wrapped her arm around his waist, momentarily taking his attention off the threat inching its way toward them.

Gwen screamed when the creature touched her foot, but it came out as a muffled whimper with Aurius's hand still over her mouth.

The creature shifted closer to the sound. It seemed to take up the entire width of the tunnel. Gwen's instinct was to run. To get away from the threat. But Aurius held her firm against the stone wall, shielding her and willing her to stay put.

Just as all her muscles bunched to burst into a sprint, a muffled bang echoed through the tunnel.

The creature stopped its advance. Frozen. Waiting for another sound. Bang, bang, bang. It sounded as if someone had hit a metal spoon against a cauldron. The creature retreated toward the sound.

After many long minutes, another creature popped into their vision. Aurius grabbed him by the throat, but after realizing it was their guide, he quickly released him.

Rat rubbed his throat for a second and narrowed his eyes at Aurius. He took a tentative step away from the goblin and motioned for them to follow. Aurius looked at Gwen. She shrugged. What choice did they have?

Minutes went by, and the inky fear shrunk away, dissipating into the depths. The tunnel brightened with its retreat. Gwen gestured to her mouth, asking if it was safe to speak.

Rat nodded his agreement.

Gwen kept her voice low. "What was that?"

"A scraper." Gwen had expected the answer from Rat, but the whispered words came from behind her. Barely a breath away from her ear.

"Care to explain?"

"It resembles black fluffy gelatin. But it can instill fear in its victims. It grows to the size of its enclosure. They sweep through tunnels and help to keep them clean."

"It scrapes gunk from walls," Rat added.

"Let's not run into that thing again."

Rat shook his head and put his finger back to his lip. And everyone froze, waiting for his command.

He nodded and motioned for them to follow again.

They took a few silent, tentative steps. Their feet squished sound into the sludge at the bottom of the tunnel.

Moments later, Rat stopped and held up his fist. His head moved from side to side. Then, just one word chilled her bones. "Run!" Rat's voice was an urgent whisper.

Gwen followed as best she could as he turned left, then right and straight for a few steps. A steady rumble became closer. Until the noise swallowed all other sounds. The moisture in her mouth dried, but the cavern floor seemed to become slicker as they approached the roar. Her hands shook, wanting to reach for a weapon.

Hope swelled in her chest that perhaps they were running toward safety. Gwen covered her mouth; her eyes widened at the thought. A spark of energy zapped through her body. She released the tension with a whimper. Somewhere in the tunnels behind them, a monster hunted them, but in front of them, and equally dangerous, was the hopeful roar of rushing water.

Just as the hope blossomed to life, the darkness claimed Rat. Gwen continued to pursue him. A firm hand wrapped around her arm just as her toe touched the sharp ledge. Aurius pulled her back against him.

Had Rat screamed? The roar had drowned all sounds except the beating of her heart in her eardrums.

Aurius's lips were on her ear. "He fell, but you can still save him."

The clasp of the necklace clicked behind her neck as Aurius removed it. "Reach out to him with your magic."

She didn't have time to think about it. Closing her eyes, she focused on the signature of magic everyone had inside them. The golden glitter of magic popped into her mind. It stood out against the darkness. Aurius's magic roared to life beside her. It was a blazing inferno. She stepped away from him. Then she felt a tiny dot of magic zipping away fast. Not through the tunnels, but down.

She felt the tug from the center of her soul. Within her, the gates that kept the well of magic from flowing out all at once broke open, answering Gwen's vital need. She allowed her magic to flow from her. Over the ledge and down the cavern. An extension of herself, she urged it to hurry. This chasm couldn't go on forever, and there wasn't much time. Her magic raced toward the falling speck. Reaching further than ever. Just as she thought it was too late, that the little light racing to the bottom of the chasm would be out of reach, she gave it a little magical push and latched on to it.

Then pulled. If she thought pushing the magic out was difficult, pulling it in was far more so. Pulling it in with someone else in tow made the effort slow. When Rat reached the ledge, she let him down to the ground next to her. His body slowly crumpled.

Gwen realized she was holding Aurius's hand. The muscles in his body were rigid. Gwen's fingers popped away from his, and he sucked in a long gasp of air. He stumbled back and lowered himself against the rock wall.

Gwen knelt beside him. "I was mistaken." She thought she heard him say. Though she barely heard over the roar of the waterfall. His eyes glowed green again. He waved her away. "Tend to the boy," he groaned.

Reluctantly, she turned to Rat. She felt for a breath and listened to his chest for a heartbeat.

Both were working fine. She didn't know how to wake him or what to do next.

Aurius joined her.

"Are you alright? What happened."

"It's just fright."

Gwen tilted her head and pressed her eyebrows together. She had never known Aurius to be frightened of anything. Except fairies, and that seemed to be just a general dislike.

"The boy. He's just frightened. He'll wake soon."

Gwen didn't see any sense in pushing him to answer her question about himself. It was too loud, and Aurius wouldn't say anything until he was ready.

The boy stirred at their feet. "Am I dead?" he asked. His voice groaned with the strain of using it after such an ordeal.

Gwen put her hand on the back of his head and helped him to sit up. "No, you aren't dead."

"Gwen saved you," Aurius said.

The boy said nothing. His arms flew around her waist, and he snuggled in against her chest. She patted his back. When he pulled away, his eyes were wet.

"Is it safe to go on?" she asked.

The boy nodded and rose to his feet.

He didn't speak, but motioned with a wave for Gwen and Aurius to follow.

She leaned toward Aurius. "Don't think I'm forgetting about what happened."

He opened her hand and placed the locket in it.

"I wouldn't dream of it, but we'll talk about this later." He closed her fingers around the magical trinket. "Put this back on. Do not take it off again."

"And if I need to use magic?"

Aurius grumbled. "You won't."

"How can you know that."

He didn't answer, stalking away from her in pursuit of the boy.

The tunnels seemed to tilt downhill as if they were going deeper underground. The roar of rushing water had diminished, and now it was a low, distant rumble. As the trio trotted lower, the darkness receded marginally. The tunnels filled with a glow from the space around a corner. Their feet crunched over dark gravel.

A few more steps later. Rat stopped by a glowing lake, similar to the one she and Avonlea had swum in before.

"This boat will take you to the castle," the boy said. The water slapped against the wooden hull of the tiny craft, beating out a gentle rhythm.

"Is it enchanted?" Gwen asked.

"Yes. It goes by itself to the castle and back."

Gwen and Aurius jumped away from the feminine voice that was behind them. Aurius immediately reached for the knife on his hip.

Princess Avonlea

"Avonlea?" Gwen pushed around Aurius. The princess wasn't dressed in her usual flouncy dress. Instead, black leather pants and a tight leather tunic covered her body and down her arms. Her hair was pulled tight against her head and braided down her back. A leather band covered the plait.

The princess pushed off the rock. "Gwen. I'm glad you've come. Though I don't care for the company you keep."

"He's a friend," Gwen said.

"The dark prince is hardly your friend, Gwen. I understand you haven't had many, so you would search for them in the lowest of pits."

Aurius growled in response.

"I consider you a friend as well," Gwen replied.

Avonlea pulled a corner of her lips up and tilted her head away from Gwen. She looked her up and down. "It's nice to see he's fed you at least."

"Are you here to stop us from entering the castle?" Aurius asked.

Avonlea raised her lips in a shocked sneer. "No. Of course not. I would be no match against two magic users."

"Then why are you here?"

"To escort you," Avonlea said.

Aurius's deep voice responded. "Why?"

She folded one arm over the other. The movement allowed Gwen to see the long sword strapped to her friend's back. "Why me or why am I escorting you?"

Aurius glared back at her attempt to goad him. "Uncle George said you would need some help navigating the underground lake. I'm here to help. We thought a familiar face might be best."

"We?" Gwen and Aurius said together.

Avonlea shifted her eyes between them. "Drake, George and I. We couldn't include Ryland. He's bent on taking down the barrier and destroying Mystrim. Last I heard, he was about to breech it, but somehow it only got stronger."

Gwen's mouth dropped open, and a small whimper escaped her. "I thought my aunt negotiated a truce?"

Aurius growled at the slip about her lineage.

"Aunt?"

"Nevermind. Why is Ryland attacking Mystrim?" Gwen asked.

"Because you didn't choose him." Her eyes shifted toward Aurius. "Did you?"

"I.." The words caught in Gwen's throat.

Avonlea's voice lowered. "It wasn't Ryland you saw in the pool was it?"

Gwen's head bowed. "No."

Avonlea stepped toward her and reached for her hand. Aurius stepped between them, causing Avonlea to take a step back. "It's ok. I understand why you lied."

Gwen nodded and wrung her hands. She couldn't bring herself to raise her eyes and face the princess. "I did lie a lot. But there was much I was just ignorant about."

"Stepfather didn't give you much choice. And Ryland is…" She didn't continue. Whatever she thought of her brother, she couldn't bring herself to say it out loud.

"Why is Drake helping? He hates me."

"He doesn't hate you. He just didn't think you were being completely honest with us. Turns out he is very good at his job."

Gwen shook her head. "I'm sorry."

A growl reminded her that Aurius was still between them. "Don't you dare apologize to her Gwen," Aurius said. "They took you from your home and threatened to kill you if you didn't do as they said. They don't get an apology."

Gwen put a gentle hand on his forearm. "She is my friend Aurius."

His voice remained low, forcing her to pay close attention. "Friends don't force you into a lie and then make you apologize for it."

"He's right. You don't owe us an apology. You couldn't have known that we would have helped you. How could you?"

"You would have helped me?" Gwen asked.

"We've been plotting against the king for ages. We would have found a way to let you escape."

"Drake did let me escape."

Avonlea and Aurius pursed their lips. Aurius whipped his head toward her as Avonlea tilted hers. "Did he?"

Gwen shrugged. "But George convinced me Ryland needed me."

"George does have a soft spot for Ryland. But I think he's beginning to see that this can't go on any longer," Avonlea said.

"What's happened?"

"Stepfather has used the kidnapping to fuel some innate rage in Ryland. He can't seem to stop himself since the wedding."

Gwen exchanged a look with Aurius. His said I told you so. Hers said I can't believe he's acting like a dragon.

Aurius narrowed his eyes at Avonlea, challenging her to back away. The princess stood her ground. "We need a moment," he said through clenched teeth.

Avonlea froze for a moment longer, lifted her hands and took a few steps back to the cavern wall. "Don't take too long. The window to get into the castle undetected is closing."

Aurius drug Gwen to the side. "I don't trust her," he whispered.

Gwen nodded. "It is sketchy. I'm surprised she would go against Ryland. But we knew she knew that I knew about the tunnels. And George sent us into the tunnels."

Aurius lowered his voice further. "This is a trap."

Gwen nodded and looked around him to Avonlea. She was sharpening a dagger on a stone as if that were the most important thing she had ever done. How long had she been training, Gwen wondered. "An elaborate one," she agreed. Gwen put her hand on his forearm. "What are we going to do? Just leave without the sword?"

His heavy sigh came out more like a feral snort. "We need a better plan."

"This is what we've got." she said.

His eyes cut to hers. "Do you trust me?"

Gwen dipped her chin. "Aurius. What are you going to do?"

"Just do everything in your power to get the sword." He winked.

Aurius turned to Avonlea. "We accept your offer."

She clapped her hands together and batted her eyelashes. "Oh good." Her voice turned flat. "Everyone into the boat."

Avonlea turned toward the boy.

"I'll take it from here, Rat."

The boy shook his head. "I want to stay with Gwen."

Avonlea's eyes shifted back to Gwen, then she lifted her chin. "It seems you are quite good at making friends."

Gwen knelt before the boy. "Rat. I love that you want to stay with us and I normally wouldn't have it any other way. We need all the friends we can get, truly. But this next part is going to be very dangerous. I don't want to see you hurt."

The once-confident boy nearly turned to tears. "You'll die?"

Gwen smiled and booped his nose. "Any moment might be our last. A rock over head could fall from the ceiling and kill me dead. This is no more dangerous than walking through dark tunnels with will-sucking monsters."

The boy wrapped his arms around her neck again.

"Well met, Rat." She squeezed around his thin waist.

His tiny voice tickled her inner ear. "My real name is Rathford."

"Thank you for telling me." She pulled away and placed a fist over her heart. "I'll carry it with me always." She gave him an encouraging smile.

With that, he pushed away and disappeared into the shadows.

Avonlea had already sat at the helm of the boat. Aurius lifted Gwen's hand and helped her into the middle seat. "After you, Princess," he said.

Gwen gave him a withering glare.

The boat pitched to the side as Aurius stepped over the edge with one foot and pushed off with the other. He quickly found his seat to keep the boat from capsizing.

"So want to tell me about it? Or should we play twenty questions?" Avonlea asked.

"I think for now the less you know the better," Gwen said. The boat gently rocked as it steered itself to the deepest part of the river.

"You still don't trust me?"

"I don't trust your stepfather. He would torture information out of you just to get to us."

She nodded and sighed. "I can usually out maneuver that threat, but it is getting more difficult. I wonder what his obsession is with you."

"Aric is a dragon," Aurius said in a flat tone as if that explained everything.

Gwen cut her eyes toward Aurius. Expecting his brown eyes to be focused on her. But they hadn't returned to their normal brown. They remained mossy green. Had they run out of time?

Avonlea didn't seem shocked by Aurius's statement at all.

"Of course he is," she said. "But he lost his magic, along with everyone else, twenty years ago when Rumpelstiltskin was swallowed by the Earth."

"Yes, except dragon shifters are cursed with greed. The curse is still active," Aurius said, ignoring the use of his father's name for the first time since Gwen met him.

Gwen turned her attention back to the princess to ask a question she had been burning to know since Aurius had dropped the dragon bomb on her. "Avonlea. Is Drake a dragon too?"

"Of course not. He's a changeling."

Gwen noticed Aurius went predator still. The muscles in his throat bobbed. "A changeling?" he asked.

The air around the boat suddenly seemed unsettled. Gwen wound her arms around her stomach trying to ease the knot that had formed.

Avonlea nodded her affirmation. "He was born in Mystrim. Before our kingdoms were enemies. The queens exchanged children. It was common practice. So that children could experience other kingdoms courts. My mother had a child with someone other than my father. I don't know who, but my father wanted him gone. One night my father held the baby over the ledge of the castle tower. My mother pleaded with him to reconsider. She already had an agreement with Queen Helen to trade Drake for the child. But when Drake arrived he wasn't treated as a prince. He wasn't told about his lineage. He simply thought he was an orphan." Avonlea stopped abruptly. "That's his story to tell. I've let my mouth run away with me. It's been so long since I've had anyone I can talk to."

"How long ago was this? Have you told Drake?" Gwen asked.

"Drake is twenty-five years old?" She didn't sound sure. "Give or take a month. He is aware of his lineage now. Mother's been gone for years and I felt it was unfair for him to think he was a captain when he is really a prince."

"And then she had you with your father?" Aurius asked.

Avonlea lifted her chin. "Yes. He died not long after I was born."

"How do you know this?" Aurius's voice had dropped an octave. All the color had drained from his face and neck. Gwen had never seen his skin so white.

"It's in the family archives. The ones Stepfather doesn't want anyone to read. He tried to destroy them, but some were protected and he couldn't do anything to them. When I've really upset him, I'm sent to my room, but as you know I have secrets." She smiled and winked at Gwen. "I'm able to visit the archives without anyone's knowledge."

Gwen smiled and nodded, still trying to gauge Aurius's reaction to this new information.

"Then Stepfather hinted at it not long ago." Avonlea's eyes dulled with sadness. "He was considering our marriage, but decided against it."

"And that's the reason you're helping me?" Gwen asked.

She shook her head. "I'm helping you because you need my help. If it also hurts my stepfather then bonus points to me. I'd also like to see Ryland out from under his influence."

Gwen couldn't read Aurius. He looked as if a fish had just jumped out of the lake and kissed him on the cheek. Her eyebrows pushed together as tried to fit his reaction into the puzzle.

The boat lurched to a stop, sending the members of the boat flailing forward and back. Gwen put the Aurius puzzle out of her mind. There wasn't time or energy for it, and he would tell her when he was ready. She scanned the new location. It looked much the same as every other place in the underground tunnel: dark, grey and rocky.

"Where are we?" Gwen asked Avonlea.

Avonlea exited the boat and turned to face them, crossing her arms over her chest. "Before you go to the castle there is something else we need to do," Avonlea said.

Gwen stood nearly jumping out of the boat. "We are running out of time, Avonlea."

"I wasn't aware of a deadline for rebellion."

"I can't explain. But there is a deadline."

"Gwen, if you want me to trust you, you are going to have to show me a little bit of trust."

Gwen narrowed her eyes. "Your uncle just taught me that the first lesson of leading is to trust no one."

"That is his experience. He has a lot of people depending on him. Trust is a risk. You have to decide what that risk is worth." Her tone brooked no argument.

Gwen considered it. She looked at Aurius, who was still recovering from Avonlea's news about Drake, lost in his own thoughts. This was the only way into the castle, and they had to get into the castle. If it were a trap, it had already been sprung. There was no way out now. She sighed and nodded, looking over her shoulder at Aurius with a raised eyebrow.

He followed her out of the boat as if pulled by a string. The crunching sound their feet made on the sharp slate gravel echoed. No one said a word as they followed Avonlea to a doorway twenty feet from the water's edge. A natural cave water had carved out during a time with much more water.

Aurius finally shook off the apparent shock of Drake's news and halted in front of her. He clasped Gwen's wrist, encircling it with his thumb and forefinger. "Gwen I need to tell you before we go in there."

Gwen turned away only to be pulled back toward him. "Aurius. We need to hurry. Your time is running out." Her eyes shifted to the cave room.

"I know." His rough hand encircled hers. "But I was wrong about your magic."

She tilted her head and pushed her eyebrows together. "I don't understand."

"I didn't either at first. But you aren't..." he swallowed. "You aren't a catalyst. At least, not like we thought."

"What do you mean? If I'm not that, then what am I?"

"It doesn't have a name but your magic can take magic from others."

"I know. The lady, the night at the barrier, she showed me how my magic works," Gwen said.

He shook his head. "I should have listened to you."

One thing Aurius never did was apologize. And this sounded a lot like an apology. "Aurius, what are you talking about?"

He took her hand and held it firm. "Your magic. It's familiar to me. I didn't question in at first. Your magic has always complemented my own."

The point where their skin touched was like a burning inferno. She couldn't concentrate on exactly what he was saying. Gwen tugged against him, but he held her firm.

"You weren't born with catalyst magic. Your magic is more powerful. And it rarely gets used up because it searches out magic from other places."

"So that means." She tried to pull away again, but he drew her closer.

He shook his head. "You were a baby. You didn't know." His thumb slid across her cheek. "You couldn't control it."

"My mother, Aurius. That's what she was talking about. That's why I locked away my magic."

Aurius let go of her hand and grabbed both of her shoulders. "What happened?"

The moisture in her eyes threatened to spill over. "She said it wasn't my fault, but that I had locked down my magic because I thought it was."

He shook her a little, his talons pressed into the flesh on her upper arm. "You didn't kill her."

A sob ripped from her throat. "She died because of me."

"You didn't kill her," Aurius repeated.

"It's the same thing."

He let go of her shoulder. His arms wound around her. "No. It's not."

Gwen wanted to collapse. Aurius's arm slid to her waist before her knees could buckle. "Why did she let me? Why would she let me slowly drain her magic from her. That had to be the worst type of death."

"She was protecting you," Aurius said into her hair.

Gwen couldn't keep the tears from flowing. "From what?" she sniffed.

He pushed her back and met her eyes. He swiped a curl from her face and behind her ear. "From a life of being used for your power, Gwen."

"How is starving to death in a hovel better than that?" she asked.

"I don't think that was her intention. She was doing what she thought was right."

"She gave her life and all she did was create a different prison."

"I didn't tell you this so that you can go nihilistic." Aurius's voice was low. "Why?"

"You can detect magic with your power. Just like you did earlier saving Rat. Your magic seeks out the magic in others. Without thinking or training you took my magic and used it for your purposes."

She gasped and covered her mouth with her hand, trying to pull away, but he held her firm. "Oh my word." Gwen stepped in and put her palm over his heart. He covered it with his. "Aurius. I'm so sorry. Are you hurt?" The tears formed for her mother turned to tears for him.

He shook his head and offered. "No." His voice was firm. He wasn't going to baby her. "You gave it right back, again instinctively, which is how I know you didn't kill your mother."

Gwen pulled her hand from his and pushed her fingers into her hair on either side of her head. She squeezed her eyes shut.

"Your magic is instinctual, but you can learn to control it."

Gwen's fingers went back to the locket around her neck. "So this isn't to protect me? It's to protect everyone else."

Aurius shrugged. "Maybe both. I think it has weakened a bit as you've grown. Certainly now that you have discovered and used your magic."

Gwen took a step away from him and released a long, deep breath. "No wonder Papa was ready to get rid of me."

"Gwen," Aurius growled. But she held up a hand, cutting off whatever else he was about to say. Taking a page from Avonlea's book, she lifted her chin and squared her shoulders. No use in wallowing. There were bigger problems. The least of which was what they would do if they found out the type of magic she possessed. If she was dangerous with two types of magic... She shut her eyes and opened them again, finding Aurius watching her with his head tilted.

She offered a brave smile. "Ok. What do we do now?"

"Use your magic to search for the sword."

She took a deep breath of the cool, moist cavern air. "That is helpful," she nodded. "Now we know I don't have two types of magic, so no need to." She drew a line across her neck and clicked her tongue.

Aurius growled as he did every time she talked about dying. "You have powerful magic Princess Gwen of Mystrim, Miller's daughter. Use your power to save your kingdoms." He bent to meet her eyes and caressed her cheek. "While I'm going over strategy, you reach out with your magic to search for the sword."

She bobbed her head and wiped her eyes.

He narrowed his eyes and lifted her chin. "Remember to trust me."

She gave him what she thought might be a reassuring smile.

He squeezed her hand. "It's instinctual. Just let down your walls and let it do its job," he said, pulling her through the door into Avonlea's hideout.

Rebellion

Avonlea strode around the stone table and sat at the head. A true princess in every sense of the word. In just a few months, she had gone from court manipulator to battle strategist.

Maps were strewn about the table. A large map of the two kingdoms. And then smaller, more detailed maps of the areas within the kingdoms. Gwen stretched to look at them. Places she knew, like her village and the felled woods, were easy to find. Many places were unknown to her. Little pieces dotted the maps, leaving Gwen wondering what that meant.

Avonlea flicked her hand over her shoulder toward Aurius. "Captain. This is the Dark Prince. He doesn't like that name, though, so you'll have to ask him what he want's to be called."

Drake lifted his head from where he hovered over the maps with a raised eyebrow. "I didn't know goblins gave out their names so readily." He didn't seem overly concerned that the Dark Prince had arrived at their underground rebel base.

It earned him a glare from Aurius. "You could call me the Goblin King, but that is a mouth full. My friends call me Aurius."

"He does have a name?" Drake leaned back, crossed his arms over his chest and raised his eyebrows.

"You are not Rumpelstiltskin?" Avonlea asked.

Aurius cut his eyes away from Drake toward the princess. "He was my father," he admitted.

"Well, now that introductions are out of the way. We'll begin." Avonlea motioned to the captain. "Drake."

Aurius held up a finger. "I don't think the changeling was introduced to me," Aurius said, placing the tips of his fingers over his heart and bowing slightly at the waist.

"Aurius." Gwen's tone held a warning. He only raised an eyebrow and let a bottom incisor poke out over his top lip, imploring her silently to remember to trust him.

Drake glared. "Obviously, you heard my name is Drake."

"Oh good. At least he knows he's a changeling." Aurius tilted his head and pouted his lips. "How does it feel to be rejected by your mother?"

A sword was at Aurius's throat before Gwen could blink an eye. "I was trapped here by the curse your father created."

"I think you will find that it was your mother who erected the barrier. And she could have crossed it at any time to retrieve you."

Drake moved closer to Aurius's face. "What do you know of my mother?" He snarled his words slowly.

Aurius leaned away from the blade at his throat but didn't seem afraid. "Oh a great deal. It was she who raised me after my father died."

Drake pushed Aurius against a nearby wall. Gwen could hear the breath rush out of him as his back hit the damp stone wall between two flaming sconces. It didn't stop him from smirking, though.

"Do you think you can best me with a sword?" Aurius asked.

"Yes."

"Confidence. I like that, but can you beat me with magic?"

Drake narrowed his eyes. The point of his sword pressed into Aurius's shirt. "I don't have magic so of course not," he growled.

Aurius tilted his head and pushed his lips up in the middle. "Aw. The changeling from the magical land of Mystrim doesn't have magic," he said, his tone mocking.

Avonlea and Gwen poised to step into the fray, but neither moved.

Drake pushed him harder against the wall and growled. Then he stepped back and put his sword in its scabbard, returning to the stone table in the center of the room.

Aurius pushed himself away from the wall. "Shall we do an experiment?"

he said. As everyone else in the room grew silent.

"We've had enough of your games," Drake said.

"Oh but the games have just begun," Aurius trilled.

Gwen leaned the fronts of her legs against the table. Her hair had mostly come undone. Strands hung loosely over her shoulder as she looked at the maps, ignoring whatever Aurius was doing.

"Gwen, can I borrow your locket?" Aurius asked.

Gwen's hand instinctively reached for the keepsake. "I don't think that's a good idea."

Aurius's eyes shifted slowly from Drake to Gwen, reminding her of the conversation five minutes earlier. He was buying her time to find the sword. That was the look she couldn't resist. She couldn't help the little hitch in her mouth at the thought of those green eyes boring into her. Still, she hesitated to let him have the trust he asked for.

Aurius shifted from the wall and stood behind her. "It's ok, princess. Let me play," he whispered. His fingers grazed her shoulders as she nodded and lifted her hair. He released the clasp and caught the locket before it could fall an inch.

"Drake hold this." The locket flew through the air, glittering in the light from the chandelier over the table.

"Why would I..." but the locket was in his hands before he could get the words out. He doubled over, wrapping his arm around his waist. Sweat poured from his face, which had turned a dark shade of red.

His eyes widened as flames flashed across them. "What is happening?"

"Let it out Drake. That raging inferno you keep buried just beneath the surface. All the insults from people beneath you. Let out that rage." Aurius taunted. He shoved Gwen in the shoulder, and she landed in the corner away from Drake. Aurius gave her a look, saying she should use her power right now. But did he expect her to extract Drake's magic or look for the sword?

The look on his face said both.

She used the corner for support and let her magic out to search for the magic of the curse-breaking sword. She willed it through stone walls and under doors. Once the mission was clear, the magic responded on its own.

Searching. It even had a sense of urgency. Knowing there wasn't much time to accomplish its task. Then Gwen divided the magic without physical movement. She reserved some to stay with her, surrounding Drake with a bubble of protective magic. Something she didn't even know she had. Had she taken it from someone? There wasn't time to examine that.

"Aurius help him."

To Gwen's surprise, it was not her voice commanding the Goblin King.

Aurius stepped away from Drake, allowing Gwen's magic between them. "As you wish. But favors from goblins come with a price."

"Since you are the one who caused his distress the only one paying the price will be you." Avonlea's voice was steady, and her expression brooked no argument.

"Fine. Fine." Aurius lifted his hands in defense and turned his attention to Drake. "I think I know who your father was. I can't be sure though."

Veins popped on Drake's neck. His jaw was locked and his teeth were gritted.

"You're trying too hard to keep it in. You need to let go." Aurius said. His tone was even and calm. The playful mockery had vanished. "Let the fire burn."

"I will... destroy everyone." Drake ground out the words.

"It just so happens you won't."

"No," Drake moaned.

"Then you will continue to suffer," he lowered his voice. "And die."

"Auirus," Avonlea warned.

Just as he turned to respond to her, the inferno burst from Drake, drawing his attention back. Gwen's magic absorbed the magical flames that raged for minutes. Sweat dripped from her brow. She struggled to control the inferno.

Just as she was about the drop the shield magic, the flames finally died down, and Drake stood in awe. There was a small flame in the palm of his hand. Gwen struggled to get her breath. Fortunately, all the attention was on Drake, and she could focus on regaining control of herself. The dark corner helped to shroud her struggle.

"There. Was that so bad?" He nodded to Gwen. She funneled her magic back into searching for the sword.

"Yes," the others in the room said in unison. A smile played on Aurius's lips. Gwen had known he could manipulate a room; she just hadn't seen this side of him in a while.

Avonlea covered her mouth with both hands. "You have fire magic." She giggled.

"Yes," Drake said. "It seems that I do."

"It looks as though your dad was the candle maker in Mystrim. The only man in Mystrim I know with fire magic."

"So I'm not a prince?" he asked.

Aurius placed his chin between his thumb and forefinger. "Queen Helen is definitely your mother. Looks like you might have been a minor accident though. It would have been tough to give you up, I imagine. Being royal requires some hard decisions. She wouldn't have been able to be queen with an illegitimate son, though."

Drake's eyes turned dark. Gwen recognized when he shut down at the thought. "I don't want to talk about this," he said.

"That makes you Gwen's cousin by birth."

Drake whipped around to find Gwen standing in the corner.

She gave him a little wave. "Hi. Turns out I'm a princess after all."

He took a step toward her. "I have..."

Another step.

"Family."

He closed the distance between them and gathered her in his arms. She barely had time to think before he was swinging her around, unable to help the giggle that escaped her.

She put his arms around his neck and squeezed him back. A low growl escaped Aurius, but he didn't interfere.

"I can't believe we're related," Drake said, placing her back on the ground. He took a step back.

Gwen smiled. "My father, King Nolan, and Queen Helen were siblings." Drake gave her another squeeze and searched her eyes with a new appreciation.

Avonlea interrupted the reunion. "That explains the message we intercepted a few days ago," she said flatly and opened the door, whispering to a young man standing outside and shut the door again. Moments later, the door opened again, and a messenger brought a letter.

"This is addressed to you Gwen." She motioned for the letter to go to Gwen.

"Why would a letter arrive for me here? Helen wanted me to go to Aurius."

"Interesting. Perhaps you should read it," Avonlea said.

Gwen unfolded the letter and pulled at the edges.

Dearest Gwen,

Since the curse is not broken. I can only assume you haven't married Prince Aurius after all. I'm hoping this letter finds you. As Prince Ryland is trying to break through the barrier into our kingdom, I might assume you chose a different course altogether. If that is the case, let me remind you what is at stake. If you are captured, you will be imprisoned.

Worse, Aurius will turn into a goblin, which will unleash the worst kind of mayhem. I do not wish to see that kind of fate for him.

And perhaps worst of all, the barrier will fall and all the magic of Mystrim will succumb to the curse.

You have little time and a duty as a princess to set everything right.

My eternal Love,

Aunt Helen

"Interesting indeed," Avonlea said as she read over Gwen's shoulder. "It seems that Aunt Helen thinks you are the savior of us all."

Gwen folded the letter and threw it into the nearby fire. "That's what she says."

"And are you, our salvation?" Avonlea asked. Drake, having returned to Avonlea's side, looked over her with renewed interest.

"I'm doing my best. But I need to do this my way and not the way everyone thinks I should. Marrying Aurius will only satisfy the contract our parents signed for us. We don't think it will break the curse."

"But you think you know what will."

Gwen exchanged a look with Aurius. A look that held their entire mission in limbo. Do you trust me she asked? Aurius lifted his chin and pulled back the corners of his lips. Gwen took that as a sign to plunge ahead.

"We're looking for a sword," she said quietly.

Drake and Avonlea looked at her as if she had lost her mind. "There are plenty of swords just in this room."

"It's not an ordinary sword. It will," Gwen paused, not sure she should divulge all the secrets. Still not sure where Avonlea's loyalty would be. "We think it's magic might solve our problems."

"And you think this sword is in the castle?" Drake asked.

She dipped her chin. "I know it's in the castle."

Aurius's chest lifted a little, proud that she had accomplished her task.

"And where in the castle do you think it is?" Avonlea asked.

"In the middle of the dungeon there is a room. Magic is seeping out from it." That was as far as her magic could get, but she wasn't going to let the room have any more information about her magic than was necessary.

"The kings vault? The sword is in King Aric's vault." Drake said.

"It's impossible to get into that vault. It is protected by immense magic." Avonlea shook her head.

"Difficult sure... Impossible probably not." Aurius drew attention to himself.

"As soon as you arrive at the vault the king will be alerted. There is no way you can get around that."

Gwen smiled. "Thank you for letting us know."

"You're going to attempt it anyway."

Gwen met eyes with Aurius to see if they were still in agreement. He held her gaze. "We've come this far. We're going to see it through," she said.

Drake and Avonlea exchanged another look.

"We've shared our plans. I think its time for yours," Aurius said.

Drake nodded to Avonlea.

Avonlea put both palms on the stone table in front of her. Her single braid fell over her left shoulder. "We have been planning this since we were young. It wasn't always serious but with Ryland taken over we needed to take action."

"What's happened?" Gwen asked.

Aurius stepped beside Gwen. Instantly she felt more comfortable with his supportive presence nearby. "He is cursed but not in the way everyone thinks. Marrying Gwen won't solve it."

"He's been manipulated by the king. He's not cursed," Avonlea said.

Aurius shook his head. "All dragons are cursed. Just as all goblins are cursed. It's not something we can deny. Your stepfather is manipulating him, yes. But he's using the curse to do it."

Avonlea narrowed her eyes in a glare from across the table. "Respectfully, you don't know anything about Ryland."

He pressed his lips up in the middle. "I know about dragon curses."

Gwen clapped her hands, momentarily distracting them from their argument. "Ok. Moving on. Let's hear about this plan."

Avonlea shook her head as if coming out of a trance. She blinked a few times and looked over the maps. "We've been turning the people against the king. Using propaganda to turn the people to you, Gwen. Uncle George thought the idea was splendid. King Aric was going to use your kidnapping against Mystrim and the White Witch. But we used it against him."

"Wouldn't that turn the people against you as well?"

Avonlea shrugged. "I'm fine with that as long as King Aric is not on the throne."

"Will Ryland be fine with that?"

"It's really not up for debate. It's already been set in motion. The point is that we have a rebellion brewing. We have conscripted armies ready to defect and turn to the other side. Militia all over the kingdom ready to rise up and put the rightful king on the throne."

Gwen took a deep breath. Aurius brushed the side of her hand with his pinky. A small sign of support, encouragement, and a reminder that he was with her. He was for her.

"We can be your distraction," Drake said.

"While King Aric is away stamping out rebellions. You can get to the vault," Avonlea agreed.

The silence in the room was stifling. Did Gwen want people to die just so she could break the curse?

They all exchanged glances. This was the best way, the only way, forward. She bowed her head to acknowledge the future deaths. To mourn people she had never met, but would die for her cause. With a nod, she sealed their fate. It was a few men fighting for freedom or a kingdom dying without hope. The sacrifice was heavy to bear. She would carry it in her heart forevermore.

Silence sat heavy in the room. The next move would start a rebellion, and no one wanted to take that step lightly.

Gwen swallowed the lump in her throat just as the door burst open, pulling the occupants from their paralysis.

"What is it?" Avonlea asked.

"Ryland has returned from the front lines," the messenger said.

"He's home already?"

He wrung his hands and looked at his toes, stammering in response. "He's... something isn't right."

"Because he's a dragon," Aurius reminded them.

All eyes flicked to Aurius. "We know," they said together.

Aurius pouted innocently. "Well, alright so long as you know."

"Tell us what's happened," Gwen said.

He shook his head. "I can't explain. You'll have to see for yourself."

Gwen stepped back from the table and stood beside Avonlea. "We don't have much time. The sword is our priority."

"If we don't know what is happening with Ryland and why he's returned, it will be too dangerous." Avonlea pulled a cloth from the object in the corner closest to her. Immediately, the room grew brighter. Gwen recognized it. The mirror from George's dress shop.

"A magic mirror. Not many of those about. Impressive." Aurius said, pushing his lips up in the middle.

"It can only see certain people," Avonlea said. "It was a way that George could keep an eye on us as a promise to our mother."

Aurius cut his eyes to Gwen. Had she picked up on the magic from this object? She moved her head to tell him no.

Avonlea touched the mirror's edge. "Adspicio." As soon as the word was uttered, Ryland's image appeared on the silvery surface.

His normally perfect hair was messy and unkempt. His hands folded into fists as he stomped through his suite. Dark grey smoke billowed from his nostrils. His normally icy blue eyes turned dark and reptilian. He roared at nothing, lifted a sofa and threw it across the room.

The mirror went black.

Avonlea had certainly practiced keeping her emotions off her face.

She turned to Aurius. "Tell me what is happening to my brother."

"My guess is that he has dragon sickness," Aurius said.

Drake again had his sword out. "My guess is that he is a war dragon. When they go through their first shift a rage builds in their mind. Rage is part of their physiology. It fuels the shift, allowing them the ability to change and masks the pain."

Aurius tilted his head toward Drake, his eyes questioning.

"I wouldn't be a good captain if I didn't know who I was protecting."

"You knew he was a dragon?" Avonlea asked.

He held up a finger. "Suspected and now confirmed."

"But Ryland can't shift," Gwen said, bringing them back to the problem at hand.

Aurius shook his head.

Avonlea lifted her head and stared at Aurius. "So what will happen?"

"Hard to tell. But certainly it will get worse unless he can release the dragon within him."

"So we need to either break the curse or get him to Mystrim," Avonlea said.

Aurius nodded.

"Or both," Drake said.

Aurius shifted a chair away from the table. A scraping sound broke the quiet murmurs that had sprouted throughout the room. "Breaking the curse will suffice. No need to turn the dragons loose on Mystrim."

Gwen turned to Avonlea. "We need to get to the vault sooner rather than later."

The princess flipped her braid over her shoulder. "I guess we're starting the rebellion sooner than I had planned. I hope we've rallied enough people."

Gwen squeezed her hand. "It will be enough," she said, reassuring her friend.

"How can you be so sure?" Avonlea asked.

She shrugged. "If it's not, we're all dead and it won't matter anyway."

Drake stood. "I'll go to Ryland and see if I can calm him and buy you some time. But as soon as he or the king realizes the vault is compromised." He took a deep breath and shook his head. "You need to be gone before that happens."

Avonlea lifted her hand and motioned to the messenger by the door. "Get me the kings troop movements now." The boy bowed and raced out the door.

"I'll leave you. I hope to see you again AFTER all this is over," Drake said. Gwen didn't miss the small squeeze he gave the tip of Avonlea's fingers. Gwen's eyes shifted to Aurius. He hadn't missed it either.

Drake stepped through the doorway, barely avoiding the messenger as he raced back into the room with rolls of off-white parchment.

"Here are the reports you requested Princess." He bowed and left the room.

She took the scrolls and spread them on the table.

"This isn't terrible news. It looks as if my stepfather is in the northern part of the kingdom."

"Perhaps he heard reports of our crossing there," Gwen said.

"How? We didn't notify anyone. And there was no one in sight when we crossed," Aurius was surprisingly suspicious.

"There was a disturbance in the barrier. That could have tipped him off," she reasoned.

"How would he have known where it came from unless he is connected to the barrier in some way?"

Their eyes met. "Or someone he knows is connected."

Avonlea dismissed their discussion. "That doesn't matter right now. It's good news. It will take days for his portion of the army to return here."

"But Ryland."

"We can focus on Ryland and securing the castle. Maybe a skirmish in a nearby town will draw him away. Here." Her finger landed on a town Gwen had never heard of.

Avonlea nodded to the man who had joined them after Drake left. He moved with fluid stealth, carrying out Avonlea's silent orders. Gwen never saw his face and made a mental note never to get on Avonlea's bad side.

"We need more troops," she whispered to herself.

"I can send word to the elves and others in Mystrim," Aurius offered, "but unless the barrier is brought down there isn't much they can do. They don't have charms to protect their magic."

Avonlea nodded. "Send for them anyway. It will be better to have them prepared on standby should the curse be broken."

He scribbled out the note, whispered a word, and flicked it up between his fingers. Another nearby courier stood next to him and retrieved the paper from him.

"Release this in sunlight. It will find its intended recipient."

"Yes, your highness."

Aurius raised an eyebrow.

The courier's voice trembled. "I mean…"

"Its fine Gerald. He is the dark prince." Avonlea's eyes raked over Aurius. "Soon to be the king."

Gerald bowed and rushed out of the room, presumably to find some sunlight.

Aurius moved toward the door and looked over his shoulder. "Gwen its time to do our part."

Gwen wrung her hands and shifted her eyes to Avonlea.

"I won't let you down," Avonlea said.

Gwen dropped her hands and nodded. "I trust you."

One Way In

Gwen clutched the splintering wooden seat on either side of her to keep her hands from trembling. The longer the boat skimmed over the water, the further she slumped in her seat. She looked over her shoulder into the darkness beyond the back of the boat. Strands of hair, pushed by the breeze, tickled her cheek. Her face fell. Even if she wanted to go back, there wasn't a way. The boat contained no paddles, powered only by magic and the force of the current.

She could commandeer control, but did she want to? Yes, she thought. She wanted to go back. But she wouldn't.

"Chin up, Princess." Aurius's voice echoed against the low cavern wall. "This will all be over soon."

Her lips pulled back into a small smile. Gwen turned her shoulders back to the front of the boat.

In the distance, water dripped from the stone ceiling into the cavern pool. The moist air made it difficult to breathe. The water below them glowed as the boat rippled the cloudy water. Darkness yawned beyond the boat.

Bubbling sounds appeared in the distance. The sound of a large object cutting through the water. "Did you hear that?" Gwen asked.

Aurius nodded once.

"It's coming toward us."

Aurius nodded again and put a finger to his lips. She pressed her lips together.

The boat tipped to the right slightly. Gwen held a scream from escaping. Something was under their boat.

The water rippled around them. Gwen's fingers wrapped around the boat railing. Her golden curls hung over her shoulders. Her roved back and forth over the glowing water beneath her, searching the waters, waiting for the beast to show itself.

"Avonlea said there were no creatures in this water," Gwen said. She had assured her many weeks ago when they went for their secret swim.

"I think she lied," Aurius said.

The water tinkled as it parted on their left. Both their heads snapped toward the sound. The only evidence that something had been there was a few ripples in the water. On the other side, a splash had them searching the water again on the opposite of the boat.

Aurius rolled his sleeves up to his elbows. "It's toying with us," he said.

"Why?"

His eyes met hers. "It wants us to be afraid."

"Mission accomplished," she mumbled.

"Show yourself beast," Aurius demanded.

"Aurius... why would..." Gwen's words died in her throat. In front of their boat, a serpent rose out of the water. Overlapping iridescent scales reflected the blue glow of the bioluminescent creatures all around them. Sharp teeth punctuated a long snout, with lips pulled back in a snarl. Large black disks reflected the fear of the members of the boat in front of it. Gills spread behind its head to make it appear even more menacing.

"There you are," Aurius said as he raised his hands. Magic sparkled in his fists.

The beast flicked its tongue toward Gwen, reared its head back. The strike would be a killing blow.

"Aurius no magic!" Gwen yelled as the creature's head slammed toward her. She squeezed her eyes shut and threw her palms over her head, waiting for the strike, but it never came. Slowly, she opened one eye and then another to see the serpent now turned toward Aurius.

Its body followed its head in the way of serpents, and rose out of the water, slithering toward the half-goblin. It held him in its gaze, coming nose to nose with him. The Serpent's tongue flicked over Aurius, and the magic in

126

his hands died. Silence crept on for a few more moments. There was no magic that she could detect, but the beast held Aurius frozen in its thrall. The boat wobbled as Gwen lifted herself and wrapped her hand around the beast's gills. She pulled. Her grip faltered on the slimy skin of the serpent, and she fell back into the hull of the boat. The wooden planks dug into her spine. She had narrowly avoided smashing her forehead into the boat rail. The beast shook its head, then cut its eyes toward Gwen. A moment later, its body folded over itself and disappeared below the surface of the water.

The boat lurched forward. Aurius sat and folded his hands between his knees, fingertip to fingertip, elbows on his knees. With his sleeves rolled up to his elbows, it was hard not to notice his physique had broadened.

Gwen shoved her hair away from her forehead. "What was that about?"

He was silent for so long, she thought he wouldn't answer. But his throat bobbed. "The water dragon was... someone I knew," he said. The words were quiet. Water lapped quietly against the boat as it resumed its slow progress forward.

"How do you know?"

"Instinct is hard to ignore."

"Do you know who it was? Maybe it was magic to make you think you knew it."

"No. I'm a goblin.

"Half-goblin," Gwen corrected.

Aurius lifted an eyebrow and tilted his chin at the correction. "Either my magic will not allow me to be spelled like that. I just know I should know her. She was someone important. To me."

"She?"

"The dragon. She's trapped in her dragon form."

"She said that to you?"

"No. She didn't speak into my head. I just feel it."

"I wonder why she's down here?" Gwen said, ignoring a twinge of jealousy. Could the dragon be someone he once loved, she wondered.

"It wouldn't surprise me if someone trapped her down here. And when I find out who she is and why she is down here there will be a price to pay."

His hands balled into fists. The muscle in jaw ticked a couple of times.

Gwen hooked her fingers together. "Do you want to try to get her out?" she asked. Her soft voice was barely audible over the rush of the breeze and water.

Aurius's eyes snapped to hers. He held her in his gaze for a few moments. Then his eyebrows relaxed, and he lifted his chin. "She's safe for now. Let's get this sword."

Gwen clutched the rail from where she had fallen in the hull of the boat. Wind whistled through her hair. Aurius reached for her as the cave became darker. "Gwen there is only one reason water speeds up."

She wrapped her fingers through his, and he pulled her next to him. "What could it be?" Her voice was barely audible over the roar of the now rushing water.

"There is a waterfall and soon. Hang on to me." He tightened his arms around her.

The boat raced toward the darkness. There was no time to be frightened as they tipped over the edge and fell into the water below. The boat broke apart under the weight of the water crushing down on it.

Gwen squeezed Aurius's hand with all her strength, but it was no match for the might of the water crashing around them. It reached its icy tendrils around her waist and drug her away from him, loosening her fingers as it moistened their grip on each other. Her feet kicked powerful thrusts. It was pointless. The dark blue current rose to meet her, or was she sinking down to it? She couldn't tell. Just that it was squeezing her. A burning in her chest reminded her she needed air. Her hands shot out in the direction she thought was up, but she wasn't sure. Soon it wouldn't matter.

The dark blue turned to black. Peace. Finally, peace. Death had stood at her doorstep for weeks, and now his patience had finally paid off. Her eyes slid shut, ready for her last moments. The deep blue water grew darker as the depth increased. Gwen remembered to kick her feet, but the pressure was too great to overcome. She opened her mouth. The last breath slipped over lips and escaped as a bubble to the surface. Her eyes slid closed as the icy chill crept through her body. But just as the icy tendrils of death embraced her, something else clamped onto her arm.

She fought. Death was supposed to be easy. She had assumed it wasn't painful. The fight was instinctive. A survival reflex triggered by her impending doom. Her body thrashed back and forth, working to get away from whoever had claimed her. Warm lips pressed against hers and forced air into her mouth. Hot air replaced cold liquid. Her eyes shot open.

Aurius pressed his arms around her and kicked hard to the surface. His muscular legs overcame the pressure of the water with just two thrusts. They broke through the surface. The icy liquid left Gwen's lungs more violently than it had entered as air replaced it.

Aurius pulled her close to his body. Steep cliffs on either side of the river made it impossible to escape. It didn't pull them back down, but allowed them to float along as if they were nothing but debris.

"Stay close. Don't let go," Aurius said. Gwen could only nod.

"Can't swim." Her blue lips trembled as the words slipped through them.

The steep cliffs narrowed into a tunnel, then spilled out onto the underground lake. Aurius pulled her to the shallows where she and Avonlea had swum. Gwen clung to him. Every part of her was drenched and dripping. Her hair hung in clumps, clinging to her face. Her clothes did much the same. The water sloshed around them as she trudged through it.

When they reached the shore, Gwen dropped to her knees and heaved. Every breath was an excruciating reminder she was alive.

"Why?"

Gwen turned her head from her place on the ground. His face was a blank mask as he glared at her through narrowed eyes. They were dark. His body was open, ready for anything, but his hands curled at his sides. Was he angry?

"Why what, Aurius?" she said through painful breaths.

"Why didn't you use magic to save yourself?"

"I" she took another breath and rolled her body to sit on the rocks. "Didn't think of it."

His nostrils flared. He crouched in front of her, and his face filled her vision. The sharp, moist scent of water overwhelmed her.

He tilted his head. "You wanted to die."

The accusation was offensive. It had also been true.

She nodded. "I've anticipated it for some time now."

Aurius's eyebrows pressed together. Confusion warring with anger.

Gwen sighed. "If I am going to die, that was a pretty peaceful way to go and..."

"What Princess? After everything you were just going to give up?" His voice echoed through the cavern, forgetting they were sneaking into the castle.

Gwen pulled her head into her shoulders. "Why do you care?" she said softly.

His anger didn't recede. "I think I've made it pretty clear why I care," he snapped. His fingers curled into fists.

"No." She lifted herself off the rocky bank. "You haven't. You growl and grumble and steal memories. But not one of those things prove why you care whether I live or die."

"So saving your life at least three times, discovering and keeping the cottage for you, providing for you. None of that proves anything?"

"All so I would fulfill your father's contract. You are bound by it as much as I am," she said.

Aurius lifted his chin to growl, but sighed instead. He pointed in her face. "You are bound to me by the contract. I am not bound."

Gwen stepped back. "What?" Her arms wound themselves around her stomach as her shoulders dropped forward. The familiar sting of tears pricked her eyes. She hadn't wanted to be contracted to marry anyone, but it was something they were both bound by. "You don't need to fulfill the contract?"

"The contract requires me to marry you to prevent the change, but I am not bound. I'm only required to require you to fulfill it. And yet I've forbidden it. I've looked for ways to release you. Even now we're searching for the instrument that will be my doom. I'll be the Goblin King without a bride to temper the magic, without an heir to share the curse. It will probably be the doom of the entire realm, but I'm sacrificing all of that for you, *Princess*." He returned to throwing the title in her face.

130

"But we're searching for the sword so that we can free you from the goblin curse," she said, her voice barely audible over the lapping and drips of the cavern lake.

Aurius raised an eyebrow. "Are we?"

"Yes."

"You are going to have some hard choices to make soon princess. And I don't know if you are ready for it."

"What choices Aurius?"

His feet crunched through the slate gravel toward the stairs.

"What choices?" she asked again.

He glanced over his shoulder. "The sword can only be used by a catalyst."

She shrugged her shoulders and looked down at herself. "Doesn't seem to be a problem."

The crunch of the grey stones echoed in the cavern as he paced over the smooth rocks. "And it can only be used once. It takes thousands of years to recharge. Which is probably why it was cast in the vault and forgotten." He ranted as if he had forgotten she was there.

"But it will break all curses when I use…"

He lifted a single finger. "No. It will break one curse. You cannot save me and save Aurum."

She straightened her back and wrung out her shirt. The water splashed against the rocks. "Fine. Then I'll break the Goblin curse. You'll be free."

Aurius raised an eyebrow. "We could just get married and accomplish that. But if there is no Goblin King the curse on Aurum remains."

"We'll lift the curse on Aurum, get married and the goblin won't surface."

"And never have children?" He tilted his head. "If you don't break the contract, you'll be bound to me forever. I will not pass this burden to another generation." His eyes slid closed. His chest rose and fell at a slow steady pace. "But Aurum will be free," he said quietly.

Gwen reached for his arm. "I don't care if our babies are half-goblins."

His eyes examined her fingers where they met his mottled skin. "You will and soon."

"I want to do this," she insisted.

Aurius pointed in the direction they had just come from. "Do you think it is right to free me from my prison and leave them in theirs?"

"But…"

He yanked his arm away from her. "Forget it Princess. I know the path we're on. Let's just get this sword so you can get on with it."

He left her standing with her mouth hanging open on the shore of the underground lake. Drops of water still dripped from her garments and hair as she watched him step toward the doors. What did he want from her?

"What are the chances you know where all these doors lead?" Aurius asked.

Gwen's chest heaved up and down as she recovered from the sucker punch Aurius had just landed. She held up a finger together with her thumb.

"I know… a few doors…" she pulled a deep breath through her nose and released it through her mouth, lifting her chin. Something her father had taught her at the mill. When her chest no longer ached, she spoke again. "I have no idea which one leads to the dungeon."

Aurius's hand went to the top of his head. Fingers tapped out an inexact rhythm. His anger seemed to have gone as quickly as it had arrived. "Which way to the dungeon?"

Gwen pointed to the doors she knew. "The garden is there, Avonlea's suite, my former rooms. She said Drake would sometimes join her from that door."

"Naughty princess."

Gwen gave him a withering look. She hardly noticed how hunched his shoulders had become.

"Speaking of the princess, why didn't she warn us of those nasty obstacles?"

Gwen shrugged. "Maybe she didn't know."

Aurius cut his eyes at her. "Or maybe she did."

She wrapped her arms around her stomach. "We knew it was a trap," she murmured.

Aurius raised his eyebrows. "Now we know who we can trust."

Gwen's eyes met Aurius. For a fraction of a second, they turned back to their warm chocolate brown. She couldn't help but trust him.

"If I were building a dungeon with a secret entrance. I would want it accessible by the captain." Aurius wandered to Drake's door. His boots crunched over the rocks.

"My plan had been to sneak through the castle to the kitchen," Gwen said. He shook his head. "Too risky."

"How do you know there's a secret dungeon entrance?"

If Gwen hadn't been mistaken, she might say that his skin looked a little green. But of course, that had to be light from the glowing lake and the fact they had just survived an attack of a water dragon and nearly drowning. The stubble on his chin had grown. Not yet a full beard. Her fingers twitched with the idea of how soft it might feel to caress that chiseled jaw.

Aurius ignored her question, choosing instead to focus on finding the mysterious door. Aurius's fingers danced over the etching next to the entrance to Drake's office. "Do you see any magic here?"

"No."

"Me either." He placed both hands on the stone. "Maybe," he said with a groan, "We can just push it open." He put all his weight against it. The veins in his neck bulged with the effort. The stone moved a fraction. He continued to push. The loud scraping of stone on stone rewarded his effort. He finally stopped when there was enough space for them to slip through.

"This was certainly only meant to be opened by someone with great strength."

"There's that goblin humility I've missed." She winked at him.

"I was actually thinking of dragons."

"But goblins are better than dragons in all the ways that count."

Aurius returned her wink. The earlier argument of curses forgotten, apparently. He turned back to the door, and his smile faltered. "It's time Princess."

Gwen's eyes rounded, and her breath caught again.

Aurius was at her side. A muscular arm wrapped around her waist.

"It's ok. I will be with you the whole time," he whispered.

"Now that we're here, I don't want to go back there."

He nodded. "I know it's a lot to ask."

Her eyes widened, and she tried to take a step back. His muscular arm held her in place. "I almost died in the dungeons, Aurius."

"You almost died in a lot of places Princess. I know. I was there."

"But the dungeons were the first place."

"No the miller's house was. He almost let you starve to death, Gwen and yet you still want to go back there."

She tilted her head and pushed her eyebrows together. "You called me Gwen."

He turned to face her. His hands suddenly gripped her shoulders. Moss-green eyes examined her golden hair, a mess of strands waving wildly around her head as they dried. He moved a strand of hair out of her face and tucked it behind her ear. Tilting his head to examine it as if he were trying to remember the most precious thing he had ever seen. His fingers then traced a path down her neck and the backs of her arms until they intertwined with hers. He pulled her body into his. His lips brushed the top of her head. "We'll face it together, your highness."

She squeezed his hand, took a deep breath, and nodded. Aurius let go of one hand but kept the other firmly gripped as he squeezed through the space between the stone, pulling Gwen behind him.

As soon as she was through the opening, stone slid against stone. The heavy silence pinpointed the finality. The darkness engulfed them again. Gwen felt Aurius step around her and tug at the stone to open again. After a few moments, he took her hand and grumbled. "Well, there's no way out but forward."

Dungeon

They stepped onto the dark path, hand in hand, feeling their way along the rough stone walls. It wasn't long before their movement caused the glowworms in the niches to react. It was exactly as she had remembered it. There was no doubt that this was a path that led to the dungeon. It surprised her that the little creatures hadn't died of malnutrition. It didn't look like anyone used this path often.

Soon, the black doors of the dungeon began appearing in the walls on either side. Gwen chewed the inside of her cheek, wishing their pace could quicken. She kept her eyes wide, waiting for the next trap to spring. There had to be something just around the corner, though probably no one expected them to get this far.

Their footsteps, though light and slow, echoed through the corridor. Otherwise, silence greeted them.

"Why can't we hear the prisoners?" Aurius whispered.

"Sound suppression spell," she said.

"Very lonely."

"Yes."

The green glow of the glowworms wasn't comforting either. Considering they were just as much of a prisoner as the human variety. Her stomach clenched, but she tried to ignore it. Her left hand gripped Aurius's wrist while she still clung tightly with her fingers threaded through his. They were continuing along as quickly as the light would allow them. The glowworms' light didn't pop on immediately as it had in other places where they were well fed.

From behind her, Gwen felt a tickle of air.

Then a sudden sound. Not loud. A whisper. She could feel it brushing against her ear. "Geeeeetttt oooooooout." It groaned.

She jumped and pushed herself closer to Aurius. "What was that?" she squeaked.

"Ghost," he said as if ghosts existed and it was as natural as seeing a stag in the forest.

"And doesn't that creep you out at all?" she asked.

"You thought someone could escape punishment by dying?"

"Well yes."

He shook his head sadly. "Doesn't work that way in most cases."

"I'm glad I didn't die in here then. I might have been more inclined to live in that moment."

He wagged his finger. "No dying in the dungeon allowed. You might never escape."

"No dying in the dungeon. Let's make that happen," she whispered.

A few steps later, they came to an intersecting path.

"Ok Princess, it's time to make a choice. Which way do we go?"

Her eyes widened. "Why are you asking me? How am I supposed to know?"

He raised an eyebrow. "Because you have the magic that can sense the sword," he said.

"Right, right. I still forget I have magic at all."

"The locket is masking it. If you had more control I don't think you would need it."

She slipped it over her head and into her pocket. "If it worked for Drake then do you think it would work for Ryland?"

Aurius shook his head. "We're not going to find out."

Gwen flinched. "Why not?"

"Because Ryland is volatile. So if I can help it you are not getting close to him."

Gwen narrowed her eyes.

"The sword princess."

"Right." She closed her eyes. Feeling her way, the magic led her. She turned left. "We need to go left. We're close to the center of the dungeon."

Gwen allowed her magic to lead the way through the corridors.

"This is it," she said.

She stopped them twenty paces from the vault. Avonlea had been right. There were magical tripwires. If they went further, the king would be alerted, and the two of them might face unspeakable obstacles.

"Gwen, this is going to be a lot to ask," he whispered.

"Am I going to have to fight dragons?"

"Let's hope not."

"Ok. What could be worse than that?"

"You need to recall the magic from the vault. Your a conduit. You can use the magic and channel it somewhere else."

She nodded, agreeing to the plan. "Where am I going to put it?"

"Into me."

"What? No. That could kill you. You can't contain that much magic."

"It has to go somewhere." They continued whispering.

"Then I will put it back into the land."

He shook his head. "I don't know if you are strong enough to do that yet."

She squeezed his hand. "I can do this."

He paused for a moment to meet her eyes with his. "Alright. I'm right here with you," he said.

Gwen closed her eyes and allowed her magic to unravel from the center of her soul. It flowed through the dungeon like smoke and pushed through the magic surrounding the vault. The magic had a golden shimmer, like all magic, but this was bright. It wrapped around the room like a sleeping dragon.

Her magic caressed the edges, looking for an entrance, then moved toward the center. As her magic made its way deeper, she could feel more of the magic throughout the dungeon. Little tiny lights popped up in her mind through the miles and miles of corridors surrounding the vault. There were spaces above, below and for miles around. Gwen could feel everyone in the dungeon. They hadn't tripped any magical traps yet, but it was much bigger than Gwen had imagined on her first visit, having only seen ten cells that day.

Gwen gasped with horror that some of these people were innocent victims of King Aric's tyranny.

The magic of the vault responded to Gwen as if she had insulted it. When the magic lifted its head, she pulled with everything she had. She felt Aurius's hands land on each side of her hips to help keep her stable. The magic she pulled from the vault she channeled through her feet and into the ground. But Aurius had been right. She wasn't strong enough to keep that going. The ground buckled under their feet, resisting Gwen's forced disturbance. Her hands trembled as she pulled the magic from the vault with one hand and pushed it through the stone and earth with the other.

A peal of thunder shattered the silence of the dungeon.

Gwen couldn't control it any longer. Every molecule of magic rushed toward her. Too much at once. Gwen's head fell back and her chest thrust forward. Magic flowed in through her mouth like lightning and out through her arms, hands, down her legs and out her feet. She couldn't direct it any longer. It followed a path on its own. Where she had tried to control it, now it overwhelmed her.

Despite the pain of raw magic rushing through her, she could still feel Aurius's grip on her hips. "You have to control it Gwen. You use magic, it does not use you."

But she didn't know how. She hadn't practiced enough. There hadn't been time. She was trying to save him and rushed to do it. Now, instead of saving him, she condemned them both.

His hands slid along her outstretched arms and folded over hers. He whipped her around to face him. His cheek pressed against hers, forming a connection. She barely felt the coarse hair of his unshaven face. Once established, he took control of the magic. He pushed her against their nearest wall and pressed his body against hers with as much pressure as she could stand. "Let me take it Gwen," he whispered into her ear.

"How?" she groaned.

"Let go," he said.

For another second she tried to direct the magic into the floor below them. Trying to do this on her own. Aurius threaded his fingers through hers. She allowed her muscles to relax. Her shoulders drooped, and her arms bent. "Together," he said.

The magic changed course, flowing through her and into him. He orchestrated every spark of energy, redirecting it through cracks and crevices. The torrent slowed to a gentle stream, finally dissipating to a trickle. She couldn't follow it any longer.

Aurius swallowed and took a breath. His forehead touched hers. "Are you ok?" he asked in a gruff tone.

"I will be in a minute," she said through rapid breaths. She didn't open her eyes. Afraid of the destruction she surely caused.

She felt Aurius's fingers in her hair. Combing through it. Calming her. "You're ok," he cooed.

Gwen took a deep breath in and let it out slowly. She nodded to affirm that physically she was indeed okay. Her legs and arms were still a little shaky, and she felt the need to move. Instead, she clutched the back of Aurius's white shirt. It bunched over muscles that seemed to have grown overnight.

"Gwen, open your eyes."

She lifted her eyelids and allowed her eyes to meet his. They held a promise. He would get her through every moment. They would face this next part together.

Her fist released his shirt. As he tilted his head and lifted his eyebrows. Asking without words if she was ready?

She nodded again, and he took a step back. Releasing the pressure against her body. Immediately feeling the loss, she wanted to rush back into his arms. But there wasn't time for her to be weak and needy. They had a job to do.

Gwen rolled her shoulders and lifted her chin, preparing to survey her work. The door to the vault stood open. Though she couldn't see anything inside. There were no glowworms to light the way.

"Well, it looks as if we took care of the magic around the vault," she said.

"It's not really going to matter. Everyone within fifty miles probably felt that," Aurius whispered.

"What do we do now?"

"Get in and out as quickly as possible. Can you still see the sword's magic?"

Her hands formed fists, then her fingers spread out again. After doing that twice, she lifted her chin and squared her shoulders. She didn't want a repeat of what just happened, but would not be closed off from her magic again. As she closed her eyes, her magic took a little peep outside. She let just a trickle out. "Yes. It's a lot easier with all the wards gone."

"Layers and layers of wards, added by each generation of dragons. You just dismantled it in a span of about thirty seconds."

"They're coming aren't they?"

"If they didn't feel the earthquake you created, they definitely felt the disconnection with their magic."

"Then we need to hurry."

"Agreed."

After a few steps, Aurius held up a hand to check for magic again. Gwen bounced on her toes, waiting for the all-clear she knew was coming. Still, they took tentative steps into the open vault, both realizing there was magic that could escape their notice, like with the mirror in Avonlea's rebel chamber.

As they passed the threshold, the vault lit up from front to back. Gwen knew from the magical boundaries that this was going to be a big room, but walking inside was different. The walls were set with white stone, which formed sculpted arches through the room. Alcoves dotted the outer walls. Gwen's mouth dropped open at the sight of mounds of gold piled haphazardly floor to ceiling. The king had enough money to fund hundreds of years of wars. The other side of the vault held the golden spools Aurius had spun for her. Gwen could see the sparkle of the illusion now that she knew what she was looking for.

Along each side of the vault, were spaces just wide enough for a person to walk. But barely a step could be made without tripping over a piece of gold or a pile of coins. Gwen counted ten mounds that peaked well above her head through the center of the vault. Jewels and golden objects made up the mounds as well.

"This is…" Gwen said.

"Excessive," Aurius finished for her.

"He certainly didn't need me to spin gold for him."

Aurius shook his head. "Need isn't in a dragon's vocabulary."

"What would drive anyone to this?"

"Greed. The dragon's ultimate curse."

"Do they know the sword breaks curses?"

"If they did they don't care."

They stepped around the piles. The clinking of metal against metal drew their attention behind them. They had been careful not to disturb the pieces, difficult as it was; they made little noise.

Both Gwen and Aurius crouched behind a mound of gold, waiting for the king or his guards to crowd into the room. Nothing happened. Until the sound of moving metal clinking against other metal grew closer. Aurius wrapped his fingers around Gwen's wrist. He shifted onto his toes.

A flash of gold flew out of one of the piles. Aurius pulled Gwen behind him and blocked the onslaught with his back before it could hit her. But the gold mass only used Aurius as a launch pad, flew over him and pounced right onto Gwen's chest, knocking her to her back.

Her hands went to the creature now attacking her. Her head moved back and forth to avoid its jaws. Only it wasn't attacking her.

It was licking her.

Aurius grabbed the creature by the scruff of its neck. It squirmed, doing everything in its power to get back to Gwen.

"What is it?" she asked, righting herself.

"A dragon." His tone implied the obviously.

She reached for the dragon with raised shoulders, while her voice went up two octaves. "It's so cute."

Aurius moved the dragon away from her.

She put a hand on her hip. "It's not going to hurt me."

"It has sharp claws." The little golden dragon snapped its teeth at Aurius. "And teeth." He held it at arm's length.

Gwen put her fingertips on his shoulder. "It's ok."

He turned the dragon to face him and met its eyes. "You will not hurt her or anyone she loves." The dragon stopped wiggling in his hand. Its tongue lolled out, and she looked as if she nodded her head. Aurius relented and slowly moved the dragon closer to her.

Gwen reached out and took her under the forearms, pulling the little dragon into a hug. The dragon licked her cheek.

"Hey little one. We're looking for a magic sword. Do you know where it is?"

The dragon nodded its snout and launched off into the mounds of gold.

"What kind of dragon is she?" Gwen asked.

"A guardian likely."

"They leave her down here?"

He lifted his hands, palms up. "She protects the gold."

"Hardly an excuse for leaving her down here by herself," Gwen grumbled. Aurius agreed with a nod.

Moments later, the golden dragon's big black eyes popped into view from a few feet away. Her mouth opened, and her tongue hung out to one side, then slithered up to her black eye, cleaning a liquid away from it.

"I think she's expecting us to follow her," Gwen said.

"How could you know that?"

Gwen shrugged. "Just do."

Aurius didn't look convinced but held his arm out and bowed his head anyway. Gwen stepped past him and followed the dragon, who bounded over mound after mound of gold, until she reached the very back of the vault and the biggest mound of gold. The top of the pile crested mere inches below the ceiling.

"There." Gwen pointed to the gold pommel of the sword. "That's it. I can feel it."

They both climbed the pile, sliding down with tides of coins as they went. After making several attempts, Aurius put a hand on her arm. "It's too volatile. And we don't know what's under this mound."

Gwen's shoulders slumped. Any minute, the king's men could come pouring through the front door. They needed to be out of here. It had taken too long already.

"How are we going to get it?"

Aurius tilted his head toward the golden dragon. She had sat on her tail with her back legs out beside her, watching the commotion. "Ask her?"

Gwen shook her head. "How can she even bring the sword?"

Aurius didn't respond.

"Fine. I'll ask." She knelt beside the little dragon and patted its head. The dragon nuzzled into her hand. "Hello. My friend and I need that sword. Do you think you could get it for us? Or maybe just slide it down to us."

The dragon had moved before she finished the last word.

"That's a yes."

Aurius's eyes slid to her again.

"What?" Gwen asked.

"How do you talk to dragons?"

"I don't know. It's not really words. She doesn't say things to me. It's just a feeling."

The sword slid down the mound and clattered at their feet. Followed by the golden dragon, who sat adorably at the end with her head tilted and little pink tongue lolled out between her pointed teeth.

Gwen stooped to pick up the sword. As her hand touched the hilt, the distant clanging of metal armor reached them.

"Time to go," she said, scooping up the dragon.

"Leave the dragon. There isn't time," Aurius said as they both sprinted toward the door.

"I can't. She doesn't want to be by herself any more."

Aurius responded with a growl.

The dragon let out a cute little growl of her own, which Aurius ignored.

Gwen let go of the dragon, and it bounded beside her. "Ok, but stay close." Gwen said. She fastened the sword around her waist as she ran.

Aurius poked his head through the opening in the door.

"There's at least twenty at the far end of the corridor, marching rather slowly, this way." Aurius whispered. "I would guess there are more coming from the other direction as well."

"I have an idea," Gwen said and stepped into the corridor. She closed her eyes, allowing her magic out. It spread to all the black metal doors in the dungeons. Wrapping around the sound suppression spells. She yanked the spells away from the doors and pulled them back to her.

She wrapped a spell around each of them. Then she silently broke the glass of the glowworms. The little worms inched out of their homes and toward the sounds of the marching soldiers.

The three of them were now bathed in shadow and silence. She tapped the corner of Aurius's eye and pointed. Telling him to lead the way. The little dragon wound its way up her body and rested on her shoulders like a shawl.

Aurius gripped her hand and took silent steps down the only path available to them. A spiral staircase deep in the dungeon's heart. Their silent trek back went unnoticed by the guards sent to destroy them. The ascent was slow and methodical. Each step of the spiral could hold a surprise guard. Aurius's fingers curved into gnarled claws with pointed black nails, ready to fight if necessary.

When had that happened? Gwen wondered briefly.

Gwen followed Aurius up the staircase. She barely avoided planting her face into his back when he halted in front of her.

"What's wrong," she whispered.

"I think I know what happened to the magic."

"What do you mean?" She stepped around him.

His eyebrows arched over wide eyes.

Her mouth dropped open. "How could it have caused this?"

Thick, thorny stems blocked the light in the corridor. The castle had always seemed gloomy. Now shrouded in darkness, the eerie feeling grew.

The tiny dragon slipped from around her neck to the floor and bounded to the window. Her lips peeled back into a sneer and a growl.

"The garden has always been attracted to your magic."

"What do we do now? Can you shadow us out?"

He shook his head. "Even if I wanted to, I couldn't with the sword and the dragon it would take more than I have right now."

144

"I'm not leaving her behind."

Aurius nodded, finally agreeing. "You need to redirect the magic some-where else. It is too concentrated. The same way you did in the dungeon. Focus on the exit and remove the magic just from there."

Aurius turned her toward him, catching her eyes. His fingers wrapped around the top of her arm.

"You can do this." he assured her.

She nodded. "Let's get closer to the garden entrance. So we can run as soon as it is open."

"You still mean to go back through the lake?" he asked.

"We have no other option."

"You can use the sword and break the curse on the land," he clarified.

"You told me I would have to make a choice. And I'm making it."

"Gwen, we came for the sword to break the contract, but we can't leave the world to suffer while we run free."

She stepped in close; fire danced in her irises. Her eyes met his. "Your freedom is the only outcome I can accept. I'll burn the rest of it down to make it happen, but we have to escape this castle first." Her brows pushed together. "What happened to not forcing people to do things?"

Aurius groaned, but nodded and motioned for her to lead the way.

Gwen raced around corners. Right, then left. Recognizing when they were close to the grand stairway, she slowed. There was only one more turn before they reached the garden entrance under her old suite. There hadn't been a single guard to greet them. A byproduct of the rebellion Avonlea had promised to start, perhaps? Had she drawn everyone away? Or had every guard entered the dungeon?

She grabbed Aurius's hand and rounded the corner. "Almost free," she whispered.

Ryland

Ryland stood in the center of the hall. Alone.

His feet were set wide, head tilted down. Both hands hung in gloved fists at his sides. His face was a mask of rage. A sneer on his lips. Fierce eyes trained on Gwen and Aurius, flashing with fire and a promise of retribution.

"Gwen." A single word in a breathy whisper. Ice formed in Gwen's veins. She hadn't seen him since their wedding day. So much had happened since that moment.

He took a step toward them. "You look… different."

Gwen found her voice and lifted her chin. "I am."

His eyes flicked to their joined hands. "You've made your choice?"

Gwen looked toward Aurius. She could tell he wanted to step in, intervene, protect her. A shield when she needed it. He stood ready to fight if he needed to, but sudden moves weren't advisable with a volatile dragon in a confined space. He set his jaw and nodded, reminding her of what he wanted, encouraging her to decide.

Her heart leapt into her throat at the sight of Ryland. The pained look on his face. The shadows under his eyes. His dirty blonde hair was a disheveled mess. This wasn't the prince she had met months ago.

Her eyes bounced between Aurius and Ryland. All the burdens she had carried for weeks tumbled over and over in her mind.

She knew Aurius was right. They couldn't damn them all to the curse while she and Aurius lived free. What had changed his mind? All he had ever focused on was her. All he had ever encouraged her to do was make a selfish choice. Until... the water dragon. That was the moment he altered his ideas about what to do with the sword. He tensed beside her as the silence grew on. The dragon must have been very important to him. She squeezed his hand as her heart splintered.

She sighed and released him.

She turned her attention back to Ryland. "I have."

"I'd like to hear the words from your treacherous mouth."

Gwen lifted her chin and squared her shoulders. "I've chosen Aurum."

Aurius let his hands rest at his sides and lowered his brow, ready to defend her choice.

Ryland's eyebrows lifted in surprise. "So you are willing to marry me?"

"No. I'm willing to break the curse that hangs over us all."

Ryland's fist flexed and relaxed. "The only way to do that is by our marriage."

"That curse is a lie," Gwen said.

"Hmph, Why should I believe you? You've done nothing but lie since the moment I met you."

"My mother defeated Rumpelstiltskin. The chasm between our kingdoms opened and swallowed him, but since his son was not of age to inherit the Goblin Kingdom, his magic began absorbing all the magic in the land. With the barrier in Mystrim it couldn't dissipate across all realms, the curse started absorbing the life force of the land in Aurum. This sword is the only way to break..."

Ryland interrupted with a scoff. "Gwen, that is ridiculous. The death of a goblin can't cause all that."

"Respectfully, you don't know very much about goblins," Aurius said.

Ryland narrowed his eyes at Aurius, then shifted them back to Gwen, warning Aurius to stay out of the conversation. "How are you going to break this curse?"

"He's stalling," Aurius said out of the side of his mouth.

Gwen gave Aurius a pert nod.

"I'm going to use the sword from the vault to break the curse on the land." Her hand moved toward her waist. She patted her hip. The sword. It was gone. Her eyes widened, fearing she had dropped it.

Ryland stepped in front of her. "The treasure is off limits. It. Is. Mine. As are you," he said, grabbing her wrist.

"I don't belong to you or anyone else, Ryland." She yanked her hand out of his grasp.

A sword swooshed out of a scabbard and pressed against Ryland's throat. How had it ended up in Aurius's hands?

Gwen stepped next to Aurius and put a hand on the sword. "Aurius. This isn't the way."

"He threatened you." Aurius's voice was garbled as if he were speaking through too many teeth.

Gwen ignored it. She didn't want to take her eyes off Ryland. "Move aside Ryland."

Aurius pressed the sword harder into Ryland's throat. Aurius's skin had turned a light shade of green; incisors had extended. His frame was heftier. Where Gwen's fingers pressed a warning against his arm, muscles grew in seconds. Time had run out.

"No more games," Aurius said.

Gwen sighed, and her head fell forward. "Ryland. Meet The Goblin King." She leaned toward Aurius and whispered, "You can use your magic now. You can shadow us out of here."

"No shadows. We fight." The Goblin King said. "It will be a good fight." He announced.

Guards filed into the corridor at either end. Gwen searched for familiar faces, but she recognized none of them. A familiar uniform caught her attention. The black pants and crisp red shirt. For a moment, Gwen felt relieved the captain was among the throng of soldiers. He was on their side after all. But as she looked closer, it was not Drake who wore the captain's uniform. A new captain had been appointed in Drake's place. Where was Drake? The question flitted across her mind as she surveyed their situation.

Someone else was missing. The king had not returned. Gwen released a small sigh of relief when she didn't see Avonlea either.

Ryland, too, looked ready to take on the Goblin King. Gwen knew the fight would be rather equal, except for the guards at either end of the hall.

Gwen twisted her hands together. If the Goblin King had arrived, perhaps they wouldn't need the sword after all. The curse should have been broken. Everyone should have their magic back. Ryland should be able to shift into a dragon.

None of those things happened. The constant draining feeling didn't lift. They needed more time for it to take effect.

"It's not the only way. I'll buy us some time," she whispered to Aurius, then turned to Ryland. "If I choose you, will you allow the Goblin King to live?"

"Yes," Ryland responded quickly.

The Goblin didn't remove his sword. Instead, he tightened his grip on the hilt. "Gwen. Don't do this. I'm the hideous Goblin King but I know you don't want to marry Ryland either." For a moment he sounded like Aurius again, reserved and self-assured.

She took his hand, stroked the back of it and lifted it to her mouth. Pressing a kiss to the broad green hand, his veins were more pronounced against her lips.

Her eyes met his. She had to make this believable. "The past few months have been beautiful Aurius."

"Don't call me that," he said.

She smiled.

"But we both knew it was going to end this way. I can't marry the Goblin King," she announced.

Aurius squeezed his eyes shut, unwilling to watch her walk away.

"If you do this. Your life is forfeit and the life of your first born," he said.

Her eyes flicked to the sword. "And if I don't, yours is." Gwen's eyes met his then darted around the room, noting all the soldiers that continued to fill the corridor. Two against two hundred were overwhelming odds, even when one was pure magic. That number continued to grow. After the display in the dungeon, did she trust her own magic not to take everything? She could kill everyone in the corridor, including Aurius and Ryland. It was better for her to sacrifice herself until a better plan presented itself. Until the curse was removed from the land. What was taking so long? Maybe it just needed more time? And did they want to be cooped up with Ryland in a castle when he suddenly became a war dragon? Gwen assured herself that this was the best plan for the moment.

Gwen stood beside the dragon prince, lifting her chin. "Ryland, Prince of Aurum, I choose you as my marriage partner. But I have to warn you. There is a contract between Aurius and I. Our first born will be blood bound to him."

"You made a contract with the goblin?"

"My mother made a blood contract with his father. I am betrothed through contract to the Goblin King."

Ryland wrapped an arm around her waist and slung her behind him. "That's ridiculous. No wonder you've acted as you have. You and your mother were tricked by a Goblin. It's about time you come to your senses." He nodded to the new captain of the guard. "Arrest the Goblin King."

The king's knights quickly surrounded Aurius.

The Goblin King didn't struggle. His head hung low. The captain easily took his hands and placed them behind his back. The cold metal cuffs clicked into place around each wrist.

"No! You said you would let him go." Gwen screamed. Her arms flung over Ryland's shoulders as he wrapped his right arm around her waist. He lifted her easily.

"I said I'd let him live, not that I'd let him go."

Her fists landed with hard thuds against Ryland's back as he carried her away, her screams echoing through the corridors. The golden dragon Gwen had nearly forgotten chased after them. She jumped toward Ryland with her mouth open. The bite landed just above his ankle. Crimson blood gushed onto the stone floor.

Ryland roared, stopping to shake her off. He flung the tiny dragon across the hall. "Where did you find the guardian?" he asked. The golden dragon lay motionless in the corridor.

Gwen barely heard the commotion as she fought for her own release. She watched the guards march Aurius in the opposite direction. Aurius didn't lift his head or look back. His stance and the small steps he took gave him away. The Goblin King was defeated the moment he appeared. The only being that could turn straw into gold was captured by the Dragon Prince to be used and discarded if they had fashioned a way to hold him. Would they attempt a capture if they didn't have a plan to hold him?

Gwen closed her eyes as the tears slipped over her cheeks. This was not what she had planned to happen. With Aurius in shackles, Gwen would have to follow through on her choice to marry Prince Ryland. No one would rescue her. Aurius wouldn't even want to, assuming she had chosen the dragon over the goblin. She didn't blame him if that choice hurt, even if it was only to save him from death. But it had all been for nothing. Her sacrifice only resulted in his imprisonment. The fight left her as Aurius faded from view.

Ryland deposited her into the suite shared by the secret door. "You are not to leave this room. Our wedding will be tomorrow."

"So soon." Her voice was barely a whisper.

Ryland froze. His jaw clenched along with his fist. His eyes looked everywhere but at hers. Until they did. His eyes had returned to their normal icy blue. The reptilian slits had disappeared, finally under control. Perhaps Aurius had broken the curse after all. "Wouldn't want you running off to rescue The Goblin King now would we? You've caused enough trouble."

She looked down at her folded hands. "I never meant to hurt you Ryland."

"I'm not hurt Gwen. I'm embarrassed. But now that you've chosen me. All will be forgiven." He straightened his lapels. "There will be a guard at this door."

Gwen opened her mouth to protest as Ryland held up a finger to stop her. "Not Drake. He has gotten himself in a bit of trouble. I have to see to him now that I've secured you and The Goblin King."

Gwen took a single step toward him. "Is Avonlea ok?"

He ground his teeth, causing the muscles in his jaw to flex again. "She will be as soon as Drake wakes up." His voice sounded as if it had been sifted through gravel. Perhaps she was mistaken about the curse being broken.

"What happened?" she dared to ask.

Ryland took another deep breath, getting himself under control. "Not that

151

it's your concern, but Drake was cursed with a sleeping sickness. He pricked himself on the enchanted roses that are now covering the castle."

Gwen's fingers covered her mouth. "Is there anything I can do to help?"

"You've done enough." He walked out without a single glance backward. The lock clicked in the door behind him.

She waited a few seconds before running to the secret door to the underground caves. It wouldn't budge. She then checked the door to Ryland's private rooms. It clicked open. Surprised, Gwen hesitated to step through into Ryland's suite. She steeled her nerves and made her way through the short, dark passage. The exit released her from behind a large tapestry.

She had visited Ryland's suite only once. The day after the dungeon. After that night, it was a respite. Now, a heavy dread hung in the air. Dark curtains coupled with the enchanted vines — it seemed as if midday had turned to night. Splinters of every single piece of furniture littered the room. Food trays lined the walls haphazardly. She might have been the first to enter the room in weeks. A musty smell permeated the air until she retreated a step to the hidden door.

Holding a hand to her nose, she refused to go back. Surely, Ryland's suite would be the answer to her escape.

A few more steps took her to the center of the room.

The door burst open, and Ryland stepped through. Gwen froze. His lips pulled into a sly smile. He crossed the space in two strides, his hand slithering around her neck. She clenched her teeth, ready for the death she had expected for weeks.

"A princess only comes to her betrothed's room for one reason, Gwen." His eyes roamed over her face and down her neck. "I don't think you're ready to find out what that is."

She narrowed her eyes but remained silent, not wanting to stir up the dragon causing this personality change.

He sneered and drug her back to the tapestry by her arm. "Go back to your room. I don't want to see your face again until you are standing at my side saying your vows," he said, pushing through the tapestry she had just left. She took a step through, and the door clicked behind her.

Ryland's voice was muffled through the door. "Stop trying to escape Gwen."

She froze. That was the voice she remembered, the one she could have fallen in love with. One step back, then another as she backed away from her last resort. Her body dropped onto the cushions.

"Get some rest," he said.

The tap of his shoes faded.

"I'll never rest until Aurius is released," she vowed.

Captured

Aurius's back bent in a cruel curl that only the creature he had become would find comfortable. His green mottled skin stretched over corded muscles. Black talons grew into razor-sharp points. His wiry black hair hung over his face. A bit of drool gathered at the corner of his mouth where his incisors protruded.

Guards roamed the corridor in front of his cell to ensure he didn't escape. Someone had done their research. The cell was as bright as the midday sun. There were no shadows to step into. There was no furniture; it wasn't even possible for his body to cast a shadow, not that he could manage to step into his own.

Silver shackles wrapped his wrists, ankles and neck. The silver didn't burn his skin, but the magic that normally raged in the core of his body, fighting to be let out, had slowed to a trickle, barely noticeable. He huffed a sardonic laugh. All he had needed to battle the goblin all this time were some strands of silver. Then his thoughts turned to Gwen as they always did. Is this how she felt when she wore the locket?

He knew what was coming next. Perform the magic they wanted or be shackled, possibly tortured, forever. He had sorely underestimated the King's greed.

But it didn't matter now. He would do what they asked. He would make the fake gold and spells and whatever else they wanted. Gwen was all that had mattered, and she chose Ryland. He had seen it. As soon as the Goblin arrived, Gwen would give up and marry the dragon. And try as he might, he couldn't hate her for it. He loved her all the more. Finally, she put herself before others. Finally, she did something good and right for herself, for the sake of being comfortable.

It was as he told Emyr weeks ago; true love doesn't exist. If it did, Gwen certainly didn't feel that for him.

He studied the floor, which had grooved patterns in the stones. Those grooves ran together to the center of the design. It circled a hole in the middle of the floor, covered by a slotted metal plate. The floor, with its groove designs, sloped downward. Around the center of the circle, metal loops protruded from the floor at evenly spaced intervals. The silver chain that bound him twisted through the loops and over his shackles. Someone had designed this room for torture. He was so caught up in his thoughts and misery that he hadn't heard the approaching footsteps on the cobbled floor.

The metallic whine of metal sliding against metal echoed over the damp torture chamber. The bright light flooding the cell gleamed off polished black boots. These were not the boots of a torturer. They were the boots of a prince.

"Look at me you filth," Ryland said. Disgust laced his tone as his eyes roved over the heap of the goblin crouched before him.

Aurius continued crouching and tracing the patterns of the grooves with his eyes.

"I can't believe your hands were on her," Ryland turned slightly to speak over his shoulder. Perhaps guards that were beyond Aurius's field of vision. "Order the princess to be scrubbed until she is raw. I will not have this goblin filth taint my betrothed."

Clicking of the guard's feet scurried away as they ran to carry out the Prince's orders.

"You will not touch her," Aurius ground out in a low rumble.

Ryland bent to hear the words Aurius spoke. His face lowered until it was in front of him. Ryland's golden reptilian slits met Aurius's moss green eyes.

He stood up straight. "She's mine. She will always be mine. And she chose me," adjusting his cuffs. "But she needs some reminders of her choices and the consequences of such."

Aurius's lip curled into a sneer.

155

"Don't worry I know about the little contract. You get the first born. And when the bastard arrives we'll turn it over to you. But Aurius that's months away. Maybe even years." The prince removed his coat and rolled up his sleeves. He tilted his head. "What will we do with you until then?"

The metal chains clanked as the silver scraped against the metal loops and shackles. Aurius fell against the hard stone. The blow wasn't a surprise. The force behind it was. Dragon sickness. It was the only answer.

Aurius's palms were flat against the stone floor. His body trembled against his restraint. The silver shackles had dampened his magic, but they did nothing for the goblin's mass. Instead of fighting back, though, he let the prince rage against him. He let the warm trickle of blood drip into those grooves on the floor. If nothing else, it would save Gwen from a similar fate. She wouldn't survive the dragon's wrath. Even the tiny amount of magic he could now feel would heal him quickly.

The fists finally slowed the onslaught. The prince heaved above him, his rage taking its toll on his body as well. He straightened and wiped the back of his hand across his sweaty brow.

"Tell me the cure for the roses." The Prince buttoned the cuffs of his sleeves. His pinky slid through dirty blond coifs. The polished boot landed in Aurius's ribs. "Drake is a brother. You will tell me how to cure him."

Aurius's lips parted. "He's no more a brother to you than I am."

"Have it your way. We will discover the cure and when I do it will be a dark day for you indeed, Goblin King."

The prince turned from the heap on the floor. The barred door squeaked open again and clanked shut with his exit. He stood in the darkness outside the bars. "You will comply with our demands or Gwen will face the consequences."

The words hit harder than fists. Truth rang through them.

He let his body relax into the sticky stones as the Prince's footsteps faded. It would take a miracle to get out of this situation. Goblins didn't get miracles.

A guard stopped in front of his cell to jeer. "Dark Prince, ha. He doesn't look anything like a prince."

Aurius didn't growl or respond. He sprawled on the stained burgundy floor, disheveled and monstrous.

"He's not a prince. He's the Goblin King," another guard said. Elbowing him in the ribs. "You'd best move on. He'll curse you as soon as look at you."

Another voice, more feminine, but more commanding, joined them. "Move and unlock the cell you uncouth baboons."

Both guards straightened in their jackets. "We are under orders from the king. We can't open this cell for anyone, not even the princess."

"Those were your actual orders? Word for word?"

"Yes, Princess."

She sighed. "That's too bad. I didn't want to have to do this."

The hilt of her sword hit the second guard in the back of the head and the first between the eyes. They crumpled like rag dolls. Internally, Aurius laughed at the sound of the bodies hitting the floor. Externally, he showed no emotion, but continued to stare at the cold stone floor.

Keys jangled, and metal creaked again. The princess was back in her royal finery. No hint of the fighting pants she had worn a few hours ago.

"Aurius I need your help."

He lay motionless.

"Drake was pricked by the thorns that have overgrown the castle. I need your help waking him." She crossed the cell to stand beside him. He didn't move.

"Come with me. We need you."

When he didn't move a second time, she pushed on his shoulder. If she noticed the blood and the bruises, she ignored them. "If you don't come he could die."

Aurius rolled himself into a hunched position in the center of the room, then uncurled himself, stretching his legs to his full height. He was now two heads taller than the princess and much wider. Her eyes widened as he looked down at her.

"Why should I help a betrayer?"

"What are you talking about?" Avonlea's voice was steady, but her shoulder twitched toward the cell door, revealing her nervousness.

He narrowed his eyes. "The boat went a little off course." He lifted a crooked finger. "Water dragon." Then another. "Waterfall."

Avonlea took a shaky step backward, toward the cell door. "There are no water dragons. They died twenty years ago."

Aurius lifted a bushy eyebrow and huffed.

"I didn't send you that way," she said. "I have no control over the magic of the boat."

The Goblin King growled. "Who does?"

"My mother was the last to control it. She died long ago."

Aurius tilted his head and lowered himself back into a crouch. He was quiet for a long time.

"My crimes are kidnapping, breaking and entering, and performing magic without cause," Aurius said, breaking his thoughtful silence.

She clicked her tongue. "This is wrong. My brother has no right to hold you."

She stepped back and tapped her finger on her lip. "Those are ridiculous charges," she said, pacing in front of him. His eyes followed her like a predator ready to pounce.

Aurius grunted in response for the first time.

"Fine. I'll free you, in return you will tell me how to wake Drake."

"No," he hunched back in his spot.

"No?" she repeated.

"I understand you don't hear that word a lot," Aurius said.

"I will do anything to wake Drake from this illness that has assaulted him."

Aurius twisted away from her, exposing the back Ryland had shredded. "I can't help you."

Again, Avonlea ignored the blood. "You don't know how to wake him?"

Aurius shook his head.

"I see, but you do know how to find out."

He didn't move.

"Good. I'll allow your escape. You find out how to wake Drake and send me a message like you did with the elves."

Aurius lifted his head and said one word. "Gwen."

"I'll get her out too. Don't worry."

158

"She chose him."

Avonlea rolled her eyes. "Please. If there is anything I know on this planet it that Gwen Miller loves you and sacrificed herself for your freedom." She looked around at Aurius's predicament. "She made a few miscalculations, probably hoping you would rescue her as you always have. But don't worry, I'll help her rescue herself."

Aurius narrowed his eyes, skeptical of Avonlea's assessment of the situation. But what if she was right? He nodded his acceptance of her terms. He couldn't help her by sitting in this cell.

"Well, it will be hard to sneak you through the castle. Can you use magic?"

He held up the silver cuffs. "Only the witch that made this chain can break it."

Avonlea lifted an eyebrow. "Do you know the witch?"

"Yes."

The keys jingled together again. "Well, it just so happens she made a key for the chains." He rubbed his wrists as the handcuffs fell away. There was never a better feeling than freedom.

"Help me with the guards."

He lifted one by a leg while Avonlea grabbed the other's by the lapels. She squinted her eyes at him.

He shrugged. "It's not my fault I'm so large." The guard swung back and forth, dangling from Aurius's raised arm.

Avonlea nodded while tugging the other guard through the cell door. "Just put him over there. And don't hurt him."

Aurius moved him to the place she indicated and opened his fist. The guard's body crumpled like a rag doll.

"This way," Avonlea directed, ushering him through the cell door. "I'm putting a lot of trust in you. Don't let me down," she said.

Aurius froze in the shadows. His broad fingers wrapped around her wrist. In seconds they were in her suite; her mouth gaped open.

"You don't need my help escaping," she whispered, frozen in shock.

"I don't like using shadows," he said.

Avonlea blinked and finally took a breath. "You can whisk Gwen away

159

right now and we'd never see either of you again."

"Why do I have to keep saying this? I don't make people do things."

"You can ask her to go with you."

Aurius lifted his upper lip. A low growl escaped. "She made her choice."

Avonlea rubbed her head and pressed her eyes closed. "Right, right." She shrugged. "Not much of a choice when you are surrounded by hundreds of guards, but sure I see your point."

"Do you want my help?"

She stopped her babbling. "Yes. I need your help."

"Then do not speak of Gwen again."

Avonlea sighed. Her eyes cut to the secret underground passage. "Fine. I'll get you out. My brother will not be far behind. Get as far away from here as fast as you can." Avonlea pressed against stone to open the door to the tunnels.

"If I see your brother. I will kill him," he said and disappeared into the darkness.

"Just tell me how to cure Drake," she whispered and shut the door behind him.

Betrayed

Avonlea sat across from Gwen with tea and cookies. "I've come to make your day." She placed them beside her on the round tea-table. The maids had polished it so that the finish reflected her image even in the dark brown stain.

Gwen looked out the window. Still covered in thorny vines, the room was shrouded in darkness. "I don't think cookies are going to fix what happened," she said. She slouched in the chair, hand to her chin, refusing to look at the princess.

Avonlea sat her cup down heavily and allowed the china to tink loudly. "It was your magic that kept me in the castle yesterday. What were thinking causing the enchanted garden to overtake the castle like that. And the sleeping sickness the thorns cause." She shook her head and scraped the spoon along the edge of the teacup. The tea slurped over her lips, and she swallowed. "Drake, the idiot, decided to investigate instead of completing his task. He immediately fell asleep and no one can wake him."

Gwen sighed, knowing it was true. Not that she could help it. "I'm sorry he's hurt and I'm glad you're ok. But you double crossed us."

Avonlea's eyebrows pushed up in the middle. "Just because a mission failed doesn't mean I double crossed you." She stood and crossed to the bench by the window. Gwen shifted her gaze away. "In fact I came to share some information. The reason I was sent here actually. Do you want to hear it?"

Gwen shrugged. "Might as well?" she mumbled.

"The wedding has been postponed."

Gwen sat up and looked at the princess for the first time. "Why?"

Avonlea crossed her hands and laid them over her skirt. "Well there is the whole thing about the Goblin King escaping."

"Aurius escaped?" She whispered, hardly allowing herself to believe it. Her trust in the Aurum royal heirs had fully eroded.

She nodded. "Yes. He escaped and was last scene traveling toward the barrier and the enchanted forest."

Gwen nodded and slumped again in her chair. "That's good. I'm glad he's finally given up on me."

Avonlea took another sip from her teacup. "Well, that might be true if not for the fact that you are in love with him."

Gwen opened her mouth to protest, but the words wouldn't form.

"Just admit it."

"Yes. Fine. I love him. But what good does that do us now?"

Avonlea ignored the question. "And Ryland being the hot headed dragon he is, went in search of him. Apparently the thorns don't affect him. He easily escaped the castle." Avonlea stood and moved closer to Gwen. She met her eyes. "And there's this sword," she said, pulling Inauratus out from under her skirts. "You went through so much trouble to get it I thought you might want it, or need it for something."

Gwen didn't trust herself to move. "Avonlea, what's going on? Why didn't this sword go back in the vault?"

The teacups rattled as Avonlea slid the sword over the white tablecloth. "Can't say really. It's just that nothing has worked out for Stepfather and Ryland lately. They lost their guardian so they didn't trust the sword to be in the vault. Then somehow they forgot all about it." Another sip of tea. "I can't imagine why that is. They might actually be cursed."

"They are definitely cursed." Gwen steepled her fingers. Her eyes went back to staring out the window through the thatched giant rose stems that lined the outside of the castle. Even with the sword, there was nothing to do now.

Avonlea sat her teacup down. "Everything went so swimmingly yesterday. I'm surprised you aren't happier."

Gwen cut her eyes back to her supposed friend.

"We were trapped in the castle. Aurius was captured and taken for torture. You were supposed to start a rebellion to keep their attention off of us. Yet ended up watching over Drake in his room. Not to mention all the trouble before we got to the sword."

"None of this was my doing. I do not control the boat as I mentioned to Aurius. But it was a minor set back." She put her forefinger and thumb close to each other. "Because of your overuse of magic, but the rebellion is still on."

Gwen cut her eyes toward Avonlea. "Little good that does us now." Gwen looked down at her fingers spread wide in her lap. "And I'm still learning to control my magic. Just when I think I know what I can do, it changes." She stayed slouched on the chair, pulling her thumb to her lips, biting the nail.

Avonlea sighed and stood. "Do you need anything?"

Gwen hadn't moved from her place. She fixed her eyes on the windowpane in front of her. "Do you think you could get me a horse?"

The princess nodded. "Your horse is still in the stables."

"Fantastic." Her voice held no excitement.

Avonlea's skirt swished around her legs. "Should I send up dinner for you? The chef for one is excited you have returned."

"No need for dinner. Good luck with Drake."

"You wouldn't know how to wake him would you?"

Gwen shook her head over her steepled fingers. "They aren't my roses. They were your grandmother's. If anyone knows how to combat the sleeping sickness it would be the one that created it. We just redirected an enormous amount of magic which caused them to grow. I just told it where to go."

Avonlea looked down at her hands. It was the first time she had ever looked downtrodden since Gwen had known her. "Perhaps there is a remedy in your grandmother's books, or a draught from another plant in the garden," Gwen added.

"Thank you. I'll start there. Good luck to you too." Avonlea hesitated at the door like she wanted to say something else, but remained silent, smiled and left the room.

Gwen sat frozen on her settee for a long while after the princess left. Every second of the last few months ruminated in her head. How had it gone so wrong? How did she end up right back where she started?

She lifted herself, stretched her aching muscles, and crossed to the window. Maybe she could work a way through the vines. Or she could get them to part for her. She jiggled the handle. "No, not where I started." The window was locked. "I was a miller's daughter. Now I'm a princess locked in a tower."

Hearing rustling at her door, she grabbed Inauratus and pressed herself into the wall next to the entrance. Two voices drifted through the wooden wall.

"I'm just delivering the princess's dinner," one said, as a tray clinked at the door. "What errand have they sent you on today?"

Gwen rolled her eyes. Of course, Avonlea hadn't listened to her about dinner.

"We've been trying to track down that devil," another said.

Gwen tilted her head, leaning in to hear the staff gossip about their duties. "What did the king do when she burned the gold in the vault?"

"The guardian?" Gwen whispered.

"His face turned the deepest shade of red I have ever seen, then he stomped out of the castle after Prince Ryland." Surprise laced her tone, but also a bit of humor.

"I didn't even know gold could be burned like that."

"Of course it can be melted, but all the gold that had been spun by the princess just, poof, went up like a candle."

"So it wasn't gold?"

"Seems it was a trick. It just looked like gold."

Gwen lowered the sword and let her head rest against the cabinet. "Well, that cat is out of the bag," she whispered. It wasn't a secret she had wanted revealed for Aurius's sake. She shrugged and weighed the consequences of that knowledge. Perhaps it would save him the trouble of being captured again or hunted down for his ability. She smiled at the thought of Aurius being free.

The conversation continued outside the door. "The princess just made it look like gold to trick the king."

"I wonder if she has magic at all."

"Hush your mouth, of course the princess has magic, how do you think we got all these vines trapping us in?"

"Why would the princess want to trap everyone in?"

"Maybe she didn't mean to do it."

"That's the understatement of the century," Gwen whispered.

A hand rapped against the door, startling her. She jumped away, readying the sword to attack.

"Dinner princess," the servant said.

"What am I doing?" Gwen mumbled. "I can't attack servants. I'll have to figure another way out." Gwen hid the sword under the cushions next to the window bench seat and straightened her dress.

She sat on the bench by the window. "Come in."

The lock clicked, and the door slid open.

"Thank you. Just set the tray." Gwen stood beside the window and directed the ladies.

They did their work, curtsied and left quickly. Their voices faded away down the hallway.

Food didn't appeal to her. But she noticed the cloche was askew, so she examined it closer. When she peeled back the lid, her golden locket was coiled in the middle. Avonlea had returned it.

She clutched it to her chest. Immediately, she felt the difference as the metal touched her skin. Though her magic felt dampened, it wasn't completely gone as it had been for twenty years. It was there, but it felt as if someone had turned the burner down to low. Her magic had become too strong for the locket to contain. She crossed the room to the dresser and opened the clasp. Looking in the mirror, she lifted the locket to her neck.

Hesitating as she held the locket in front of her. "The locket didn't dampen Drake's magic. It released it." She ran her fingers over the metal. "Because it dampened mine."

Gwen opened the necklace with the pictures of her parents. Her mother, the queen of Mystrim; her twin almost; and her false father, a miller, a commoner - stared back at her. Their eyes bored into her, willing her to understand.

"The locket doesn't hide my magic, it nulls it to a degree. When Drake held the locket, my magic was nullified. He could access his own."

Gwen folded the locket closed and slammed it onto the dresser.

"It's not Rumpelstiltskin's curse that is reaping Aurum of magic. It's me." She stepped back from the dresser as the full weight of the statement hit her. Their forgotten conversation came back into her mind. "I drained my mother of magic." A single tear slid down her cheek. "I'm the reason she died. It is my magic that fuels the barrier. The barrier that's robbing Aurum and other places now too."

Her mouth gaped open. A scream built in her throat but came out only as a weak whimper. Backing away from the dresser and the locket, she knocked into a chair and then a table. Locked in the room with no way to escape. Nowhere to run from herself.

She finally fell onto the bench beside the window. Her tears stained her cheeks and her dress. She barely registered the hard object under the cushion, but pulled it out and absently held in her hand in front of her. The tip of the sword rested on the stone floor in front of her. Had her mother known? But everyone thought it was Rumpelstiltskin. Even Aurius, his own son, had assumed until the dungeon.

She shook her head. It didn't matter now. She had to get to the barrier. It had to come down, and there was only one way. The sword in her hand glimmered in a ray of sun. Inauratus could only be used once every hundred years. There were too many curses to choose. Aurius and his goblin curse. Ryland and his dragon curse or Aurum, cursed by her magic.

But none of that mattered if she couldn't get out of the room. Returning to the dresser, she rummaged for a pair of riding pants. It hadn't occurred to anyone that a princess might not want to wear dresses all the time.

She threw up her hands with a frustrated groan. Never one to give up, she tried the door handle again. The ladies had diligently locked it behind themselves. "Did they forget that Aurius can travel through shadows?" But she suspected they thought, as she did, that Aurius wouldn't be returning for her. Her choice had included breaking Aurius's heart.

As she was about to throw herself at the window and hope the enchanted rose bushes would break her fall, the sound of stone scraping against stone resonated through the room. The dark passage to the underground lake opened.

She was across the room, and the sword was in her hand before anyone appeared. Raising the sword to be ready for the intruder. The space remained dark.

Perhaps the water dragon would reappear to finish the job she'd started in the tunnels, Gwen wondered.

As the thought popped into her head, a golden blur swirled around her legs, up her torso, and nestled on her shoulders.

Gwen giggled as her friend found her way onto her shoulders and settled there. "Hey girl. Where have you been?" she asked as she petted the dragon's little snout. "Causing trouble I heard." The dragon lifted its head and snorted. She didn't even produce any smoke. Gwen wondered if the dragon was the kind to breathe fire at all. But of course she had to have been the one to light the gold aflame.

"You found me just in time." She said to the dragon. "Did you bring any pants with you?" Did the dragon just roll her eyes? "Of course I know that dragons don't care about clothes."

"Are you talking to the dragon?"

Uncle George stuck his head through the secret door. Rat followed. The dragon huffed and jumped off of Gwen's neck as she rushed to George and the boy.

"Rat, George. I'm so glad you're ok." She wrapped her arms tightly around them.

"Of course, we're fine," George said.

Rat said nothing. He just smiled and stood beside the underground opening.

"You would be more worried about us, even as we are here to rescue you."

Gwen took his hand and rushed with the sword to the secret passage. "There's no time. We must get to the barrier. I know how to break the curse."

"They've flooded the tunnels beyond the castle. We barely made it through."

"Are the castle gates open?"

"Yes the guards couldn't close them because of the," he sighed. "You'll have to break through overgrown rosebushes."

Gwen nodded. "I need to get to the stables. Can I get through underground?"

"Yes." She rushed toward the secret passage again with his confirmation of her escape route. He held up a hand to stop her. "But wait. Gwen."

"George there really isn't time."

He lowered the satchel she hadn't noticed in her haste to escape. "But I've brought you a new wardrobe." He pulled back his lips into a mischievous grin.

George opened the satchel and pulled out the clothes he had brought her. It wasn't a dress, but certainly not what she had in mind. The outfit was soft white. Not the black she wanted for blending into the shadows. Two pieces unfolded in his hands. Trousers that would probably cling to her legs and a shirt in a style she had never seen before. It looked as if it would do the job of a corset. The fabric was stretchy and smooth.

Gwen groaned. "Why does your armor never cover anything?"

George cupped her cheek in his soft hands. "No more hiding Gwen."

She shrugged. It was better than the corset and gown she wore now. She took the items from his hand and drug her feet to the changing screen.

She changed her clothes, grabbed the sword and rushed down the steps. Rat, George and the golden dragon were behind her. George held out her locket to her. "Do you need the locket?"

She looked over her shoulder. "No." He placed it in his waistcoat pocket. Of course, he had dressed impeccably, even in a crisis.

"How did you know to come?" she asked.

"This little guy," George pointed to the dragon as they jogged down the stairs.

"Girl," Gwen corrected.

George dipped his head in agreement. "She Found us and led us to you. The message went out to start the rebellion. But when the enchanted garden overtook the castle, everyone kind of just scattered. No one knew what to do."

Gwen nodded. "We need to reorganize," she said as her foot hit the last step.

"Avonlea is working on it."

Gwen nodded and stopped at the door to the garden. "I need you to get her a message."

"Whatever you need."

"She's likely in Drake's room. I know she's trying to wake him, but this is more important right now. Tell her to get her rebels to the barrier as quickly as she can. There's no time to lose."

"What are going to do?"

"Take it down."

George and Rat looked at each other. George lifted his chin, and Rat scampered off.

Gwen ran up the stairs toward the garden, leaving George in the glow of the worms. She pushed open the door and wove her way through the overgrowth of the garden, careful not to touch anything. She made it only a few steps. Every single plant wanted attention. "I hope to return and give you the attention you deserve, to bring back magic to the entire kingdom. Then this place will not need protecting. You will have a lot of visitors. Will you help me?"

Stems twirled and bent away from the path. The steps led directly to the French doors, which were surprisingly unlocked. She followed the same path she had the night Drake had let her escape back to the stables. Her horse was already saddled and waiting for her. The stable was entirely devoid of straw. Someone was helping her. Presumably Avonlea.

She mounted her horse and rode away without a word to the attendants.

The thorny vines parted for her as she rode through the castle grounds. The castle gates were indeed still open. Heavy metal chains clanked against stone as the portcullis lowered with the vines out of the way. She raced under the dropping gate. Dust flew up behind her as the gate slammed onto the stone path with a heavy thud.

The guards, who had begun the gate closure days ago, were fast asleep where the thorny vines encased them in slumber. She whispered her thanks to the roses as they closed back over the opening.

Sacrifice

Gwen lowered her head and pushed her horse into a gallop to the barrier. It wasn't difficult to find the battle. The army of Aurum had built roads, which couldn't have been difficult as the army had cleared most of the forests years ago.

Aurum's troops numbered in the tens of thousands. King Aric wasn't on the battlefield. Perhaps he was relying on Ryland to handle the battle. Brilliant gold-plated steel covered the heads and torsos of each soldier. They held a golden spear in one hand and a shield in the other. The men looked identical.

Most of the small army of Mystrim waited on their side of the barrier. Perhaps Queen Helen thought they would never get through the barrier. But if Aurum did, Mystrim would be wiped out. There was no need for men to pass through the barrier to fight. They waited for the fight to come to them, except for a few who had crossed to support Aurius. Ones without magic, Gwen assumed. Who would volunteer to give up their magic to support a goblin? Or perhaps it wasn't the goblin they supported, but Aurius. He had been a prince in their kingdom for years.

Men were arranged into regiments, a few feet separating each one, dotting the landscape with rows upon rows of rectangular groups of soldiers. Three rows back were contraptions separating the rest of the infantry. Three rows after that were men on horseback. There were only two rows in that group. Gwen wasn't sure if they would give chase if they saw her riding through their ranks. She allowed her horse to rest at the top of the hill while she weighed her options.

She didn't think she could call her magic back from this point. She needed to get closer to the barrier.

As she decided, the men at the contraptions moved them into place. In succession, one man pulled a lever while the others covered their heads. The contraption released its ammunition, a large boulder, toward the barrier. Five boulders hit the barrier rapidly. With each hit, the barrier shimmered with a golden ripple. Likely, none of the soldiers could see the magic. They had just seen a boulder stop midair and fall to the ground, but Gwen could see the iridescent force field, and it was nowhere near breaking.

The troops didn't move a muscle, waiting for the command from their prince, who was locked in battle with the Goblin King. One of the boulders fell from the barrier and landed feet from the battling royals. Aurius, embroiled in a battle with Ryland, didn't notice the two hundred and fifty pound boulder nearly dropping on his head.

If it weren't for Ryland's dragon blood, the Goblin King would have the upper hand. Aurius had lost his shirt. Likely, it had become too small when his physique changed. He was no longer the Aurius she knew. The goblin was in complete control. His muscle mass had increased tenfold overnight.

Gwen wanted to watch their steps. The battle was like a dance. But there wasn't time. Ryland wouldn't stop until he could access his dragon. And he couldn't do that until she removed the barrier.

She raced through the middle of the army toward the barrier. A few men on horseback chased her through the ranks, but they couldn't catch her before she reached it.

With Inauratus clutched in her fist, she leapt from her horse and sent it on its way.

* * *

It was the riderless horse that drew Aurius's attention. And cost him. Ryland's sword slashed through the muscle in his arm. Aurius pushed him away and left the battle.

"Coward," Prince Ryland seethed.

The insult was suddenly background noise as he focused on the one thing, no person, that would always take precedence. She was here on the battlefield. Had she come for him or Ryland? Aurius shook his head to clear it. That didn't matter anymore. He would protect her with his life. Even if she had chosen another. He was hers through and through. Even if she wasn't his.

But she wasn't looking at either of them. In fact, she was completely ignoring the battle altogether, standing in front of the barrier with sword raised.

Gwen whispered to the sword. "I swear to use this sword for good and not evil. Inciare."

She was going to use the sword on the barrier, but the curse on the land was still active, and he had to stop her. He raced toward her, Ryland right behind him, skidding to a stop.

"Gwen! Don't you'll destroy Mystrim," Aurius said. His voice had deepened and grown rougher. Two protruding incisors made it more difficult to articulate.

Gwen held out a hand to keep him back. "No, Aurius. You don't understand."

The sword glowed. The familiar shimmer of magic swirled around the sword and Gwen's hand, but instead of flowing out of the sword, the magic flowed into Gwen, up her arm, into her middle. Her golden hair lifted as magic roiled around her and raced into her abdomen. Her body absorbed the magic of the sword. She floated as if she were in an invisible bubble of water.

Too late. He was too late.

"I know what I'm doing Aurius. Trust me please," she spoke softly and slowly.

The Goblin King lifted his chin, his lips flat with determination. He narrowed his eyes. A rough growl escaped. With a single nod, he allowed Gwen to make her choice. Surprising even himself. Choices weren't something goblins typically allowed. But for Gwen, he would do anything.

"Gwen what are you doing?" Ryland asked. His chest heaved from the exertion of the battle and the run.

Gwen's eyes shifted from Aurius to Ryland. "It's me. My magic is draining Aurum."

Ryland stepped toward her to stop her. Gwen took a step back, and Aurius stepped in front of Ryland, facing him with a hand up. The prince stopped his advance with a low growl.

"If she's right and she succeeds, you are probably going to need some space."

Ryland raised his sword in response, but didn't make a move forward.

Aurius, satisfied the prince would not advance, turned to Gwen again. She had turned her back on them and approached the barrier. "She's going to take it down."

"Gwen stop! What are you doing?" Ryland screamed.

Aurius was silent.

Ryland turned to the goblin he had been fighting moments ago. "Will she die?"

Again, Aurius was silent.

Ryland stepped toward her again. "I can't let her do this."

Aurius grabbed him by the throat and slammed him into the ground. He put a knee on his chest. "You've been threatening her life for weeks. She almost died three times because of you. You will not interfere if she now chooses this."

"NOOOO!" Ryland roared. "She is mine. You can't take her from me." He struggled under Aurius's grip.

"She is not an object for you to possess. She is the sun, the moon and the stars. She is the breeze through the forest trees. She is the Earth. And she… Does. Not. Belong. To. You."

"She doesn't belong to you either."

Aurius struggled not to detach the head from Ryland's shoulders. For Gwen's sake, he restrained himself.

"No…. I belong to her."

* * *

Gwen put the battle behind her, out of her mind, with a deep breath, and stepped up to the barrier. Magic hummed inside of her, waiting for her to command it and mold it to her will. She lifted a steady hand to the unseen wall separating the two kingdoms. Her fingertips brushed the barrier.

Immediately, the magic reached out to her, wanting her for itself. The magic from Inauratus flowed and mingled with her own. She felt it swirling at her core. This was her gift. It was a catalyst for power. Pull the magic from one place and feed it into another. But Inauratus was a curse breaker, her opposite. Where she could strengthen magic or make it last longer, the sword's magic was a reagent. It stopped the magic. She stepped into the barrier, allowing it to pull from her, opening herself to the magic.

And it pulled. Her head fell back as she allowed her magic, her soul, to be scourged from her body. She tried to hold the scream, but it ripped from her body along with her magic. The pain of losing a part of herself was too great. Gwen thought she could live without it. She was willing to sacrifice her magic for the two kingdoms. But would she live through the taking? Now she questioned whether she would. Without her magic, would she be able to live at all? The barrier took every drop she had. The spell's design was to take, to feed itself, to become stronger and more indestructible.

For the first time, Gwen noticed Queen Helen looking over the hill from Mystrim. She expected her to be furious, worried maybe. But that wasn't what her face told. No. As the barrier held the heir to the Mystrim throne in place and drained her magic, Queen Helen was satisfied. That was what Helen wanted. Her heir to be weak and magicless, perhaps even dead. The people of Mystrim would follow no one without magic. From Helen's viewpoint, Gwen was allowing her magic to strengthen the barrier.

But the barrier wasn't finished. It reached into Gwen to get every fragment of magic. It needed it all. And it took it from the one whose magic matched its own. But this magic was different. While Gwen's magic was a bright gold, this was a dark red. And once the barrier started pulling, it couldn't stop. The dark-red curse breaker had infiltrated the barrier's spell. Instead of strengthening it, it made it weaker.

The barrier tried to stop, but it was too late. It folded and broke in on itself as the Inauratus' magic infiltrated the spell. Mile by mile, the barrier collapsed. To those without magic, the dust cloud would be the only evidence that anything had happened. The magic users in Mystrim would have seen the barrier fracture like a frozen lake in spring. Mystrim's soldiers covered their ears to protect against the sharp groaning and pops. Leaders screamed orders to move into formation and prepare for battle.

The barrier collapsed into the earth below it. The chasm between the lands closed over, leaving only a thin line of scorched earth separating Aurum and Mystrim.

Queen Helen's bitter smile fell, and she turned away from the barrier. She urged her white horse toward the castle.

Gwen crumpled to the ground, finally released from the magic and unable to keep herself standing.

"GWEN!!" Aurius's scream ripped from his throat, calling toward her.

Men in golden armor surged over the barrier, blocking his view of Gwen. The army of Aurum breached Mystrim for the first time in twenty years. The small army of Mystrim did not falter despite being sorely outnumbered. They crouched ready for the blow from Aurum. Their queen had deserted them, but they would not forsake their duties. They were good soldiers.

The elves, Prisma, fairies. All the realms of the enchanted forest had answered his call. Now engaged in their war to protect Mystrim from the dragon royalty. They pushed the front line back across the barrier line.

As the barrier collapsed, the spell released its magic that had been building for twenty years. The stolen magic rushed back over the land. Those in Aurum who hadn't had magic suddenly felt its pull.

Beneath Aurius's knee, scales rippled along Ryland's body. He jumped away. Ryland dealing with his first shift on his own would give Aurius the time he needed. He raced toward Gwen's body, covering it with his own.

He kissed her lips and shook her, but nothing happened. He searched her, looking for something to help him help her. Holding her hand, trying to will her to take his magic. He had plenty to spare.

Strong hands gripped his shoulder. "Aurius," the Elf King said as gently as possible.

He tore himself away from his friend with a growl. "No."

"There's nothing you can do."

"You know nothing," Aurius growled.

"Aurius come away."

"I will not."

The Elf King huffed a sigh and stood.

The ground vibrated under his knees. A hoof tapped and took the place the Elf King vacated.

"Let me help Aurius," Prisma said.

Aurius didn't move.

"I can help but you must step back."

Aurius's eyes shifted to the unicorn. They exchanged a moment, then Aurius placed a kiss on the fingers he was holding.

The unicorn pranced around Gwen's body and lay next to her. Somewhere in the distance, a dragon roared. Aurius faintly registered there were two now in the sky.

The unicorn nuzzled Gwen's lifeless cheek. Her horn glowed with iridescent light and pressed against Gwen's forehead. The light disappeared just below the surface of her skin.

Prisma rose.

"She'll be fine. Her magic is depleted. Take her to a place with plenty to spare so she can replenish hers. The imbalance is too great here."

The Elf King lifted his chin toward the forest and patted Aurius on the back. "Go. We'll finish this."

Aurius scooped her up and ran toward the enchanted forest. Toward her cottage, the haven he set up for this occasion. The roar of an angry dragon followed him, but he didn't dare look back. He crashed through trees and brush, disappearing into the forest.

* * *

Ryland's head, in dragon form, rose fifteen feet above the Earth. His black and red scales showed he was indeed a war dragon. The rage that had been building released from his mouth in a stream of molten fire.

The Elf King shook his head. "Dragon. I should have known."

"Dragons." The murmur could be heard through the crowd.

Emyr raised his sword and shouted to his soldiers. "Formations! Protect the forest at all costs." He tilted at the hip, one leg back, front knee bent. His sword was thin and lightweight, but everyone knows elf swords are without equal, the strongest swords made.

His soldiers crouched in the same stance. The army pushed off with the back feet and raced toward the dragon.

Dozens of Aurum soldiers, who now had magic, were learning quickly how to use it. And whether they were rebels or soldiers, their orders were to protect the prince.

They threw magic sporadically at the elves to keep them from harming Prince Ryland. The Elf King only smirked and covered himself with an invisible shield. Protecting himself from the magical onslaught. Each of his soldiers did the same.

But as they approached, Ryland's long neck swiveled away from them. Toward his own castle.

It wasn't long before Emyr, with his superior vision, could see why. Another dragon could be seen in the distance. His wings flapped slowly, but his roar said he was coming to join the battle.

Emyr was confident his soldiers could take on one war dragon. He wasn't sure about two.

"Fall back. To the trees."

* * *

Ryland flapped his powerful wings for the first time. He rose only a foot off the ground before he fell and shuddered at the earth. His men fell off their feet, then scrambled to a standing position and ran from him. The middle of a battle was not the best time to learn to fly. Still, he had to protect Gwen from his stepfather.

He beat his wings harder. Dust flew around him, and he rose above the tree line. His back ached, but he pushed through the pain. King Aric would kill Gwen if he found her. Flying was purely instinctual after the takeoff. He had probably attempted that in the worst way possible, but there was no time to second-guess his new skills.

His stepfather was an enormous black dragon; Ryland was almost as big. King Aric had experience on his side. It was obvious he had learned to fly before the White Witch erected the barrier. To think it was the barrier that had robbed them of their abilities. He would make that witch pay. But he shook the thoughts out of his head. That would have to wait. Now it was time to protect the true queen.

Ryland rose in the air, level with his stepfather. He could see the forest for miles, but Gwen and Aurius were covered by the canopy, so he couldn't mark their progress. He growled at the thought of Gwen in Aurius's arms. And shook that thought away as well. The only thing that mattered was that she was alive and safe. For now.

Ryland's intention was to intercept his stepfather before he could join the battle. Before he could find Gwen. He needed to focus.

King Aric peeled upward into the clouds with a screech. Flapping his black wings harder to gain altitude. Ryland watched him rise, treading his wings in the air, but he didn't give chase. The clouds lit with bursts of flames the color of grass. Fire that Ryland realized too late it had come from his stepfather. Green flames rolled across his back and over his wings. His scales protected him, but the fire on his wings was torture. He roared in pain.

Crimson flames flowed from his own mouth, evaporating the clouds above him. Brimstone rained onto the ground, charring circles into the field below. He would need to be more careful.

A whoosh of cold air rushed underneath him. And he turned his attention in the direction it had come from. The Elf King had his hands raised. The fire was going out.

The wind whistled from his right. Ryland screeched and flapped his wings faster. The pain was a shock through his back, to his tail. Even as determination propelled him, exhaustion pulled at him. He flapped harder. The prince of Aurum would not let something like pain stop him from protecting his betrothed.

He opened his wide maw. His sharp teeth glistened as the sun broke through the clouds. The coppery taste of blood rolled over his tongue as he closed his mouth over his stepfather's tail. His teeth pierced the scaled plate dragon armor. He locked his jaw, then folded his wings. The king's claws kicked at him. A deep gash etched Ryland's dragon scales, but it didn't draw blood.

The king had experience, but he didn't have enough strength to keep himself and Ryland aloft. Locked in a deadly embrace, the two dragons tumbled head over tail through clouds and mist. A crater of dust and trees rose around them.

Crimson mist swirled around Ryland. He couldn't hold on to his dragon form any longer. Sharp aches accompanied every movement. He lifted himself, still fully clothed in his armor, to standing. Dust still hung heavy in the air, and he had to climb over flattened trees.

But his stepfather was stronger. So, he found himself face to face with an angry dragon. There wasn't enough room for the dragon to lift off in flight.

Ryland drew his weapon. The dragon seemed to pull its lips back into a smile. Was that a laugh?

The dragon swatted his tail. Ryland jumped over it, bringing his sword down at the same time. The metal rang as it made contact with the plated armor, but didn't even make a scratch.

Ryland's shoulder still stung where the king's claw had pierced his scale. Perhaps the only thing that would damage a dragon is another dragon.

But he didn't have time to worry about how he was too exhausted to change again. Another slap of the tail had him jumping and rolling away from the dragon.

His only weapon was his other form. Inexperience and exhaustion limited his choices.

Maybe he could reason with his stepfather. It hadn't worked in the past. It was his only hope now.

"Stop this!" He didn't recognize his own voice, but it felt laced with extra power.

The dragon froze before him.

"She is not yours," Ryland said.

"Stupid boy." The dragon hissed through giant pointed teeth.

Ryland lifted his sword. "I'll never stop fighting you."

The dragon king laughed. "I'll deeeessssstroy you, boy." His right leg moved, breaking free from whatever temporary hold Ryland had on him. "The girl is ussssseeless now. She musssst die…"

"That will not happen."

"The Goblin King issss…. who I want."

"He'll kill you if you even think of getting close to her."

The dragon moved another foot as if breaking out of strong stone. He laughed. "He can try."

Without warning, the dragon's strong tail whipped against Ryland's back, knocking him into a nearby tree. He flopped onto the ground. Only able to move his eyes, helpless to do anything else, he watched his stepfather climb to the top of the canopy in one step. Branches cracked and snapped under the weight of his talons. The force of the wind pressed against him as King Aric flapped his wings and lifted himself back into the sky.

The Dragon King

Ryland was immobilized and out of options. He lay there watching the king rise into the sky, chasing the one person he thought he loved. Was it love? Or infatuation of a dragon nature? Regardless, he was compelled to protect her. Dragon scales rippled along his arms, but his body would not respond.

Dragon. That word flipped itself around in his head. His life suddenly made more sense. Still, being able to change your entire body into a beast was life-altering. He put those thoughts aside for another time. There was work to do, and lying here wasn't getting it done.

Moving from this location was impossible. He focused on a foot. "Move." He commanded it. It didn't. There was no pain either. While that might seem like a blessing to some, it was not to Ryland.

Helpless. He didn't do helpless very well. He roared. The only thing he could control. A cry for help. Minutes passed that seemed like an eternity. Everyone had their own battles and no time to run to help, despite his being the crown prince. He swallowed hard and tried again to adjust his body. "Is this where I die?" he wondered softly. Moments after the thoughts swept through his mind, footsteps pounded out of the woods.

Men surrounded him. Not just any men. An army of elves. Spears pointed at him. Silent.

He wanted to shrug his shoulders. If dragons could exist, why not elves? Ryland moved the only part of his body he was still able. His chin. Readying himself for the killing blow. He would die with dignity if he couldn't die with honor. As he prepared himself for death, the circle of soldiers parted.

A woman emerged. He could only tell it was a woman because of her long hair, braided and folded over one shoulder. And her body shape was different from the other soldiers. Otherwise, she would have blended in with them. She wore black armor and carried a spear. Her silhouette grew darker as she approached, but as she crouched beside him, he could make out the features of her face.

"What have you gotten yourself into brother?"

Ryland's eyebrows creased. "Avonlea?"

She turned toward the elves behind her. "Can you do anything for him?"

One of them tilted his head and shrugged a shoulder.

"Can you try?" They remained stoic, spears pointed at the broken dragon prince.

Ryland recognized the indignant attitude. He had attacked them, called for war, so why should they help him? "Forget it. Avonlea. I've done... Just let them kill me," Ryland protested.

She shook her head. "No chance, brother. I will take on their whole army and die here with you if necessary."

He swallowed and groaned. "Where is Drake? Why aren't you with him in the castle?"

She ran her hand through his dirty blond locks. "It's rather hard to lead a rebellion from inside stone walls."

"Father," he gritted out.

"Stepfather," she corrected.

"He's after Gwen."

She smiled at her brother. "Mother's taking care of it."

"Mother?" Ryland groaned. Blood dribbled from the corner of his mouth.

"There's a lot you'll need to catch up on once you're healed."

The ground rumbled. Tiny pebbles danced over the hard-packed dirt.

Crevices opened in the ground. The elf soldiers moved one step back, but they didn't look surprised.

The ground broke apart. Water bubbled up between the cracks. Small at first. The water rushed toward him. There was nowhere to go; he couldn't move. Would drowning be the worst way to die? But just as the water reached the leg of his pants, the ground burst wide open and water rushed out of it in a geyser. A huge fountain of water cleared the treetops. At the top of the fountain was a beautiful iridescent beast. She roared and leapt from the water fountain into the sky.

Ryland tracked her until she was out of sight.

"Mother?" he asked.

Avonlea grinned and nodded. She stepped back and allowed two elves to place a hammock beside him. They lifted his body onto the gurney. It floated from the ground in front of them.

"Don't argue. The elves have magic. They can heal you."

His lips pulled back into a regretful smile. "Not much I can do about it."

Avonlea nodded toward the elves who guided the bunk through the woods. "I hope that isn't the last I see of him," Avonlea said as she watched her brother's blond hair disappear through the trees.

"He will be healed and sent on his way."

She turned to the Elf King, who looked down and into her eyes. "You won't keep him prisoner?"

His knuckles brushed hers. She couldn't tell if it was by chance or on purpose, but she chose to ignore it.

"Not this time, no," he said. A horse was brought to him; a young elf handed him the reins and held the bridle as Emyr mounted. "I'm going to find your other brother. Would you like to ride with me?"

Avonlea stepped back. "I have too much business to finish here. But please send him my regards and remind him of his promise."

Emyr nodded and nudged his mare into the woods. One by one, the elves disappeared into the shadows and woods, leaving no trace that they had ever existed. A little voice in the back of her head told her it wasn't the last she would see of the Elf King.

* * *

King Aric flapped his broad black wings higher, higher into the sky. Away from the carnage he had left of his stepson. At least he wouldn't be a problem anymore. And he had found the Goblin King's weakness. It was just a matter of capturing him and exploiting it.

He ducked as he pushed his wings down, and he lifted himself into the sky higher still. Above the clouds was best.

On the ground far below him, the Goblin King held Gwen against his chest, growling at every obstacle that blocked him from getting her to where she needed to be.

King Aric, easily twice the size of Ryland, crushed the trees in front of him and blocked his path.

Aurius held Gwen in one hand and allowed magic to swirl around the other.

"In what world can a goblin beat a dragon?" the dragon asked with gravel in his voice.

"In every single one."

A tendril of smoke curled out of the dragon's nostrils. His reptilian lips widened into a smile. "Come with me and I won't kill the girl. You're the one I want."

A searing ball of magic Aurius had formed hit the dragon on the side of his face. He reared and swiped his hand over his snout. His tongue slithered between his teeth, and he flung his head back and forth, trying to shake off the magic spell.

When he had succeeded, he searched the woods for his prey. Finding the clearing empty, he prepared himself to launch back into the sky. His muscles bunched in his legs as his wings pressed down. As his feet left the ground, something barreled into him and knocked him back to the earth.

A water dragon wasted no time in immobilizing him. She wound herself around his neck and pressed claws into his wings. The thick leathery membranes parted with a crisp snap under her talons.

Avonlea raced to the clearing where her mother had pinned the king. He was struggling under her hold. They needed him to shift for the plan to work. She had hoped her mother's appearance would shock him back to being human. By the looks of it, they were going to need another plan. Plan B had been Ryland's command. As the true king, he could command the

185

dragon to do anything.

The king wasn't moving. Wasn't trying to move anyhow. For a moment, they had the upper hand.

The elves left under her command surrounded them. Her own rebel soldiers served as backup. It would hold. It would have to do.

Avonlea approached the king. "Return to human form."

"No," he growled.

The water dragon stretched his neck and pressed the king's face into the dirt. "It's over," Avonlea said.

"You can do nothing to me," he hissed.

She shrugged. "You can't hold the shift forever."

"And you can't command me." The dragon huffed a haughty laugh. Puffs of dust and smoke swirled above his head.

"Ryland will…"

"Be dead my morning." The dragon's serpent tongue flicked between his reptilian teeth with each word.

Avonlea shifted her eyes to the Elf King approaching on horseback. He handed the reins of both horses to a boy nearby.

"Aurius came this way. Have you seen him?" Emyr asked.

Avonlea shook his head and pointed toward the fight between two dragons.

The water dragon holding the king in place pressed a claw into the king's neck. The scales bent under her claw, but they did not break.

Emyr placed his hand on his snout and whispered a few words no one could understand.

The dragon shrank back into his human form. His body appeared fully clothed and limp on the ground. The water dragon released him.

Light shimmered from her body. King Aric's hand rose, covering his face, as the magic took over the water dragon. Others around him shielded their eyes as well, unable to watch the bright magic fade from the water dragon.

He lowered his hand. Who was this dragon who had defeated him so successfully?

The sharp point of a blade cut into the skin on his neck. A trickle of blood seeped from the tiny wound.

"You are under arrest for treason," Avonlea's mother said.

The king fell to the ground. "Aurora. How could I have known you would have been stuck in your dragon form?"

She lifted her chin. "You knew. And when the True King is well, you will be sentenced for your crimes."

He tried to rise, but the blade pressed into his neck further. "You have no right."

"I have every right," Aurora said.

Avonlea directed two of her soldiers to place the cuffs on him. As they approached, the king stood with the grace of a dragon, pulled a dagger from his belt and flung it toward Avonlea's heart. End over end, it flew, racing toward the princess.

"Nooo!" It was hard to tell who said it, as it seemed everyone had.

Avonlea spun out of the dagger's path as Aurora spun into it. The king's head no longer sat upon his shoulders. The princess's sharp blade came away drenched in the dragon king's blood.

Aurora, too, dropped to the ground. Her hands clutched her right side. One knee was in the dirt and the other was drawn up. She looked up at her daughter, who raced to her side.

"Mother."

Aurora pulled her fingers away. Deep red blood dripped over them onto the ground. She collapsed onto her side, Avonlea helping her to lay back.

The dowager queen lifted her bloodied hand to Avonlea's face. "It was my undying wish to see you again before I died. And now I have."

A tear slipped down Avonlea's cheek. "I'm not losing you just when I found you again," she sobbed.

Aurora's eyes shifted to her daughter's. "You'll be a great leader." Aurora's eyes closed and her body relaxed into the dirt.

"No. Mother. Please don't go," Avonlea whimpered. "I just found you." Tears slipped over her cheeks as she pressed them against her mother's hand. Aurora's body relaxed.

A hand grasped her shoulder. "Come away princess." Avonlea didn't turn to see who it could be.

She shook herself out of his grasp. "No. She's my mother."

"There is someone here to help," he whispered.

Avonlea turned to see the Elf King standing over her. He stepped aside. A white horse clopped behind him. Avonlea lifted her hand to shield her eyes; the glow was so bright. The horse's white horn emitted pure white light.

"Prisma can heal her if it's not too late."

Reluctantly, Avonlea rose and moved beside Emyr. Prisma stepped closer and bowed to the fallen queen, placing her horn into the wound. The light dulled as it entered her body, but Avonlea could trace its progress. The wound stitched itself back together. And air rushed back into Aurora's lungs. With a gasp, she opened her eyes and sat up.

She looked around the forest at those standing next to her, but eyes landed on Prisma still bowed before her. She stroked the unicorn's face.

"Thank you, Prisma."

"Your curse is broken," Prisma replied. "It is time to find your son."

"The goblin is not my child," she said.

Avonlea dropped to her side. "You don't have to hide it any more."

"He's a respectable man..." the Elf King argued.

Aurora held up a hand, silencing him. "We'll discuss this later. Ryland needs us as well."

Emyr's mouth closed, and he lifted his chin. He motioned to his men. They disappeared again into the trees.

Avonlea helped her mother to stand and turned to each of her allies. "Thank you for all you have done today. We owe you a debt of gratitude."

"Much of what was done today was payment for a debt owed," Prisma said.

Avonlea's head tilted in confusion.

"It is your kingdom, not ours that has suffered much at the hand of the curse." Prisma rose and looked at the dowager queen. "Consider us even."

Aurora bowed her head to the unicorn.

"What should we do with the king?" Avonlea asked.

"Leave him, the carrion will take care of him."

"That's rather gruesome Mother," she replied.

She shrugged. "It's what he deserves."

Avonlea pursed her lips and turned to her men. "Please deliver his body to the castle to lie in state. He was the king and the kingdom needs to see that he is good and dead."

"Very well. If it must be done," Aurora said.

Avonlea nodded to some of her men, who had just arrived, waiting for her orders. They strapped the king and his head onto a horse and led it back through the woods.

"Mother, I know you have been through a terrible ordeal, but the kingdom will be in chaos."

"Shh child. There will be times to discuss such things. First we must ensure Ryland heals and is healthy enough to sit upon the throne."

"And if he is not?"

"The order of succession is clear. Eldest to youngest in order of birth."

"So you do not want the throne?" Avonlea asked.

"I've been a water dragon for twenty years. I doubt I would be very good at ruling." She shook her head. "No. It is time for Ryland to take his place if he is up to it."

Avonlea grabbed the reins of a nearby horse and handed them to her. "Let's be off to check on Ryland then. Are you well enough to ride."

Aurora nodded and took the reins. "Does this not please you?"

She clicked her tongue to urge the horse into a canter. "It pleases me very well. I do not want Ryland's throne and I want to make my own choices."

"You mean you don't want to marry because you have to."

"I don't want to marry a noble for the good of the kingdom."

"I suppose you have someone in mind?" Aurora asked.

"Perhaps. But that is not important." She sighed. "I just found you and I don't want to leave you, but I can't be in two places at once."

Aurora lifted her hand. "I'll ride to check on Ryland. You return to the castle and ensure everything is in order. Send word if you need anything."

The princess bowed her head in thanks and turned her horse toward the castle in Aurum.

The Goblin and the Miller's Daughter

Nothing else mattered. She owned his soul, and he would serve her in life and death. He knew the dragons were on his heels, though he couldn't see them, hear them or smell them. They were there. He sensed them. One wouldn't be a problem, but if the king and the prince had teamed up? He growled at the thought and pushed on through the dense undergrowth.

The door of the cabin burst backward with the thrust of Aurius's foot. Grinhelda yelped in response. She stood in the kitchen covered in flour, her apron barely doing the job of saving her dress.

Aurius growled and pulled Gwen closer to his chest, shielding her from the witch.

Grin put her cookbook down on the counter. "Aurius what are you doing here?"

"I could ask you the same?" A growl punctuated each word.

"I came to help Gwen of course. What's happened to you? She was too late?"

Aurius's chest heaved from his run through the woods. A trek that should have taken days took only an hour in this Goblin state. He didn't know if there was any going back. He couldn't remember any reason he should want to be only half goblin. The goblin was much better suited for saving Gwen. He didn't answer her questions, turning to the stairs instead. The best place for her was her bedroom. He bounded up the steps two at a time.

"Still not much for conversation, I see," Grin grumbled behind him.

He laid her on the bed, her hair spread out around her in a halo. The white cushions barely dipped with the weight of her body.

"What does she need?" Grin asked.

"Magic," he grumbled, the single word.

"I felt the barrier break. Magic restored."

He smoothed a lock of hair away from her forehead. "It was hers. She gave it all."

"I see." Grinhelda took her hand. "You brought her here because of all the magic you stored in this place."

Aurius grunted in reply. "There's more at the castle, but it's not safe."

"Give her yours."

"No."

"It won't hurt her Aurius."

"It might."

"Her body will distill the magic. The curse won't transfer to her."

"I cannot take that risk."

"Then you risk her death."

"OUT!"

Grinhelda let go of Gwen's hand and raised hers in defense. "I'm only trying to help."

His upper lip pulled away from his teeth. "You've done enough. You should never have sent her to me in the first place."

Grin rolled her eyes and leaned against the door frame. "I was doing you a favor." She looked at her blood-red nails as if he were boring her.

"Out before I remove you myself."

Grin pursed her lips and left the room. She closed the door behind her. Aurius turned his attention back to Gwen. The bed sank under his weight. As it did, a golden coin slipped from her pocket.

As soon as it hit the fabric of the bed, the dark prince popped into view.

"Gwen it's been awh…" the hologram paused. "Oh. It's you." He sneered.

"Yes. And I didn't summon you. Go away."

Wispy Aurius turned to face Gwen. "What's happened?" he asked.

"She used the sword and brought down the barrier."

"The barrier that was protecting Mystrim and the Enchanted Forest?"

"Yes. Helen used Gwen's magic to take and absorb every drop of magic from Aurum."

"And the sword acted as a reagent, nullifying her magic in the barrier."

"Yes."

"Why is she here?"

"She needs to absorb magic or she will stay in this state of limbo."

"What have you tried?" Wispy Aurius asked.

Goblin Aurius grumbled.

"Nothing?" Wispy Aurius's eyes widened.

"I hoped just being here would work."

Wispy Aurius clutched his head. "Oh no. The Goblin has already rotted your brain." He searched the room. "The coin has the most magic. Quickly put it in her hand."

The goblin did as he was told. It was him after all. But it did nothing. "I don't feel anything happening with the coin. There's a block of some sort." Wispy Aurius pinched his chin between his thumb and forefinger. "She isn't able to absorb the magic in this state. She barely had control of her magic awake. I doubt should can control it subconsciously."

"So this isn't going to work?"

"We just need to force the magic in."

"How?"

"We have to give her some of ours."

"I will not pass the curse on to her."

"Then don't."

Goblin Aurius blinked at himself, waiting for more explanation.

"You control what magic you give her. Give her the best parts."

"Then only the goblin will remain."

Wispy Aurius frowned. "We love her."

"Yes," the goblin agreed.

"Then we must do this."

Goblin Aurius nodded and squared his shoulders. He cast a protective bubble around her.

"Will you stay with her when I go?" he asked.

"If she will have me," Wispy Aurius replied.

"It's the best we can do. I wish there were more," Goblin Aurius said, letting his hand rest on her face.

"Yes. Well there's still the contract you can't figure out how to break."

"She used the sword for the barrier, we can't break the contract."

Sadness tinged the corner of his eye. "I'll encourage her to keep looking for other ways," he whispered.

Aurius curled his meaty green hand around hers, careful that his claws did not scrape her skin. Closing his eyes, he felt for the core of his magic. He was born with so much; it was hard to identify its source within himself.

He had been avoiding using it for so many days that now pulling on it again was a chore. But it happily obeyed once it was fully awake. It flowed through him, a trickle at first, then a swirling stream of energy that he directed to flow into Gwen through their physical connection. He meant only to give her enough to help her through this and regain consciousness. Too much, and he feared she would be cursed as a wicked, conniving goblin who only ever got what she wanted, along with him. After she woke, Wispy Aurius would guide her in taking a bit of magic here and there.

The magic glided over their joined hands. But once it reached Gwen, it rushed to fill the void her magic had left when she sacrificed everything to restore the kingdom of Aurum. Goblin Aurius tried to pull back on how much magic was flowing into Gwen, but her ability was greedy, and it didn't want to let go. It wanted to pull and pull. The more magic flowed in, the faster it pulled.

"Careful," Wispy Aurius warned.

Goblin Aurius growled. "I'm... not... controlling... it."

"She has enough. Cut it off."

But even in her unconscious state, she had a grip on his hand that rivaled the strongest magic wielder he had ever encountered. Their hands were cemented together. He couldn't let go until Gwen let go. He might be long depleted by then. Wispy Aurius disappeared and moments later, reappeared. There was a tap on the door.

"Aurius?"

The door opened without his answering. Grinhelda rushed to his side. But a golden globe prevented her from interfering.

"Aurius, let me in."

"Can't," he said through clenched teeth. He was trying to pull away with all his strength.

"I can't help you if you don't drop the shield."

His eyes shifted to the witch standing inches away. Tears stung his eyes.

"I didn't want this for her."

"Drop the shield."

He squeezed his eyes closed. The shield dissipated. Grinhelda tried to pull their hands apart. It didn't budge.

She stood straight, with her hands on her hips. "Gwen. Aurius loves you and you are killing him."

She turned and walked out of the room.

The flow of magic slowed, and Aurius's magic pulled back into himself. His fingers popped away from her wrist one by one. Gwen's eyes remained closed. It would take time for her to revive. He leaned over her and smoothed the golden strands of hair again. His lips lingered on her forehead as he pressed a kiss there.

"Goodbye Gwen," he whispered and stepped into the shadows.

Gwen's eyes snapped open. She lifted herself off the bed. Her hair hung down her back. Eyes darted left, then right. "Where's Aurius."

"I'm here." Wispy Aurius popped out of the coin.

Gwen swung her legs off the edge of the bed. Her boots were still on her feet. "You are usually very helpful, but you know who I mean."

Wispy Aurius didn't meet her eyes. "He's gone to let you live your life."

Gwen raised her hands to her temples. "He's an idiot."

"Well. I don't know about that."

"Why did he leave?"

"So you wouldn't be obligated to marry him."

Gwen pursed her lips and shook her head. "I know how to break the contract."

Wispy Aurius raised his eyebrows. "Care to enlighten me?"

"The quill. The one used to sign the contract. It can reverse the agreement."

Wispy Aurius's eyes widened. "Yes. Of course."

"Well if you knew that why haven't you said so?"

"The quill was lost. We didn't think it possible. The question is how do you know that?"

Gwen shook her head. "No. Not lost. Hidden. In a cottage for her daughter to find. My mother left me the key to break the blood contract that she burdened me with. And his magic told me. Whispered it to me. Is his, your, power always so raw and rugged?"

Wispy Aurius sat down on a chair Gwen couldn't see, as if he was stunned. "You found the quill?"

"Yes, days ago." Gwen's eyes snapped to the open door, where Grinhelda had stood. "Before someone pushed me into rescuing the Goblin." She slid her legs over the edge of the bed and took a moment to catch her breath before she stood.

"Well, what are you waiting for? Go get it."

She crossed over to the closet searching for new clothes. "I don't have it. You know you could have put something in here beside black dresses."

"Gwen. What's happened to the quill?"

She scraped a hanger along the metal pole and shrugged. "A raven swooped in and stole it."

Aurius opened and closed his mouth like a fish.

"Is Grin still here?" she asked.

"Yes. Downstairs."

Gwen chose a plain black smock that thankfully didn't have a lot of length and somehow had pants built in. Wispy Aurius disappeared when she pulled the royal golden robes from her body and replaced them with the plain black clothes. There wasn't time for modesty.

"Where are you going?" he asked when she grabbed the coin and trounced across the room.

"I'm going to find the quill, then we are going to break the contract and break the Goblin curse."

"The sword can only be used once."

"I don't need the sword, Aurius. She wiggled her fingers. I have the sword's magic."

Gwen stood in front of the trifold mirror. She waved her hand over the surface. It rippled, linking her to the place she wanted to go, but she was only met with darkness.

"Where is he?"

"If it's black then he's blocking you," Wispy Aurius said.

"I need him to help me find this raven and get the quill."

"No, you don't." Grinhelda stood at the door again.

Gwen turned toward her voice.

"Good to see you're awake." She leaned against the doorjamb and crossed her arms. Her eyes darted toward the mirror. "You'll need the quill first."

"Do you know where Aurius is?"

"Skulking in a cave most likely."

Gwen faced the mirror again, still black as ink. "How am I going to find a raven in the middle of the forest?"

"There are no wild ravens left. They're all employed by kingdoms. If you see a raven it was sent by a throne," the witch said.

"Why would King Aric send a raven to steal a quill?"

Grin shook her head. "He doesn't have the magic to do it."

"So Queen Helen?"

Gwen waved her hand again. Aurius's room in the castle came into view. It had been wrecked. "What happened?"

"Looks like someone was looking for something," Wispy Aurius said.

Grin pointed to the mirror. "You have a way into the castle."

Gwen nodded and prepared to step through the mirror. A low roar rattled the cottage walls. She put her foot down just shy of the mirror.

"Once I'm ready." She turned to Grinhelda. "When I find the quill how do I find Aurius?"

Grinhelda lifted her eyebrow. And swiped a golden card off the dresser. She flipped it up. "The same way you found him the first time."

Gwen snatched the card from Grin's hands. She wrapped her fingers around the calling card and smiled. "This will do."

"Gwen if you use that calling card you will be invoking the rule of three. Aurius is a goblin now. The thing he hated most," Wispy Aurius said.

"You hate your father. And you think by becoming a goblin you will become your father."

Wispy Aurius looked at his shoes.

"It's ok. I'm willing to take that risk. Now back in the coin. You're going with me."

He nodded and blinked out of sight. She stuffed the coin into her pocket.

She raced down the stairs. Grinhelda followed her down the steps at a more leisurely pace.

Gwen's hand twisted the knob on the door of the cottage as she looked back over her shoulder. Grin descended the stairs like a queen. Her borrowed black wedding dress splayed out in a trail behind her.

"You're free to go marry your king now," Gwen said over her shoulder.

"I'm rather comfortable here."

Gwen rolled her eyes. "I'll be expecting a rent payment then."

A faint smile appeared on Grin's lips. "Oh I expect you'll be getting a considerable boon." She winked at Gwen.

Wind blew the door out of Gwen's grasp, and it slapped against the doorjamb. Dust flew up in all directions. She shielded her face from the sharp pricks of dirt, leaves and debris. Forcing her feet against the gale, she took two steps onto the porch.

A dragon the size of the cottage landed in front of her. Its head reared back in a motion ready to breathe fire.

"Grinhelda, did Aurius bring Inauratus back with us?"

"I thought you didn't need the sword," the witch said.

Gwen tilted her head. "Ryland doesn't know that."

Grin pressed a piece of cold metal into her hand. "Here."

She looked at her hand and back toward Grinhelda, happy to see the plated gold sword.

Grin made a shooing motion with her hand. "Now go. Slay your dragon and win the hand of your Goblin King."

Gwen smiled and lifted the sword in front of her.

Cursed

Gwen had never had training with a sword, though this was the second time in a few hours she had held one in her hands. She was born to it. The blade felt light and balanced in her delicate fingers, as if they had made it for her.

She shook the thoughts from her head; they had no place in this fight. Gwen narrowed her eyes at the dragon in front of her, focusing her attention.

"Ryland. I don't want to hurt you, but if you don't let me pass I will cut off your toes." She knew it sounded silly, but it was the only part of the dragon she could reasonably reach.

Ryland returned to human form. As soon as the elves had healed his paralysis, he shifted into his dragon and flew north. His head bent forward, eyebrows furrowed. Acrid smoke still billowed from his nostrils. The muscles across his chest and shoulders flexed in barely controlled rage.

"You chose him?" The dragon's growl didn't leave his voice. It only highlighted the anger he was trying to control.

Gwen's shoulders lowered, and her chin lifted. She narrowed her eyes and met his with a glare of her own. "I chose Aurum and Mystrim and Magic and the Elves and Prisma."

"You are mine. I won't allow this."

"So you are dishonoring the choice you allowed me?" she asked.

His smile was the same sweet smile she had been accustomed to. It was full of teeth and something twisted, confidence that he could have whatever he wanted. "I'm still a dragon." He took a predatory step closer. "And I claimed you."

"That settles it." Gwen lifted the sword and leveled it at Ryland. "Inciare," the word came out as a whisper, but a sparkle floated over the weapon. Inauratus lit into a soft golden glow as the magic settled into it.

Ryland took a step back. "You still wield Inauratus? It's only meant to be used once."

"I guess they lied. And today I break the curse of greed over dragons." She brought the sword down on Ryland's leg, aiming for the place that was least damaging. She hoped a flesh wound would be enough to immobilize him.

Ryland fell flat on his back. With his wounded leg straight, the other bent beneath him. Struggling, he lifted himself to his elbow. His hand went to the wound on his leg. Fingers dripped with blood.

"You've struck me," he groaned.

She stood a few feet away and focused the magic taken from Inauratus into Ryland, searching for the curse on dragons. Greed. Anger. Malice. "All healing comes with a little pain," she said.

The sword's magic dismantled the curse built into dragon magic. It blocked the connection to Ryland's instincts, natural protective instincts corrupted by darkness. She could see that even powerful curse-breaking magic wouldn't dissolve the curse forever. Ryland would be worse off than before she helped. The only way for a permanent change would be if she used her new borrowed magic to replace the curses with their opposites — generosity, love, and devotion. Her magic mended his, and she pulled it away.

Gwen stretched out her hand to help him stand. "Don't worry. You'll be fine. Do you feel any different?"

His eyes widened. He looked over his shoulder and all around. "Confused."

She groaned as she lifted him. "Come. Let's get you to a healer."

"I just left the elves. They healed my back. The dragon compelled me to come straight here."

"That would be because of the curse I just broke."

He stopped and wrapped his arm around her, pulling her to face him. His fingers brushed her cheek. "Gwen... I feel lighter."

Ryland's lips pulled back into another smile. Gentle. One that filled Gwen with hope rather than dread.

"What if I still want to marry you?" he asked.

"Do you?"

His eyebrows pushed together. "I don't know. All of my feelings and memories are still there but the need to have you all to myself is gone."

Her eyes searched his. She saw the truth in his words.

"I could have loved you," she said.

"But you don't."

"I know that you were cursed." She placed a hand on his cheek. "I forgive you." Her eyes found the golden button at the top of his uniform. "But I can't forget it." Her eyes slid back up to his to gauge his reaction.

In response, he leaned on her shoulder, turning to limp to the cottage.

After a few steps, he said, "I did my best to protect you from the worst of it."

"You started a war."

He nodded his head. "That I did."

"Why?"

"My uncle used me. Planned the assassination attempt. The kidnapping enraged me and I couldn't control the curse's affects. He used that to declare war with the backing of most of the people."

"Turns out Avonlea really is a strong leader," Gwen said.

Ryland huffed a smile and nodded. "Heh. Seems so." He groaned with every step. "How far is this healer?"

"About twenty more steps."

Ryland's face turned down. Gwen thought to reassure him he could make it, but he spoke instead. "I allowed myself to be blinded to the plight of the people. We thought they were satiated because we visited a few taverns and everything seemed fine."

"Everything was not fine," Gwen replied.

"We'll be implementing some new policies in the future. The people don't want to be placated." Another step, another groan.

"Maybe I hit you a little deeper than I meant to."

Ryland shrugged. "I deserve it. What about you? What are you going to do?"

"I have a Goblin to hunt, then deal with my aunt. Queen Helen. Not necessarily in that order."

"The White Witch is your aunt? So you are a princess after all."

Gwen rolled her eyes. "You can dress me up in pretty clothes and fancy shoes. But I'm a miller's daughter through and through."

"But the miller is not your father apparently?" Ryland pressed on Gwen's shoulders as he maneuvered the front steps of the cottage.

"No. He was a surrogate. Paid by my mother to raise me."

"But you still love him as a father, even after…" He let the question hang unfinished. They both knew he had basically sold her to King Aric.

"How could I not? He took great care of me until the end when he outed me. But the money had run out and I guess he was out of options."

"Still a pretty crappy thing to do. Sell your ward."

"Even that decision could be traced back to your uncle."

They paused a moment in front of the door. "Why did you come back to fight if you aren't even an Aurumite?"

"As I said… I'm a miller's daughter." Gwen said as if that explained everything.

The cottage door opened again, and Grinhelda stood in the doorway. Her mouth gaped at the prince's leg wound.

"Your payment for room and board for the last week will be to heal him," Gwen said.

Grin crossed her arms over her chest and lifted her chin. "That's worth a little more than room and board. How do you even know I can do it?"

"If you can't heal him, you are of no use to me. You can leave now," Gwen said.

Grinhelda rolled her eyes. "Fine. Bring him in."

Prince Ryland's knees nearly collapsed under him as he took another step. He grabbed the doorjamb and made his way to the sofa.

"I'll buy a new sofa Gwen," Ryland said with a groan.

"Just get better Ryland. That will be payment enough." She lowered him onto the furniture.

"Sure he can just get better, I have to use all my power," Grin grumbled.

Gwen crossed her arms over her chest. "When he starts living here, I'll charge him rent."

After Ryland was settled, Grinhelda leaned toward Gwen. "Who is this again?" She said from the corner of her mouth.

Gwen smiled. "I would think you would know a prince when you see one, Grin." She patted Ryland's foot. "I'll leave you to it." Gwen bent slightly at the hip and turned to leave.

"What about the sword Gwen?" Ryland asked.

"I'm the only who can wield it."

"It belongs to the crown."

"Then perhaps… the crown owes me for releasing its prince from a terrible greedy curse."

Ryland's eyes slid shut as he bowed his head, yielding the argument.

Gwen turned to go.

"Good luck with the Goblin Gwen," he said.

She froze and looked over her shoulder. "He's more than a goblin."

"You love him."

"Yes."

"Then I truly wish you the best, but I still hate this," Ryland admitted, his eyes squeezed closed in pain.

"Good rulers do what's best even when they hate it."

"I want to be good, Gwen."

"I know."

"I'm not sure I have it in me."

"You do." She turned the handle of the door. "Fight for your kingdom. They way you fought for me."

He nodded, and she stepped away while Grin worked her magic.

"There's still a few curses left to break, Princess," Ryland said when she had reached the door.

She smiled. "Then I'll crush every single one."

Mother

The earrings clicked as the dowager queen pulled them from her ears and dropped them into the ceramic bowl. She avoided seeing her face in the mirror. Her reflection was a reminder of where she'd been for twenty years. Stuck as a dragon in the depths of the kingdom, protecting her children from the dangers that lurked below. It left them vulnerable from above.

Only one had known her secret. He did his best to protect them, guide them, love them when she couldn't.

She pulled her silk gloves off her fingers one by one. It had been a long time since she had dressed in finery. Her wild dragon mind wanted nothing to do with it. Her skin itched to be back in scales, in the water where she had lived a lifetime.

She had woken from that dream to a war between her children. All of her children. Her life had gone from one nightmare to another, and it left her wondering if a witch had cursed her after all. While she hadn't chosen to be trapped in her dragon form, she had held on to hope that at least her secret would be safe. That her children would be safe.

"Hello, Mother," Aurius's easy lilt was gone. Replaced by sharp resolve.

Aurora jumped, startled by the sound of another voice in her private quarters. Her hand flew to her chest as she twisted her body in the seat at the vanity, ready to adorn herself with scales again. She quickly relaxed when she discovered who it was that had addressed her. "Aurius. What are you doing here?"

He didn't move. And didn't answer her question. "It's odd using that term.

I've never had a mother. I thought I would try it out." He rested his elbow on the arm of the wingback chair he had turned toward her, clicking the black goblin talons of each hand together. The chair could barely contain his massive size. "I'm surprised you acknowledge I'm your son at all."

Aurora turned back toward the mirror, choosing to address his reflection rather than him directly. She wasn't surprised that he had come. Who wouldn't want answers about their mother? He wore crisp black pants, a black shirt, and a double-breasted coat. Though his skin was green, his bottom teeth protruded, and he watched her with animal-like moss-green eyes, he didn't look like a goblin. "What do you want from me?" she asked, surprising herself by the steel in her voice.

"Nothing." Aurius snapped, then sighed. "Answers," he said, seeming to fight a war within himself.

As the dowager queen lifted her eyes to his in the mirror, her lip lifted in disgust.

"You need me," Aurius said.

She continued her bedtime ritual and routine, one even twenty years of solitude in a serpent body could not evaporate. "Do I?" The hand cream glided over her skin, seeping into the sensitive human skin. She found herself longing for scales again. They were easier to manage and not so... raw.

"If you want your son to marry the most powerful catalyst to ever live, you do."

Aurora pulled the pins from her ice-white hair. "I don't care who Ryland marries or what I have to do with it."

Aurius ignored her. "I will break the contract with Gwen if you tell me why."

"You can't break the contract without the quill," Aurora was certain the rumor was true. Goblins could revoke their contracts. One of many goblin secrets, she was sure.

He tilted his head. "I can break the contract. Why did you bargain with Helen to trade me for Drake?" Not an admission, but he was very confident.

"If you could break the contract why not do it months ago when Gwen asked?"

"My reasons don't concern you," he said.

She turned back toward him, looking over her shoulder. "You think you have it all figured out."

"I'm just missing the one piece."

"You were an illegitimate child. A bargain, made with the Goblin King." She looked from his toes back to his eyes.

"What bargain did you make with my father?" he asked.

Aurora turned back to her beauty regimen. Yet another reason scales were easier. Much lower maintenance. She brushed her long, icy locks into bouncy waves and began her explanation, still unsure she owed him one. Her blood ran through his veins too, though. The goblin curse might have burned her magic away, but he was still of her lineage. She examined his face in her mirror. The ridge of his nose, the shape of his eyes — they were hers. Even the square of his jaw reminded her of her father.

"Rumpelstiltskin needed a son. An heir. But he didn't want a dalliance with a farm girl. He wanted a royal heir. He approached me with a contract. It was one night and we both got what we wanted."

Aurius leaned forward in his chair, steepling his fingers between his knees. "I know and understand father's reason. What did you want?" he said slowly, enunciating each syllable through clenched teeth.

Turning in her seat to fully face her son, her voice changed. She sounded almost vulnerable. She looked at her hands as she said the words she knew Aurius deserved. The confession he wanted. "An enemy of Reginald's had cursed Ryland as a baby. Rumpel said he could remove the curse from Ryland if I had another child. I agreed and signed the contract. The fine print was ironclad, but I hadn't read it."

Aurius cut his eyes to the window. "No one ever does," he said, his tone flat.

"Less than a year later you arrived." Her voice trailed off as if guilt had choked her. "Your life in Mystrim wasn't good?"

"Oh please. Don't start catching sentimental motherly feelings. And asking questions now," he growled.

Her eyes shifted to the window, but she didn't shy away from his anger.

"It is difficult to love a monster's child."

"Fine. I'm a monster's child. Some may call me a monster myself. You didn't love me. The bargain mother. Why did you trade me for Drake? What was in it for you?" His words became rougher and louder with every syllable.

"I didn't say I didn't love you. That I don't love you. I said it was difficult. And I didn't trade you."

His eyes narrowed.

"Reginald traded you. I would have kept you and loved you as any other child." She looked down at her hands, winding her thumbs one over the other. "He found out that you were not his and..." She looked up. Her eyes reluctantly followed the movement of her head. Finally, she made eye contact. "He refused to raise you as his even after I had told him why it had to be done."

Aurius looked at his steepled hands and swallowed. "You found out about Helen's indiscretion and suggested a trade."

"I was trying to keep you safe. Reginald wanted to throw you from the tower wall. The only other option was Rumpel and I couldn't let him have you."

"The contract didn't include my father taking me as a child?" he asked.

"No. He wanted you raised as a royal. I had to find a royal household. You had to be raised as a prince."

"Why?" Aurius asked.

"The answers will only lead to more questions."

Aurora jolted at the sound of his booming voice. "My father is dead and you are the only one alive that might know."

Her throat bobbed. "I think he just wanted to give you something he didn't have," she said, giving him the only answer she had.

Aurius shook his head. Rumpelstiltskin had only ever cared about himself. "And a deal with Helen would be mutually beneficial. You would have leverage."

"Reginald thought so," she said.

"But he died and his brother knew nothing of the trade."

"Aric knew Drake was a ward, but nothing more."

"I'm not so sure you're right about that." Aurius stroked his long beard. "Then you were trapped as a water dragon for twenty years."

Aurora looked at her hands in response.

"And what about Ryland's curse? Why wasn't it lifted?"

She looked up then. "It was. Ryland is not cursed," she said.

"He has a dragon curse."

"No. Your father's machinations were very intricate. Gwen wields the curse breaker. His curse was broken."

Aurius barked a short laugh and shook his head. "I hope you learned to make better bargains."

Aurora folded her hands together and looked around the room to avoid meeting Aurius's eyes. "I regret..."

"That I was ever born."

She shook her head and swallowed hard. "No. I regret that I couldn't protect you better."

"Don't trouble yourself Mother. Helen knew who I was and what I was. She provided for me. Gave me access to the library. I learned much from the elves and regrettably the fairies."

Aurora lifted her eyebrows. "You have forest friends?"

The muscles in his jaw tensed. "Yes. And now Gwen does too."

She squared her shoulders. "You've protected her well." She sighed. "I wish there was something I could do."

"I've spent twenty years without a mother, I'll manage quite well."

"I don't..."

Aurius lifted himself from the wingback chair, crossed the room to a window and lifted the latch. It creaked under the weight of nine diamond-shaped glass panes, separated by dark wooden sash bars. A shadow danced away as the light shifted, and a cool evening breeze rustled through the room. "You don't have to worry about me anymore. Gwen chose Ryland. Unlike him, I will honor her choices."

She clicked her tongue. "Aurius don't be stupid. She chose him to save you. Even Ryland admits that."

He looked through the thorns to a couple walking through the garden holding hands.

"She had other options, and made her choice."

His mother crossed the room to stand beside him. She lifted herself onto her toes and peered through the thorny vines. The couple giggled and swung their arms back and forth. Aurora rolled her eyes, setting her heels back on the floor. "Your brother would have killed you both. He had dragon sickness. Even a goblin can't contend with that."

Her fingers lifted to touch his forearm. He jerked away from her touch.

"Don't," he growled, "you dare call him my brother. He is not, never was, and never will be."

She let her hand fall back to her side. It brushed along the light voile of her unique evening gown. "He is your brother. Avonlea is your sister. You are an heir to the Aurum throne."

"Only by half."

"The better half."

Aurius narrowed his eyes. "Debatable. But that's not really that hard to accomplish."

"Aurius. Your family needs you," she tried.

He huffed a laugh at the audacity. "I don't think the people of Aurum will accept a Goblin King in the line of succession."

"I don't want Gwen to marry Ryland," she admitted.

He shrugged. "Doesn't look like anyone has a choice. But seeing as you have provided me with the information needed and I certainly don't want to be betrothed to their future child, I'll break the blood contract."

"The contract should be broken, but not for those reasons."

Aurius cut his eyes at her.

"Not only for those reasons," she amended.

He ignored her and stepped onto the windowsill.

"Careful of the thorns. They cause a sleeping sickness. Drake has succumbed to this treachery," she said, reaching for him again, too late as he was already weaving around the three-foot thorns.

"He's just waiting for his true love's kiss. You should let Avonlea know." Aurius waved his hand, and the vines parted. "I'm a goblin, Mother. Only the goblin curse can affect me and as you can see it's run its course." He motioned down his body.

He jumped from the window ledge, landing nimbly three stories down. He crouched until his knees were near his shoulders. His knuckles balanced his weight. For those few moments, he looked more like a wild animal than a man. She had regretted the choices she had made, and all that had happened. But she didn't regret having Aurius save Ryland's life. Rumpelstiltskin lifted Ryland's curse, in the only way the curse could be broken without the curse breaker. There had been many surprises this evening. But most of all, she was surprised Aurius hadn't surmised how Rumpel fulfilled his part of the contract. Rumpel did have intricate plans, but Ryland's curse had been broken that night. He moved the curse to his own son, knowing the goblin curse would dissolve it.

The dowager queen was still looking out the window when the door burst open, soldiers filling her room.

"He's gone," she said, without a look backward.

The lead guard held a hand on the hilt of his sword as he searched the room. "Where your highness?" he asked.

"To fulfill the destiny he was born to," she said as the soldiers followed her gaze out the window. They nodded to each other and filed out of her suite in pursuit of the Goblin King.

Kinship

Gwen turned the knob of the queen's quarters. The castle had been empty and easily taken by the people of Mystrim. But no one could get past the magical barriers Helen had erected throughout the castle.

The barriers were no match for her magical ability. The ability to transfer magic from one to another.

Gwen flicked her wrist. The magic flowed freely from the traps into her. She could easily hold it, but the garden sanctuary was the perfect place for her to place it. Her father's garden accepted the magic and dissipated it through the area. Each flower, brook and tree grew just for her. As if they were there for her to use however she wanted. She felt their enjoyment of receiving her magic. When this was over, the garden would be where she spent her time.

Gwen approached the throne room, silent on the plush carpet. She had already drawn Inauratus.

Helen sat on the throne in all her finery. Every piece of jewelry she owned adorned her, and the crown glittered on her head. Her fingers stroked the head of a black crow, which turned a beady bird eye toward Gwen as she entered.

"I thought you might seek me out," she said. Her fingers played with the feathers on the back of the bird.

"Why did you do it?" Gwen asked.

"I thought you would have learned by now."

Gwen lowered her chin with a glare. Helen went on. "In our world, Gwen everything is about power. I recognized yours as soon as you were born. I saw an opportunity so I took it."

"Your taking, destroyed a kingdom. You're responsible for the deaths of thousands."

Helen's lips crawled away from perfect white teeth in an evil sneer. "That is genuine power isn't it?"

"No." Gwen stepped toward the throne. "Actual power is having the ability to destroy and choosing not to."

Helen pursed her lips. "You're one to talk. Draining the life from your own mother?"

Gwen tensed at the reminder.

"Maybe we should try you for regicide?" It was a statement more than a question from the queen, trying to show she still had the power to try her for anything.

"I was an infant. And my mother made her choices."

Queen Helen's eyes slid over Gwen until she struggled to keep from shuddering. "If I know anything about you, it's that you don't want to be a ruler. So tell me the real reason you came all this way?" she said.

"You have something of mine," Gwen said, when she couldn't find a good reason to hide it from her any longer.

The crow cawed, drawing attention to itself.

Helen's eyes shifted to her right and snapped back to Gwen. "I don't know what you think I have, but as I am still Queen, I can't imagine what you think is yours."

"This is over Helen. You're not queen of Mystrim any more."

"So you have come to claim your throne? You're kidding yourself if you think these people will follow a catalyst."

Gwen released an exasperated breath. "If I must. It is not what I want. But I will not allow people to be tormented by you any longer."

"Tortured by me?" Helen placed a hand over her chest and laughed. "It's your magic I used in the spell. I think you'll find that I'm a hero. And you think they'll let you be queen married to the Goblin King? If you wish to wed Aurius you should walk away now."

Gwen shrugged. "And I think you'll find they frown upon creating a fake curse to become a fake hero." She extended her left hand, palm up. "Give me the quill Helen. It means nothing to you."

Helen narrowed her eyes. "On the contrary. It is control. Leverage." She tilted her head. "So you don't want to marry. Interesting."

Gwen ignored her probes. "You can't be queen. But if you cooperate I might not kill you, for the sake of your son, Drake."

Helen's eyes softened only briefly at the mention of her son's name. It was enough to confirm his identity. But Queen Helen was ruthless in her endeavor to keep her secret.

"Gwen dear you can't kill me. How would that look if the heir killed her predecessor?"

She lifted a shoulder. "I don't care."

The former queen's red-stained lips formed a gentle smile. Designed to disarm those around her. "You need me, Niece."

"The quill, Helen." Gwen remained unbothered.

"Let me stay on as your advisor and I will tell you the location of the quill."

The raven hopped from the arm of the throne to the pedestal and turned its head in a jerky move.

"Helen." Gwen's tone held a warning that she was at the end of her patience.

The ex-queen's sweet facade faded. "Then you'll just have to die." She thrust her hand in front of her. Magic swirled and rushed from her fingers toward Gwen. Stolen magic. Different strands woven around each other. Each making the next more powerful. Helen had been collecting magic for a long time using the barrier. At the heart of the braided magic was Gwen's siphon magic, taken as an infant, holding it all together.

Gwen gasped at the sudden onslaught of power. Her greedy magic reached out, enticed by the amount of power ready for taking, absorbing everything Helen threw at her. Even in the middle of the onslaught, a thought occurred to her. The magic was greedy. Helen's spell woven into the barrier had stopped feeding her power and instead kept it for itself. That was why she had grown weaker. Gwen groaned as the sheer amount of power grew within her, but Helen's stolen magic wasn't bottomless. "Time to end this," she whispered.

"I revoke your use of my magic," Gwen said. Immediately, Helen's magic disintegrated into sparkling specks of golden glitter. It fell onto the plush carpeted floor. Helen's mouth dropped open.

Gwen channeled the remaining magic into the thieving raven. With a poof, black feathers drifted into the air, floating this way and that. Drifting in the breeze, onto the floor beside the throne.

Helen moved her hands in frantic thrusts, trying to get the magic to flow again. "How?" A tiny squeak escaped her throat as she snapped her mouth closed. "You're not a catalyst." Helen had aged forty years in a matter of minutes. Tremors racked her body as she took a shaky step back to the throne and lowered herself onto it. She lifted her curled fingers toward her niece again.

Gwen tilted her head to the side. "The barrier is gone. And you are cut off from my magic. There's nothing you can do Helen. Tell me where the quill is and I'll let you live."

"What are you?"

"Not the catalyst you expected to control I bet." Gwen took a step forward and raised the sword to Helen's neck. "The quill, Helen."

"I'll never tell you."

"Fine." Gwen waved a hand. Golden light encircled the ex-queen. Her shoulders twisted back and forth as she struggled, trying to escape the magical bonds.

Gwen looked towards the table behind the throne. A gilded box lay there. A key stuck out of it. Helen and the raven had given away the location of the quill. As soon as she had mentioned it, the raven had jumped toward the box as if it were protecting the treasure. Helen's eyes had also shifted in that direction.

Gwen lifted the lid to find the quill lying there on top of the empty jewelry box.

She held it between her forefinger and her thumb. Lightly. The memory she had seen before didn't grab her, but she knew this was the same instrument used to sign her fate.

Gwen smiled. "Now to find Aurius," she whispered.

A man cleared his throat. "Excuse me. Um. Princess?"

Gwen's eyes shifted in his direction, with a raised eyebrow. She pressed the quill to her heart, protecting it from any who might want to take it again.

"What shall we do with the queen?"

"Give her a proper trial. She was the rightful ruler for many years after all."

He bowed. "You will need to be crowned queen."

Gwen sheathed her sword with a smooth scraping sound. "I have business to attend. And I'm not sure I want to be crowned queen."

"But who will be rule?"

"I have business to attend," she said again. "We'll figure it out when I return."

"That will not be enough to secure your reign. You need to leave someone in charge or it will be a free for all."

Gwen sighed. "Fine. You are in charge."

The man's mouth dropped open. "I can't..."

She patted him on the shoulder. "See how it feels? But as it is I think you will be a fine placeholder. Keep my throne warm while I'm gone. I expect the kingdom to be in tact." She tossed the words over her shoulder as she left the throne room.

She stopped abruptly in the hall and turned back toward him. "Can you give me the magic horse?"

"You are the heir and princess. They are yours."

She jerked her down in a nod. "Have her saddled within the hour."

Gwen hurried down the hall, away from the horror she had created in the throne room. Away from the tragedy of Queen Helen's fate, she'd had to mete out. It wasn't a job she enjoyed or a duty she had wanted, but choices weren't abundant. Gwen shook her head, putting the sad thoughts behind her. She would have loved to have had a mentor like Queen Helen. A beloved aunt. Family. But she would live a thousand years on a poor miller's farm rather than allow a power-hungry madwoman to control her.

Gwen twisted the handle to Aurius's suite. It was a mess. No doubt

Queen Helen had been searching for her leverage. Gwen stepped over books scattered about the floor, carefully avoiding a glass lamp that had shattered. White down feathers coated every surface. It gave the room a pristine facade, despite the chaos that it hid underneath.

Her lips turned down at the corners. Not that the items in this room held any value. This was her haven for weeks. The place she had fallen in love with the Dark Prince. It was gone. Mostly destroyed. But there wasn't time for tears.

Her thin fingers brushed away the soft covering over the books that were strewn about the floor. Aurius might find all the queen's men and string them up just for disrespecting the written word so flagrantly. Pursing her lips, she shook her head. "It's not here."

She swiveled and scanned the room. Was there a hidden compartment? She suspected she wouldn't be able to find anything. Until she noticed a golden shimmer in the room's corner near the fireplace. It was small. Barely visible. She wouldn't have noticed except that she was kneeling. Obviously, the queen's men missed it.

The feathers muffled each step. She approached it slowly, as if it were some kind of trap. If it were, surely it would have sprung against the Queen's men. But you could never be too careful when it came to magical spells. Her loneliness pressed on her. This was up to her, and if she was caught in a trap, it might be days before anyone found her.

Her fingers stretched toward the golden shimmer. Her magic recognized his and rushed toward it. Strength she didn't know she possessed yanked on her magic to slow the rush.

But as soon as her magic connected with the shimmering gold, the suite exploded with light. The room faded away as if it were a curtain, and she had just pulled the string. Turning, the glamour crackled away and revealed a room full of items. Almost as if it were a storehouse of magical objects. Impossibly, the room continued for miles. The cottage was nothing in comparison. Her mouth gaped open. She didn't know where to direct her eyes.

The magic in her veins buzzed. There was too much, but her magic wanted it all. She needed to get out of this room, but she needed the book first, and it had to be here.

She ground her teeth. Magic ached to get away from her and to take from all the surrounding objects. She closed her eyes against the pain. Willing herself to focus on one thing. The one object she needed.

"Magic focus. We need the book. That is it."

But it didn't listen to her. "Take it all." it whispered. "In case we need it later." It soothed. "It will be ok."

Gwen couldn't argue with that. What if she had to fight someone again? She shook her head. Her eyebrows pressed in the middle. That wasn't right. She didn't need to store energy; she could just take it from them.

"But you would feel better," it whispered.

Gwen wiped away the thought with a brush of her hand, but it was becoming difficult to remember why she shouldn't store the magic. "Why can't I take it?"

"Gwen!" She heard her name growled from behind her. The voice was familiar.

"You don't need it," the voice said, but that made little sense. She needed it. She almost died because there wasn't enough. There was never enough, and she needed to make sure she never ran out again.

"This will always be here for you. I'll give you access. Just turn toward my voice."

It took all the willpower she had just to slam her eyes closed. All her strength went into turning her shoulder to the voice behind her. As she turned away from the objects, her magic whimpered. "Please." A final anguished plea reverberated in her skull.

"No." Gwen said. Firm in her resolve not to become her aunt.

With her back now facing the vault of magic, Gwen opened her eyes. Meeting those moss-green eyes of the Goblin King.

He reached out with his crooked green hands tipped with black talons. "You shouldn't have come, Gwen." His muscular forefinger gently tipped her chin up.

Gwen narrowed her eyes. "You shouldn't have left."

His other hand snaked around her side and pulled her toward him. The backs of his fingers gently stroked her cheek. Her eyes slid closed as she leaned into the caress. Nuzzling for more.

"Gwen."

"Aurius."

His lips rested on her forehead. "Don't look for me."

Gwen's eyes flew open. She was back in Aurius's room. No shimmering warehouse of objects. No Goblin King.

Something was different. A piece of parchment lay on the bed she had once stayed in. A familiar paper. She unfolded it, recognizing it immediately as the contract her mother had signed.

"That jerk!"

She nearly crumpled the paper to toss it, but as she thought about throwing it in the fire, she pulled her anger back. There was a better way to handle the Goblin King. A smile formed on Gwen's lips as a plan unfolded in her mind.

＊

Gwen canceled her ride on the magical horse. Instead, she sent out invitations to her coronation. Every kingdom was required to send a delegate or come in person. Most kingdoms were eager to see the princess who'd been in hiding as a miller's daughter all these years.

She waited in the antechamber just outside the throne room. Her dress rustled as her steps clicked on the floor in one direction and then equally in the other. Her new ladies insisted the dress needed four or five layers.

Peeking through the crack in the door, the light from the throne room lit a line down one side of her face. "He's not here."

"You knew he wouldn't be." The voice was sweet and steady.

Gwen wrung her hands together. "Yes. I just hoped he would come to his senses."

"It seems he hasn't." Avonlea perched on the edge of the settee, ankles crossed. Even as the leader of a rebellion, she was still the prim princess. Her childhood training wouldn't be easy to change.

Gwen paced in a new direction for a few more steps. "I hate this."

"You can change your mind and marry Ryland," she said, ever the champion for her brother.

"I don't love him, and our heir would have to marry Aurius."

Avonlea pulled a grim face. "You have the quill."

Gwen groaned. "This whole situation is backwards."

"Not too late to back out," Avonlea encouraged.

"It's a little too late. There's a room full of kings, queens and dignitaries."

"Right." Avonlea rose from the chair she'd been lounging in. "Might as well get this over with then."

Gwen pinched the bridge of her nose. "I can't do this in front of everyone."

Avonlea's eyes rounded. "This was your plan." The pitch of her voice increased.

"Why didn't you talk me out of it?" Gwen asked.

Avonlea's lips pushed up in the middle. "Making a spectacle of yourself and the Dark Prince in front of hundreds of leaders and heads of state? It seemed like a good plan."

Gwen rolled her eyes. "Fine, let's get this over with. Open the doors."

Two guards pulled open the double mahogany doors. Gwen stepped to the entrance, allowing the herald to announce her and the fanfare to begin. She lifted her chin, straightened her shoulders and took fourteen measured steps down the aisle to the dais.

Turning toward the crowd, she took the golden card from her pocket and pressed it between her thumb and forefinger. "Mr. Woolworth," she said before the man in the robes could step forward with a crown.

"I thought we had come to an agreement," Aurius said from the back of the room.

The crowd turned and gasped. This was the first they had seen of the Goblin King. Though they had heard rumors of his broad shoulders, mottled skin, and green eyes that glowed, they hadn't believed it to be true of Aurius. Somehow he had become more handsome in this transformation, at least to Gwen's eyes.

She lifted her chin and squared her shoulders. "There was no agreement."

"So you summoned me?"

"Yes."

Aurius's eyes didn't leave hers. His voice was only a little gruffer. He managed it well, and Gwen could still hear his elegant tone beneath the growl. His clothes were clean and mended. It hugged his muscles as if they were about to burst through with enough movement. He hadn't been living in a cave, at least.

"Well then, let's bargain shall we?"

She nodded in return. "What is your price?"

"Your first born," he quipped.

The crowd held its collective breath, but his nonchalant tone didn't faze Gwen. "Someone has already negotiated that price," she retorted.

His head tilted forward, and he looked up through his lashes. His voice lowered. "Then your second."

"Agreed."

"And what is it I am bargaining for? It seems you have all the magic you could ever hope for."

"Your hand in marriage."

"No deal." He turned to leave. The Elf King blocked his path with his arms folded over his chest.

"King Aurius. You have answered the call you must make a deal or forfeit your crown as the Goblin King."

He pretended to take the imaginary crown off his head. "Fine. Take it. I don't want it."

"Old friend. You know that's not how it works. You will forfeit your life, your lands. Hundreds will die."

Aurius's shoulders hunched as if the weight of the world pressed upon him.

"My life is forfeit, I don't care about my lands, and..." he looked over his shoulder. "The hundreds will be in good hands."

The Elf King's face hardened. "If I don't, this curse continues to another generation," Aurius whispered to his old friend.

Emyr raised an eyebrow. "Is it worth it?" he asked.

He looked back again at the dais. "Yes."

"You're an idiot."

Aurius growled at his friend.

"She obviously loves you. Look at the lengths she's gone through to get you in a room. And make you stay in a room."

"The crowd?"

He nodded.

Aurius turned with a sigh and raised his voice over the quiet murmur of the crowd. "You already have my condition for our betrothal."

Gwen smiled. "And I'm willing to grant it."

"It's too late Gwen."

The room was silent.

Gwen pulled the quill from her dress pocket. "This is the quill used to sign the contract between Rumpelstiltskin and Queen Liora, my mother."

The crowd gasped collectively as if they hadn't heard the gossip.

The quill snapped between her fingers. Aurius stepped forward and reached out a hand to stop her, but it was too late. "The contract is binding, Aurius. And I will hold you to it."

Aurius tilted his head toward the ceiling with a low growl.

Gwen stepped off the dais. With the Elf King behind him, Aurius couldn't retreat into the shadows. The room was too bright to allow it. He had no escape. He stiffened at her approach as she held out her hand.

"Your hand, Aurius."

Fire burned in his moss-green eyes. His hand slowly rose to her palm. She threaded her fingers through his, and he stiffened further. "I'm trying to spare you Gwen."

"I'm done allowing you to save me, Aurius. Its time you let me do something for you."

Her magic latched onto his, but it didn't pull. It searched. Searched for the curse. His back buckled and his face contorted in pain as the magic from Inauratus ate through the goblin curse in his blood and all the curses that had ever been laid on him. Gwen almost collapsed at the sheer number of things the magic found.

The green color leached from his skin. His incisors shortened. The gravel left his voice.

Sweat dripped from his brow when she finally finished. He was bent at the waist, heaving heavy breaths. When she released him, he looked up at her. The moss green in his eyes was now mixed with chocolate brown.

"You freed me," he whispered.

She smiled. "As I said I would."

"I'm still a goblin."

He flipped his hands back and forth. His skin still had a slight green tint. Pointed talons still curved over his fingertips. "That's not the part you hated."

"No. I guess not."

She lifted his hands to her lips. "Will you marry me Aurius Rumpelstilt-skinson?" she asked.

"That is a ridiculous name."

Gwen laughed. "Woolworth then?"

He shook his head. "How about the Miller's daughter and the Goblin King?"

He wrapped his arm around her waist and pulled her to him. He pressed his lips to hers as the room erupted in raucous cheers. For the first time in his life, he was just Aurius. He smiled against her lips and whispered, "Yes, Gwen Miller. I will marry you."

So, sweet girl, as you can see… Love saves the world… Just make sure you choose the right prince.

Epilogue: Home

The door creaked open. The stone walls held no warmth. Gwen crossed her arms over her chest, trying to rub heat into them. While spring was just around the corner, winter wanted to hold on for a moment longer.

"Papa?" she said as she took a tentative step inside. Her head bent around the corner of the door while her feet remained outside. But not for long.

Gwen's boots clicked against the rough stone floors. Following a worn path from the door to the fireplace. One she had walked hundreds of times. A small heap of ashes remained in the hearth. Gwen crouched and let her hands hover over the grey mass. No heat. No embers. Her father hadn't been here for days. She pulled them back and rubbed them against each other. Breathing into her hands to warm them.

She stood and looked over the cottage. Two place settings remained on the table, but dust collected on top. Had Papa finally stopped saving a place for her mother? Or were these for them both? Did he honor his loss of Gwen the same as her mother? Despite not really being her father, he had never treated her as anything other than a daughter.

Gwen took a few steps to the bedroom. Blankets lay neatly folded in the middle of the feather bed. Papa's boots were gone, and his favorite pipe was missing.

Gwen sighed. She had hoped to see him today. To make sure he was okay. She wanted to see the mill restored and working properly. But the land was still healing, and it might be a long while before the grain industry could support a working mill.

It had been hard enough to convince Captain Drake to let her come back here. Despite her title, she would never convince her retinue to let her near the tavern where she suspected he might be. Just that morning, they had received a note threatening her as a magic user. It seemed a new faction of anti-magic dissidents had risen. Ones whose magic was not restored, most likely.

Her hands slipped into her dress coat. A sheet of browned paper folded in thirds brushed her fingers. Pulling it out, she brushed it to her lips. "May you find your recipient well," she whispered and slipped it under the bowl where she would normally sit for meals.

She pulled her shoulders back and lifted her chin. Four quick steps and she was out the door again. Though the sun had now risen above the treeline, Gwen didn't shield her eyes. The brim of her hat kept her from squinting against the offending light. She adjusted her riding gloves, determined she would not let the tears fall.

A few more steps took her to her horse. A charcoal grey mare with a star on her face. The mare shook her head as the groom handed her the reins. Grabbing the horn of the saddle, she placed a foot in the stirrup and bounced herself onto the horse.

"He's not here and it doesn't look as if he is coming back," she said, adjusting herself in the seat.

Aurius allowed his horse to ease up beside her. He put his hand on hers. "Should we check his favorite tavern?" Aurius asked, his voice low and menacing.

"I think we've extended the captain as far as he's willing to go."

Aurius's eyes shifted toward the captain and back to hers. His lips pursed over his protruding teeth. "Don't use him as an excuse, Gwen. He'll obey your orders."

She shook her head with a sigh, looking down the road toward the tavern. "Papa's made his peace. There's no sense in disturbing it." She clicked her tongue and turned the horse back to the road toward Mystrim. "I think our tour is finally over. Let's go home."

As she urged her horse forward, a boy raced down the road toward them.

The soldiers escorting her intercepted him before he could approach their retinue. "Your highness." The messenger said between breaths.

Gwen looked kindly at the young man, waving for the soldiers to let him through. "I've told you to stop calling me that."

The messenger bowed and then looked at the captain. "Yes, your highness."

Gwen cut her eyes at Drake, who shrugged and made a face that said, "What do you want me to do?"

She shook her head and ignored the title everyone insisted on using. "You're needed urgently in Mystrim."

"Why?"

"The goblins your highness."

Gwen threw a look over her shoulder at the man behind her with the slight green tint to his skin. He leaned in with piqued interest, but since the messenger hadn't addressed him, he didn't speak.

"They've come out of hiding."

* * *

Reviews are the best way to continue your support of an independent author. It helps more than you can ever imagine! Please leave a quick few words so more readers can find me.

Acknowledgements

Thank you again for reading this book. Without readers, writing doesn't make sense.

To my family. Thank you for your support and inspiration, especially in the final moments of prepping this book. I know there were so many days and nights I spent immersed in a different world. It's exciting that you now get to visit this place I've created for you. I hope you like it.

Thank you to my ARC and beta readers for catching all those little things I never see.

Thank you to my Lord, thank you for your blood that breaks all curses.

Plans for the future:

Gwen and Aurius's story is done for now, but there's more to come for Mystrim, Aurum and the enchanted forest.

Lord willing, Avonlea will get her own story, a sleeping beauty retelling, and we might just explore why Aurius is no fan of the fairies. A Cinderella retelling is in the works. Follow me on Amazon, Facebook, Instagram, or Substack to hear about new releases.

Who knows where we'll go from there. I'll keep writing as long as I'm able. Hopefully, someday it will start paying the bills around here. My goal is four books written next year. I will start publishing again in 2027, unless I just can't stand to keep you in the dark.

Happy Reading.

Also By Evangaline Pierce

Sacred Series
Sacred Vengeance
Sacred Mercy
Sacred Redemption

Magic and Gold Series
A Crown of Gilded Thread
A Sword of Plated Gold

Available Now on Amazon
A Crown of Gilded Thread is also available in audiobook format through
Curios.

About the Author

Award-winning author, Evangaline wrote her first short story at the age of twelve. She has spent much of her adult life writing papers for college professors. She rekindled her love for storytelling several years later when she published her first book, chronicling her family's journey to find a missing person.

Evangaline loves crafting adventures that honor her faith and love of Jesus. Faith, hope, and love within suffering are common themes in her writing. Her main characters often face and overcome overwhelming odds.

She currently lives in Texas with her husband, daughter, two dogs, and a flock of chickens.

You can follow her on Facebook, Instagram and Substack where readers can interact with Evangaline and each other, or get exclusive content via email.

You can connect with me on:

🌐 https://evangalinepierce.com

📘 https://facebook.com/evangalinepierce

Subscribe to my newsletter:

✉ https://substack.com/@evangalinepierce

www.ingramcontent.com/pod-product-compliance
Lightning Source LLC
Chambersburg PA
CBHW051507260626
47162CB00008B/2856